THE YELLOW DOCUMENT

OR

"FANTÔMAS OF BERLIN"

BY MARCEL ALLAIN

Bibliographical Note
This Antipodes edition is a republication of the work first published by
Brentano's, New York, in 1919.

ISBN 978-0-9966599-8-7

CONTENTS

THE YELLOW
DOCUMENT

Prologue: A Monster

Dressed in a colonel's uniform of the Death's Head Hussars—the sixth uniform he had worn since the morning—William II left the card table. His mustache curled upward and a conquering air concealed the infirmity of his short left arm. With a Napoleonic gesture, he spoke with forced gaiety.

"Ambassadress, I have beaten you."

"Your Majesty was pitiless."

"Naturally, Ambassadress."

And moving away a step, he added:

"I do not hold with the French that one must never beat a woman, even with a flower."

William II pushed aside the small card table upon which he had just concluded a well-fought battle with the wife of the Russian ambassador, and continued:

"My opinion is that every charming woman is a demon. I should not choose a flower, but a sword, to beat them with."

The ambassadress bowed, smiling. William II turned on his heel and moved away, muttering, "A fool."

That evening an intimate dinner had taken place at the Potsdam Court in honor of the Kaiser's birthday anniversary.

It was in 1893. The emperor had just reached his thirty-fourth year. One glance at him would be enough to guess that he hoped great things of the future and believed in the promise of a glorious destiny.

Pride, daring, avidity—all the defects which stamp the soul of an adventurer, characterized his imperial features. One might also read there rascality and hypocrisy.

William II now leaned toward the empress, Augusta Victoria, and questioned her more than amiably:

"Does not the heat disturb you, my dear? You are very pale."

In reality, the Kaiser was quite indifferent to the health of the empress, but this show of attention was part of the role he played.

William II did not disdain from time to time to affect the virtues of a good bourgeois—at least before his guests—to give the impression of being an excellent husband.

What answer did the empress make? William II moved away from her chair without waiting to hear, and touched a Prussian general, one of his favorites, on the arm.

"Well, my dear fellow, and what about your soldiers? Do you think those recruits we were talking of the other day will maintain the prestige of our army? Are the troops of '93 worth those of '70?"

"Without doubt, Sire."

The emperor's question produced a chill in the big drawing room where the evening's guests remained silent each time he deigned to utter a word. The French ambassador grew pale.

William II noticed it.

He frequently made "breaks" with a heaviness of wit which proved a total lack of *savoir-vivre*. He wasn't disturbed, however, and shrugging his shoulders, he laughed and turned the conversation. It was his way of excusing himself. That day, however, he gave a slight shudder when he met the energetic and determined eyes of the French ambassador. He started to speak, stopped, and then questioned:

"What has happened to your military attaché, Ambassador— that Captain Bayen? Will he soon be back again?"

The ambassador articulated clearly:

"Very soon, I hope, Sire. He is finishing his studies in tactics— which enable the French army to remain what it has always been, the first army in the world."

The reply was sharp, brutal even, and the ambassador, a courteous man, must have felt pushed beyond the limit by the insolence of William II to dare it.

The Kaiser appeared not to understand.

"By Jove, I was forgetting—I must leave you for a few moments. I have some work."

And as nobody answered, the emperor, keeping up the pretense of middle-class virtue, added:

"I have my mail to sign. Ah, Germany & Co. is a great firm, and being emperor is a hard position."

He went to the door, nodded ironically and condescendingly to his guests, then left the room, waving aside the chamberlains who were about to accompany him:

"Not necessary. I shall return in a moment."

The Kaiser gained his private apartments. Certainly, it was not an ordinary worry that made him leave the drawing rooms. William II, in fact, appeared very upset. Two porters stood like statues at the door of the imperial rooms.

The emperor questioned sharply:

"Where is the officer of the portfolio?"

"In his office, Sire."

"What orders has he given you?"

"His excellency has charged us to notify his majesty's ministers that his majesty will grant no audience today."

"Very good."

William II entered the room which was softly lighted by an electric lamp encased in an alabaster vase.

"Nobody here yet?" he murmured.

But at this moment from the shadows of the room, a dim figure emerged, seemingly from the wall, and advanced with a deep bow.

William II grew so pale that he seemed about to collapse.

"Ah!" he cried in a hoarse voice. "You are here already, my private counselor?"

The emperor waved to a seat and continued:

"The porters did not announce your arrival, Doctor Krampft. You nearly frightened me."

"I beg your majesty to forgive the servants," the man replied slowly. "Nobody saw me enter."

"Did you come in through the walls then?"

"Perhaps."

The emperor nodded:

"After all, that would not be impossible to you."

He raised a warning finger:

"Do you know what they call you, Krampft?"

"Will your majesty deign to tell me?"

"My household calls you 'Fantômas of Berlin.'"

The Kaiser dropped onto a sofa and continued:

"And the title is deserved. You have the audacity and the cunning of the man they designate as 'The Genius of Crime.' The master of frightfulness."

"Is this a reproach, Sire?"

"It's a compliment, Krampft."

A grim laugh followed and the Kaiser added:

"That's enough. Fantômas, since you are Fantômas, what have you learned?"

"Nothing, Sire."

"What! Nothing!"

The Kaiser started and his voice grew violent.

"The yellow document? That cursed document. Are you going to get it for me?"

"No, Sire, it is in the hands of Captain Bayen."

"Do you know at least, if it is complete?"

"I am sure it is not, Sire."

With a gesture, silencing his master, the emperor, the mysterious individual called Fantômas of Berlin, pronounced slowly:

"Sire, your majesty will allow me to define the situation which you do not quite understand. A man, an Austrian, has invented a machine of such power that the country owning it would be assured of world supremacy. This man offered his secret to your government. Your government did not believe in him. So without hesitation, he offered it elsewhere. It was then that Captain Bayen, attaché of the French embassy, sacrificed his private fortune and bought the secret."

"Alas!" sighed the Kaiser.

"Sire, do not despair," murmured the enigmatical individual. "This man sold his secret, but he did not sell the whole of it. Captain Bayen has only the description of a machine. He has not the method of using it to get the full results. The inventor asks for millions; Captain Bayen has applied to his government for the money. We shall not have lost until Captain Bayen possesses the whole secret."

Herr Krampft folded his arms and added calmly:

"Now Captain Bayen will never know the whole secret."

"Why not? France is rich…"

"I ask your majesty's pardon. Captain Bayen will never know the secret because the inventor cannot tell him. He is dead."

"Dead?"

"Dead, Sire. He died yesterday, poisoned by his dinner."

Herr Krampft did not shudder in announcing the poisoning of the inventor, which might be called murder.

The Kaiser rose, agitated.

He took the hands of his counselor and pressed them:

"Krampft, you have saved Germany."

"No, Sire."

"No? Why not?"

"The man can no longer speak, Sire, but perhaps he has already spoken."

A glance from the Kaiser forced Fantômas of Berlin to explain further. And truly Doctor Krampft must have ben daring indeed to retain such complete calm in the presence of his master's anxiety.

"Sire, the man is dead. But he died in Captain Bayen's very house. That is where he lived. It was Mme. Bayen, the young wife of this cursed French officer, who was with him at the end."

Krampft, in a low tone, admitted:

"I am afraid, Sire—terribly afraid."

Nervously the Kaiser paced up and down the huge room where so many state secrets had been discussed, where so many infamous plans had received his royal seal. He walked and walked with half shut eyes, apparently oblivious to the presence of his private counselor.

A strange man this Krampft. Scarcely thirty years of age, he wore the court dress, but wore it badly. Beneath it he had a common air. Slender, he gave the impression of size on account of his thick and knotted limbs. The squareness of his head, added to an abundant mustache and beard, enlarged his face and hid his mouth and the most of his cheeks.

William II stopped abruptly.

"That woman must never be able to speak."

"Yes, Sire."

"Yet she must live so that if ever we secure the yellow document from her husband, she may be able to explain to us how it can be utilized."

"That is true, Sire."

"It is necessary."

William II placed both hands on the doctor's shoulders.

"Krampft, do you recall the mission I entrusted you with three weeks ago?"

"I recall it, if your majesty orders me to do so."

"Krampft, I advised you that a child would be put into your charge. I told you that you would have the bringing up of that child. I told you the child is my child, my bastard. Krampft, I gave to you then a proof of my confidence."

"Sire, I hope I have and will always deserve it."

"Undoubtedly, Krampft—well, I have another mission for you... as serious a one—"

"I am at your majesty's orders."

"Krampft, this is what I have decided: Mme. Bayen must die!"

"Die, Sire?"

"Apparently die, Krampft."

"I don't understand, your majesty."

"And yet it is quite simple. Captain Bayen is guilty of espionage in buying the yellow document here... Krampft, I shall see his wife and say to her: 'Madame, your husband will get twenty years of prison if you refuse to save him. You can save him by giving up the secret confided to you by the inventor who died yesterday. Until then, you will be my prisoner.' Madame Bayen is French. She is a woman in love—she will speak and save her husband."

"And you would release her, Sire?"

"No! never!"

There was a moment of silence.

Krampft dared to break it.

"If your majesty thinks to force this woman to speak, your majesty is mistaken. She is not only French, she is Alsatian. She will hold her tongue. Or else she will provoke a scandal. She will write—telegraph—she will escape!"

The Kaiser shook his head.

"Krampft," he murmured, "you forget my agents who open all letters, my police who arrest those who try to escape—you forget that I am the master and that I shall say to this woman: 'If you attempt to escape, Captain Bayen will run the risk of a mortal accident.' You forget something else, Krampft."

"What, Sire?"

"That Mme. Bayen is enceinte, that she expects a child—and

that the child will serve as a hostage. We shall steal it from her if necessary!"

Another silence reigned.

The emperor began his pacing again. He finally spoke:

"Krampft, a terrible struggle is about to take place for this yellow document. Captain Bayen has won the first point, I shall win the second. I hold him through his wife, and I hold his wife through her child."

But Krampft shook his head.

"You are not convinced?" asked the Kaiser.

"No," replied the counselor calmly.

Ah! It was not a question of fright or horror for the infamous plan which William II dared to expose.

But he foresaw redoubtable consequences of that plan, and these consequences alarmed him.

"Sire, your majesty seems to me too daring," he ventured, at length. "Your majesty may possibly hold Mme. Bayen prisoner by reason of her child, but consider, it is not only a question of Mme. Bayen—what will your majesty say to the captain when he returns?"

"That his wife is dead, Krampft."

"And if he doesn't believe you?"

"He will believe me, Krampft, for he will mourn at her tomb—without suspecting that his wife is in confinement, perhaps not far away. Such things are easily brought about when one is who I am—the emperor. You know that very well."

Certainly William II would have been well served had his counselor seized him by the throat and strangled him as one strangles the most odious criminal.

But Krampft merely smiled:

"May I put a question to your majesty?"

"Speak, Krampft."

"Has your majesty already chosen Mme. Bayen's jailer?"

"Certainly," replied the emperor. "That jailer will be you." And he added jeeringly:

"It is a position which belongs of right to Fantômas of Berlin."

An hour later, Krampft left the imperial palace.

But in spite of the high confidence which the Kaiser had shown in him by making him his associate in crime, Krampft appeared anxious. He muttered to himself in a low tone: "The emperor is mistaken! His majesty does not know French hearts. Hate blinds him! Whether he tortures the wife or the mother, Mme. Bayen is Alsatian and will not speak. And as for Captain Bayen, the soldier, even though he think his wife dead, even though he be condemned to silence, he will not forget—he will have his revenge."

Krampft felt chilled from head to feet.

1. A Joke

Although three o'clock had struck at a neighboring school, the heat was scarcely less intense than at noon and the buildings of the cavalry quarters of Lunéville, whitewashed, with roofs of red tile, seemed to flame under the pitiless sky.

Javot, cavalryman on duty at the barracks, questioned the quartermaster with visible anxiety:

"What's your idea, Quartermaster, is it to be war?"

For a week past the newspapers had been filled with sensational news about the "difficulties of Europe," of the "diplomatic tension," hinting by degrees that a war was not impossible, that it was likely, that it was certain.

The quartermaster shrugged his shoulders, and like the fighter he was, gripped the hilt of his saber.

"Hum! War! War! Then mobilize—and there you are!"

"Everyone is talking of it here, Quartermaster."

In fact in Lunéville, a town so near the frontier, so French, and with such hatred of Germany, war was the only topic of conversation.

Will war really be declared?

Javot, who was curious, but lacked in ideas, remarked:

"Things are stirring, but we won't get war tonight."

At this moment the men had their attention drawn to an old white-haired priest who had stopped at the gate, apparently hesitating to enter.

Javot rose leisurely, stretched himself, yawning, then buttoning his dolman, asked:

"Say, d'you think the chap in the cassock means to join us since he's inspecting the barracks?"

A hearty laugh greeted this sally.

"Doesn't look as if he'd make much of a cavalryman."

And in truth the priest scarcely suggested the type of a warrior.

He appeared to be well over sixty and wore a huge pair of spectacles awry on his nose. He leaned on a thick stick which served practically as a crutch.

Timid and hesitating, he went forward and backward, much to the amusement of the men.

The quartermaster, dragging his saber and clinking his spurs, advanced.

"He's dying to ask questions, but he doesn't dare. Have to help him."

Stepping down, he addressed him:

"Pardon, sir, but do you want anything?"

The priest immediately became alarmed. He bowed, hat in hand and stammered:

"Yes—no—that is—Colonel Bayen?"

"And what do you want with the colonel, sir?"

"I want to speak to him—I mean, I want him to know that I am at his service—or rather—"

What the devil could this priest want with the "father" of the regiment? "He'll get a quick right-about-face," thought the quartermaster. Then smilingly:

"Well, sir, it's very easy to see the colonel."

And turning to the sentry, he ordered:

"Call the adjutant on duty."

The order was carried forward and finally reached the officer, who was cursing in the canteen.

"Well, what is it?"

The quartermaster announced:

"It's about the priest here who wants to see the colonel. Shall I send an orderly?"

"Oh, give me a rest. I've other fish to fry. Pass along the priest. The colonel will see him if he wants to."

The adjutant turned on his heels and moved off with his customary cursing.

"What an outfit! Lot of loafers! I'll give them a spell of the cooler!"

He could not have said whom he was threatening. His anger was vain, perpetual, and without effect.

Now, while Javot conducted the priest to Colonel Bayen's quarters, that officer was pacing up and down in his study, his hands behind his back, and plunged in deep thought.

Colonel Bayen?

Those who formerly had met the young military attaché in Berlin would probably not recognize him now—the passing years and possible troubles had so aged him. His eyes alone had remained as they used to be, energetic and strong-willed. His gray hair and mustache, tanned face, and quick movements were typical of the highest class of officer.

He was no longer a drawing room officer. Upon his breast he wore the Legion of Honor, a distinction gained at the point of the sword.

Colonel Bayen had fought in the colonies and his bravery had advanced him while still a young man to the grade of colonel. His career had been full of excitement.

The 32nd dragoons were doubtless ignorant of his history, but his fellow officers sometimes spoke of it.

It was known that Colonel Bayen had suddenly resigned his post of embassy attaché, giving up a sure career upon the death of his young wife.

It was known that her death had occasioned him such despair that for a time it was feared he might lose his mind.

Then, suddenly, it was noticed that the officer had pulled himself together again.

He went to Algeria and won his advancement by the courage with which he punished the rebel tribes.

It was only six months ago that Captain Bayen, receiving the grade of colonel, had returned to France.

By what mysterious influence, by what recommendation to the ministry had he obtained command of the 32nd dragoons at Lunéville? Nobody knew. But certain traits of his character were better known. Strict as to military matters, he lived alone, traveled seldom and passed his time either on horseback or in his study.

Colonel Bayen abruptly stopped his anxious pacing as Javot knocked at the door.

"Come in," he cried.

The orderly opened the door and stood at attention.

"Colonel, there's a priest here—he says you are expecting him—or that he wants to see you."

Certainly Colonel Bayen had made no appointment with a priest. He seemed surprised:

"Where is he?"

"In the salon, Colonel."

"In the salon?"

A vague smile fluttered over the officer's face.

Next door to his study, a small room, narrow and dirty, encumbered with papers, was considered by his cavalrymen as the "salon."

The name was traditional and had been handed down from class to class until nobody dared to correct the pretension.

Colonel Bayen thought for a moment.

"I've something else to do than receive visits…"

He was about to refuse when suddenly he changed his mind.

"All right, send him in."

"May as well get it over," he thought. "I suppose this priest has come to recommend some young soldier. I'd better see him today—for tomorrow…"

Evidently tomorrow's events would preclude the reception of any visitor.

A moment later, the priest made his humble apparition in Colonel Bayen's study. He made a deep bow and then waited to be addressed by the officer.

Colonel Bayen, not understanding his attitude, spoke:

"Well, abbé, I am listening."

Then the priest came to a decision and conquered his timidity sufficiently to burst out volubly:

"You see I am punctual, Colonel: After receiving the visit you know about, I did not delay an instant. Alas! in these days with rumors of war in the air, one must not put off until tomorrow what one can do today. And since you have been touched by divine grace and have done me the signal honor, I who am a humble priest—"

Colonel Bayen, who had been seated at his desk, rose abruptly, interrupting the priest.

"Excuse me, abbé, but I haven't the least idea what you are talking about… Touched by divine grace? The visit you received? What the devil do you mean?"

If the colonel seemed surprised, the abbé appeared more so.

Then a quick smile spread over his face.

"Oh, pardon, you are right. I have forgotten to introduce myself. I am Abbé Jandron, second curate of the church of Saint Jacques."

"Abbé Jandron, second curate of the church of Saint Jacques?"

Mechanically and in an amazed tone, the colonel repeated the words, which didn't convey any meaning to him. Slightly impatient, he questioned:

"Forgive me, abbé, but I'm rather in a hurry. Kindly explain the object of your visit."

"But, Colonel, you know quite well why I am here since you sent for me yourself."

"I sent for you?"

"Why, certainly."

"When? How? Why?"

The priest, seeing the officer's amazement, had a sudden thought.

"I'm afraid that in my absentmindedness I have made another mistake. You are not Colonel Bayen?"

"Pardon, I am Colonel Bayen."

"Then, it is my turn to be at a loss."

And while the colonel, now amused at the evident discomfiture of his visitor, questioned him by a look, the priest continued:

"Colonel, I am very distressed at what has happened! I am, doubtless, the victim of a stupid joke—one in very bad taste. I see now you did not send for me."

"No, abbé, once more, no."

Colonel Bayen, becoming serious, questioned:

"Please explain. How did you come here?"

The priest, no longer timid, replied:

"In two words, this is what happened: An hour ago I was in my garden. I was reading my breviary when my servant came to announce that a woman, to be exact, a lady, wished to see me. Naturally, I acceded to her request, thinking she was some penitent…"

"And that was not the case?"

"No, Colonel. I found myself in the presence of a most distinguished and amiable person, who said: 'Abbé, I am sent by Colonel Bayen, commandant of the 32nd regiment of dragoons, in barracks in the town. The colonel has been suddenly touched by divine grace. On the eve of a possible war and probable death, he wishes to speak with a minister of God so that his conscience may be at rest and in peace.' And that is all that brought me here, Colonel."

The priest was silent for a moment, then continued:

"If you did not send this person to me, you see that I am the victim of a joke—and that I can only apologize for having disturbed you."

"One moment, abbé!"

Colonel Bayen had grown pale and his voice betrayed his nervousness.

"What did this person look like?"

The priest made a vague gesture.

"Alas, Colonel, I scarcely saw her—she wore a very thick veil. Still, I do remember she had regular features, very white hair and a simple but elegant costume."

The good abbé was able to add no further details, and doubtless he had never before spoken at such length of a woman, nor of what he called in the catechism, external signs of beauty.

Colonel Bayen, frowning, had appeared to listen eagerly to the priest's words.

"This woman is unknown to you?"

"Absolutely, Colonel."

"She is not a member of your parish?"

"I have never seen her."

"There can have been no mistake?"

"No, especially as she herself gave me directions for coming here."

The priest, with some curiosity, asked:

"Do you know who it could be? Among your friends is there one who might be interested in your soul's salvation?"

Already the habits of the confessor were regaining their importance in his spirit.

"Perhaps one of your relatives may have been planning an interview with me through pure christian zeal? Have you not really decided to study our holy religion? Don't you think that in view of a possible war—"

The priest stopped suddenly.

Leaving his chair, and seemingly oblivious of the ecclesiastic,

Colonel Bayen, very pale, began pacing, feverishly up and down his study.

The abbé distinctly heard him murmur.

"It's a warning—it's a warning—certain—"

"A warning from heaven," declared the good priest. "In the noble profession of arms, it is well to make peace with God before the battle. Tureune, Condé, Bayard—"

His eloquence was again interrupted.

"Abbé, one question. Did this woman actually speak of 'probable death'? Do you recall the words?"

The priest seemed to make a great effort of memory.

"No," he declared at last. "I could not guarantee the words but I very well remember this: She said, 'If war breaks out, Colonel Bayen may be killed, he must be converted, he must win to heaven.'"

Colonel Bayen did not reply. He continued his walk, growling and apparently furious:

"It's queer—it's more than queer!"

Before his anger, the unhappy curate became still more alarmed. He bowed and bowed:

"Pray believe that I am so sorry—this stupid joke—in such bad taste."

"It is not a joke, abbé."

Colonel Bayen spoke in a low voice and then appeared to regret his words. He quickly continued:

"Please don't apologize, abbé; it's of no importance whatever. I will have you escorted to the door."

It was a dismissal. The priest did not insist further. Following Javot and bowing to all the officers he passed, the abbé left the barracks.

In the meantime Colonel Bayen, alone in his study, livid, his arms folded, his head bent, reflected:

"Who?" he asked himself. "Who is the woman? And above all, who sent her? Why? For what end? Is it known, by any chance—"

He did not finish the thought.

Suddenly he shrugged his shoulders.

"All right," he murmured. "But I must decide—decide without losing a second. It is urgent—it may be even now too late."

2. A Tragic Appeal

In excessively bad humor and clanking his saber on the stairs, Louis Monet, lieutenant of the 2nd squadron of the 32nd regiment of dragoons, returned at ten o'clock at night to his very modest apartment. Louis Monet was returning from leave and was decidedly angry. While he climbed to his rooms he grumbled to himself.

"Fine business! I'll bet I'll get a brick on my head next! What the devil! When one is on furlough one is on furlough! What does this telegram mean? Why recall me posthaste? What has happened?"

Louis Monet reached his door and groped for the keyhole, cursing the while. At length he found it and entered the hall shouting:

"Hello, La Flemme! La Flemme!"

He had a good resonant voice which rang through the apartment without getting any reply.

"La Flemme! Come here or I'll give you a taste of the cooler."

And then he suddenly quieted down.

"The beggar isn't here!"

He lit a match, glanced round the room which served for sitting room and study, then went into his bedroom. He had made the round of his apartment.

"Nobody," he grumbled, "Not a soul. La Flemme is on a spree!"

He threw his saber on a sofa, then lighting his lamp, which began to smoke abominably, he broke out again:

"Good Lord! It's poisoning me. And my orderly off without leave! I'll give him four days!"

To hear him one would suppose that Louis Monet had a disagreeable character and that he was in the habit of punishing his unfortunate orderly.

Nothing was further from the truth. If he took it out of his servant, well named La Flemme, it was simply because he had to find an object for his anger. But that anger was harmless as La Flemme himself knew very well.

The officer now lit a cigarette and calmed down immediately.

"The whole thing is absurd," he murmured.

"What can the colonel want with me? Why this urgent recall?"

And for the twentieth time at least, Louis Monet reread the telegram which had been given to him some hours previously at Épinal where he had expected to get a good dinner at an old aunt's house, having a week's leave of absence. Louis Monet seemed very young. Entering Saint-Cyr with honors, he had gone from there to Saumur. He then joined the 32nd dragoons as second lieutenant and had had the luck to advance rapidly to the grade of lieutenant. He had now been a scant three months in garrison at Lunéville. His furlough, so unfortunately interrupted, was the first he had obtained since his nomination to the corps.

A charming man and a good sport. That was his reputation among his men. He did not seem greatly surprised at the absence of his orderly.

"After all, the beggar couldn't guess that I would return so unexpectedly."

And lighting another cigarette, he opened the window and leaned out.

The streets ere already deserted. The life of the small town had sunk into silence and the night. Louis Monet gave a sigh.

"Not much like the boulevards! And if it were not for her!"

At this moment his expression suddenly changed. The lieutenant became grave, serious. A shadow of melancholy seemed to veil his eyes. His imagination evoked an exquisite picture, intoxicating—a picture, the mere thought of which made his heart beat.

"For her," he repeated. "Yes, it's just for her that I came here."

A sigh escaped him.

He recalled his efforts at the ministry to effect the change from Paris to the less agreeable Lunéville.

Ah! the real joy, the gentle emotion he had felt in establishing himself in the place where she lived!

He spoke her name tenderly, a name which fitted the willful grace of her youth, the elegance of her person, the piquant seduction of her figure: Colette.

It was for Colette, whom he loved above all others, that the rich and young lieutenant came to vegetate in this hole.

And what wonderful luck it was had drawn him to this sincere and pure love that now occupied his whole heart. Colette... She was everything to him, and six months ago he did not even know her. Chance selected him to be sent to the obscure village where she lived, on a cartographic appointment. Her father, M. Ravignon, a prosperous gentleman farmer and important personage, happened to be mayor of Cirey, and it was thus he made her acquaintance. And since then, how quickly things had moved! How thrilled he was the first time he realized that Colette did not view him with indifference.

And how much greater the thrill when he would again meet her, she whom he called his "fiancée."

And yet Louis Monet sighed.

To meet her—that would not be easy.

Since his arrival in Lunéville, the lieutenant had not been able to get an hour's talk with Colette.

Naturally he had called upon the mayor of Cirey. He had also had the pleasure of bowing to Colette, who became very white on learning that he was now an officer of the 32nd dragoons. Still, Louis Monet could not help noticing the chilly reception given him by Colette's parents. He had been received; he had not been asked to call again.

He had been treated as a friend, but amazement was shown that he should have been transferred to Lunéville.

"Certainly old Ravignon doesn't look favorably on me," he muttered.

This unpleasant fact depressed him for a moment and then he shrugged his shoulders:

"After all, to the devil with him. Colette loves me. We will overcome his objections. Why should he refuse his consent? I'm richer than his daughter, I have a future, and if war should break out... War! Good Lord! These politicians are a nuisance allowing things to drag along. If Germany wants a beating, let her have it and be done with it."

Once more his expression changed.

Without doubt Louis Monet loved his profession. He loved it for its nobility and its unselfishness. He loved it because to be a soldier is not to belong to oneself; it is to be a man with a single love, the greatest of all loves—love of country.

Ah! let the signal be given, let war be declared and he will be ready!

Woe to the enemy, woe to Germany! It would be a holy mission to drive those robbers of '70 beyond the frontiers of Alsace and Lorraine.

"But war is not coming, alas!" he added.

The papers bought at the station gave reassuring news.

England was making every effort to force Germany to a peaceful attitude. Austria no longer refused to negotiate with Russia. St. Petersburg and Vienna appeared to be in accord.

"So it can't be on account of war that the colonel has recalled me. It was a private telegram I received, not an official one."

And annoyed, worried at this unexpected return, Louis Monet declared:

"I've nothing on my conscience either, no scrape, no row, what the deuce can they want with me?"

He turned his head and glanced into the shadows of the street.

At the extreme end, the cavalry barracks stretched away with geometrical precision, the buildings all alike, stables, storehouses, guardhouse.

"It looks peaceful and calm," he admitted.

"If there was anything in the wind, inspection or preparations for mobilization, I'd see some signs of life."

He threw away his cigarette half smoked, crossed the room to choose some book to while away an hour on his sofa.

Suddenly he listened.

The door of his apartment slammed and a voice frightfully off the key began to sing:

> *Allons chasseurs, vite en selles,*
> *Formez vos escadrons*
> *Dites adieu à vos belles*
>   *Car demain nons partons*
> *Tontaine, ton ton, Tontaine—Ton ton!*

Louis Monet immediately shouted:

"La Flemme!"

A hulking big dragoon, helmet on one side, saber under his arm, and an enormous pipe in his mouth, appeared in the doorway.

"Hello!" he cried.

Furious, Louis Monet shouted:

"Where the devil do you come from? What right have you to be away without leave? You'll get a week for this."

La Flemme smoked his pipe calmly.

"Lieutenant, where have you sprung from? Why are you here?"

Louis Monet could not help smiling. "Attention! and stop smoking."

"Can't, Lieutenant, can't let Josephine get cool or she won't draw."

La Flemme seemed in no wise disturbed by the lieutenant's anger. He had an excellent reason, too, for his calmness.

He had been Monet's orderly for five years and the friendship he felt for the officer had been amply returned.

If La Flemme took advantage of it occasionally to be slack in his duties, Monet's threats of dire punishment never amounted to anything in the end.

Imperturbable, as usual, he continued to smoke his pipe, continuing his questions.

"Why the devil are you here, Lieutenant?"

"No use staring at me like that," replied the officer. "I was on furlough and I have returned."

"I know that," calmly answered La Flemme.

"You know it? Who told you?"

"Why, the colonel."

"The colonel!—How's that?"

La Flemme rubbed his eyes.

"It's quite simple, Lieutenant. The colonel said to me just now, 'La Flemme, you are Lieutenant Monet's orderly?' 'Yes,' says I. 'Then go to the station and watch out for his return from Épinal. When he gets in send him direct to me, however late it may be. I shan't go to bed till I've seen him.'"

Louis Monet seemed astounded.

That such an order should be given to La Flemme must mean the matter was serious.

But what could be the motive for recalling him and for Colonel Bayen's anxiety to see him?

La Flemme was about to make suggestions but the officer stopped him abruptly.

"Shut up, idiot. Give me my saber and come with me to the colonel."

A moment later, Louis Monet, followed at a respectful distance by La Flemme who grumbled at being kept out of bed, walked down the street to the colonel's quarters.

The sentry on duty saluted.

"Announce me," ordered Monet.

As he entered the room his anxiety increased.

The study, usually in perfect order, seemed topsy-turvy. Drawers were open showing piles of documents. In the fireplace bundles of paper were burning. But what most struck Louis Monet was the attitude of Colonel Bayen.

He was extremely pale. Standing in front of the fire, he stirred the burning papers. Upon seeing Monet he murmured:

"At last."

"Colonel, I beg you to excuse me. I might have been here several minutes earlier if my orderly had caught me at the station."

"It's of no importance, Lieutenant. I suppose you wonder why I sent for you?"

"I am at your orders, Colonel."

"I will enlighten you. Just a moment."

The colonel opened the door.

"Sentry, send here the officer on duty."

The call rang out on the bugle.

"One moment," repeated Colonel Bayen. "I'll be with you in an instant. Above all, not a word of this before the adjutant."

Louis Monet became still more bewildered.

He felt some mystery in the air.

The adjutant appeared in haste.

"You sent for me, Colonel?"

"Yes, to give you an order. Take ten men, and harness the five baggage wagons that are in the courtyard. Get horses from B Stable. The guard has been notified."

The colonel turned away his face as though he did not wish to see the adjutant's surprise.

"When the wagons are harnessed, gallop them round the courtyard. It is a test I want to make. I shall come down in a quarter of an hour. Go."

Too well trained to venture a remark, the adjutant moved off.

But Louis Monet was on the point of asking himself if the colonel had taken leave of his senses.

To harness the wagons at such an hour! To drive them at full gallop round the courtyard! It was incomprehensible, it was disturbing.

Colonel Bayen turned to him:

"A moment more and I will explain everything."

A profound silence reigned in the study.

While Monet waited patiently, the colonel opened the windows wide; he then stamped down the cinders of the burnt paper.

Several minutes passed. Then abruptly a noise was heard. The wagons rumbled over the courtyard with a loud rattle and the clanging of horses' hoofs.

The colonel beckoned Monet to the windows.

"Forgive me for keeping you waiting, Lieutenant. I warrant you have no idea of what is going on?"

"No, Colonel."

"You cannot guess why I brought out the wagons?"

"No, Colonel."

"And you think my actions rather strange? Well, what I have to say to you is so serious that I had to take precautions."

The colonel paused a moment, leaned out and examined the progress of the wagons.

"Lieutenant, those wagons make a great deal of noise. Do you know the advantage of that noise?"

Louis Monet was so amazed that he did not answer.

The colonel continued:

"This noise will guarantee the privacy of our interview. One might listen at the door, Lieutenant, there might be a dictograph nearby, the very walls may have ears, but in this racket I defy any but you to hear what I have to say. You understand?"

"Colonel, I am most anxious to hear what you have to confide to me. Have you a complaint to make of me?"

"No, Lieutenant."

"An order?"

"No, it is not an order."

"What is it then, Colonel?"

The colonel seemed to hesitate. For a moment he remained silent while his face contracted under some terrible emotion."

"It is an appeal I have to make," Colonel Bayen declared at last.

Louis Monet felt the ground slipping away; he became dizzy.

"An appeal, Colonel? What appeal?"

Colonel Bayen drew near him and placed both hands on his shoulders. He looked at Monet with the eyes of a leader of men.

"Lieutenant, you are 26, you are young, you are rich, the future opens brightly before you. Well, you must give it all up. You must die, Lieutenant—die shamefully, perhaps. In any case, without glory. You must die because death is a duty—your duty—"

Colonel Bayen pointed to the flag of the regiment under its glass case, and the flag itself seemed to live and glow under the words:

"Lieutenant, in the name of France, I appeal to you to consent to die."

3. In Danger of Death

Completely staggered by the unexpected declaration of Colonel Bayen, Louis Monet
could scarcely refrain from a gesture of alarm. To die! Die for France—certainly that is what he had decided a long while ago.

The young officer had often dreamed of the glorious death of a soldier.

But the half-told confidences of the colonel had already convinced him that it was a question of something else.

A death "perhaps shameful" was what the chief had said.

And this death was unquestionably a mysterious one.

There was mystery in the way the colonel broached the subject.

"Listen to me, Lieutenant, and upon your honor, do not give a hasty reply. I repeat—what I have to say is more than serious, more than terrible? You will have to bind yourself and you must not do so lightly."

Louis Monet grew slightly pale.

He stood staring at Colonel Bayen, literally drinking in his words.

The colonel drew his attention to the extraordinary method he had used to assure the "privacy of the interview."

"Above all, Lieutenant, I desire to call your attention to this of which you must be thoroughly persuaded—nobody can know what I am saying to you, nobody by any chance can overhear my words. You agree with me?"

Louis Monet nodded.

It was, in fact, materially impossible to make out what the colonel was saying. The wagons made such a racket in the courtyard that Monet himself had to stand by his ear to catch the words. Furthermore, nobody could be hidden near the two officers who were leaning on the window sill.

The study was empty, that was sure.

"Colonel, I beg you to finish."

"Not yet, Lieutenant. I have another thing to call to your attention. I have appealed to you, Lieutenant, because you are the richest and most popular of all my young officers, also because I know you are a bachelor. But I need some further information."

The colonel's voice trembled a little.

"Is there any woman in your life?"

"No, Colonel."

Louis Monet had answered instinctively. He added:

"That is to say, I have no mistress."

His hesitation did not escape the colonel, who insisted:

"You love nobody?"

"Yes, Colonel, I have a fiancée."

The colonel's face clouded over.

"A fiancée? Truly a fiancée? Will you swear it? A young girl worthy of every respect?"

"Of every respect, Colonel."

"Well, you must cast that love out of your heart."

Louis Monet folded his arms.

"That is impossible."

"Monsieur, I ask you in the name of France!"

"Colonel, my country does not require, cannot require such a sacrifice! I am ready to die, I am not ready to cease loving the woman I love!"

The young lieutenant spoke with such feeling that Colonel Bayen realized that it was not a question of some passing affair, easy to terminate.

"Very well," he said, at length. "I see you love truly. In that case I can speak all the same. I have a mission to give you, Lieutenant—a serious mission, upon which may depend the fate of the war."

"Then you think we shall have war, Colonel?"

"War is not probable, Lieutenant—it is certain!"

"Certain, Colonel?"

"Yes, Lieutenant. And it will be a horrible war."

The colonel's voice again trembled, but he controlled his emotion.

"Lieutenant, you know very little of me and I have not much to tell you. However, this much you must know: Twenty years ago, when I was attaché at the Berlin embassy, I was the victim of a horrible tragedy. The man you see before you now is a man vowed to vengeance and devotion—"

Louis Monet, who did not understand, bowed.

"Lieutenant, chance, or rather circumstances, put me in possession of a terrible secret, a secret which is able to secure to France a victory over Germany. For twenty years I have devoted myself to this. For twenty years I have performed a prodigy. I have kept alive—I have not been murdered—so that when the hour strikes, I might save my country and my vengeance."

The colonel opened his dolman and took out a yellow envelope which he gave to Louis Monet.

"Take this, hide it and listen to me."

The officer thought for a moment, then continued his strange instructions.

"Lieutenant, I said that for twenty years I have run a daily risk of assassination. From the moment this document is in your pocket, you yourself are in danger. You will not have a moment's peace of mind, a moment's confidence or rest. Every means to kill you may be used. An accident one would not dream of prepared by others; a duel, during which a cutthroat will deliver a mortal blow by treachery; poison you could not guard against; your revolver may explode in your hand; you pass by a scaffolding and a mason drops an implement on your head; in crossing a river, the ferryman will capsize his boat. Lieutenant, you will be alone against everybody. If you should be suspected of possessing this document, you will have against you a hundred thousand German spies!"

Louis Monet was deeply impressed by the colonel's words.

Although he had never been actively concerned with espionage, he knew the terrible German organization by hearsay and from having read a critical study of it.

And will he now be tracked by these scoundrels in the pay of William II?

"Colonel," he replied in a voice he tried to make firm, "it little matters what dangers I run in the service of my country. This document will be delivered to whom you designate."

"That is not your mission, Lieutenant."

"What is it then?"

"It is threefold, Lieutenant."

The colonel spoke with difficulty. He weighed each of his words with anxiety, fearful of saying too much and not saying enough.

"Lieutenant, these are your orders—pardon, what I beg you to do: In the first place you will hide this document in a place only known to yourself, confide it to somebody who cannot be suspected. Put it where you can recover it if misfortune should overtake you. Do you understand?"

"Yes, Colonel, but—"

"Pardon… Then, upon official mobilization, you will go to the strategic bridge of Vezouse. You will walk up and down, keeping the closest lookout. If anyone suspicious appears, do not hesitate, fire, kill him."

"But, Colonel—"

"Wait! Finally, when the bridge guard has been reinforced by the territorials which will be sent without delay, you will return here to quarters—and if I should be dead—"

"Ah, Colonel!"

"If I should be dead, I repeat, you will get possession of the document, you will open it and follow the instructions which it contains."

Louis Monet was going through an agony of mind, his lips refused to emit a sound. How strange, were the colonel's instructions.

"Ah, I forgot one thing, Lieutenant. After my death you had better call upon the second curate of the church of Saint Jacques. Here is a note in which I ask him to explain to you in detail the visit he made me."

This time Louis Monet could not restrain a cry of amazement.

"But, Colonel, why speak in this way of your death? Are you in danger?"

Colonel Bayen shrugged his shoulders.

"I run the risk of every man who holds a state secret. I run the risk which you are going to run, Lieutenant—that of being murdered, and at the very time when I least expect it."

He gave a strange laugh and continued:

"Ah, pardon, Lieutenant, as a matter of fact I exaggerate. I shall not be killed without warning. They have had the irony to do that—they sent a confessor to me."

The laugh faded from the colonel's face. His affected gaiety dropped.

"I owe you further explanations, Lieutenant. I told you I singled you out because you are rich. But riches are not a proof of honesty! But I had to take into consideration that Germany would be willing to pay millions for the paper you have in your pocket. I may add that if I give it to you instead of sending it to the ministry, it is because it is too late now to communicate with the ministry."

"Too late, Colonel?"

"Yes, Monsieur, too late."

On seeing the lieutenant's surprise, Colonel Bayen explained further:

"A messenger would not reach his destination—he would be killed on the way. If I should attempt the journey I would fall before I reached the station. As for letters, it is evident that they are read in the 'private office'—not one escapes observation."

"But it is impossible, Colonel—German espionage is powerfully organized, but—"

"German espionage dares everything and can accomplish everything! And as for this particular document, they would stop at nothing, believe me."

Louis Monet grew paler. He felt dizzy and could scarcely take in what he heard.

Colonel Bayen insisted:

"You are in danger of death, Lieutenant, in terrible danger. And yet I have done everything possible to prevent eavesdropping, so that not a soul may suspect what has passed between us. You are a witness that no one has overheard our talk?"

Monet glanced round the room and then out of the window to the courtyard where the wagons were still clattering.

"Yes, Colonel, no one can possibly have heard what we are saying."

"Consequently any indiscretion committed must come from you."

"Colonel, you may be sure—"

"I know, Lieutenant."

He reassured the young officer by a look.

He had thoroughly investigated the patriotism of Louis Monet.

And he was not mistaken.

Louis Monet now felt the fever of war—that war announced by Colonel Bayen, inevitable and certain. Instinctively the young man straightened up, throwing out his chest and raising his head.

He was in danger of death.

He had everything to fear—the unforeseen accident, the treachery of murder, hidden ambush, a quarrel designed to lead to a duel.

He must fear everything and sacrifice everything to the mission he had been given.

Very well, so be it. He accepted the struggle.

Perhaps his life would he the price of success, but life mattered little in such an affair.

Louis Monet bowed to his chief.

"Colonel, a thousand thanks for the confidence you have shown in me."

Simply, Colonel Bayen wrung his hand.

"Good luck, Lieutenant. If—we should not meet again you may know that I died like a brave man, a victim to my duty."

Louis Monet was choked with emotion. He wished to speak but could not utter a word.

He was about to go when the colonel called him back:

"An instant, Lieutenant. In such a case it is not enough to be brave—you must also he clever, which is harder for a soldier. Be sure that it will be known that I sent for you in haste and that I saw you tonight. We must therefore have a pretext to throw them off the scent. This pretext I have already spread in the town."

"What is it, Colonel?"

"I have simply spread the report that you have been gaming a bit too hard and this interview is to reprimand you for your losses at the card table."

The lieutenant smiled at this likely excuse, which was also so untrue, as he rarely played.

After a moment's reflection, he said:

"Then I'd better drop in to the club now?"

"Certainly, Lieutenant."

The colonel held out his hand.

"There is nothing more to be said, and in fact, in future we had better avoid each other except during hours of service. Goodbye,

Lieutenant, and good luck. Either you or I will not go through it alive, I made my sacrifice a long time ago. I hope you will be the one to triumph."

Without a word, too upset to reply, Louis Monet started to go.

The colonel recalled him once more:

"That I may have no regrets or scruples let me be sure I have given you thorough warning. From this minute you must beware of everything. You no longer have the right to be yourself. You belong to your mission—you belong to the country! And that the country may be victorious, you must think ceaselessly: 'Death is stalking me!' Go, Lieutenant."

Louis Monet left the room.

4. Facing Contempt

Louis Monet had scarcely closed the door of the study, when he seemed to awake from some nightmare and began to doubt the reality of things.

Had he properly understood the words of his chief?

Had not the colonel exaggerated the seriousness of this mission he had been given?

"I am in danger of death," repeated the lieutenant.

But the defining of this certainty caused him a feeling almost joyful.

Fear? Anxiety? These he did not experience. He simply felt that pleasant fever which animates soldiers when the hour of battle arrives.

But while he crossed the courtyard, fresh doubts took possession of him.

He had not forgotten one of his instructions. He knew that his first duty was to hide the precious document confided to him.

"I must hide it where nobody will think of searching, but where it can be found if anything happens to me."

While he pondered this problem, another thought came into his mind.

Colette!

He did not fear for himself, but he feared for her. Must he give up his love?

The young lieutenant, as in a dream, saw the sweet face of her he loved so tenderly.

He recalled the tender meeting which led to what he considered their engagement.

Colette! At first he only knew her beauty, her slender figure and fair hair, which had intoxicated him from the moment he met her. Then once during a walk he had a chance to speak alone with her. He felt her thrill to him. And finally, shortly before he went away, he burst out with his love and tenderness.

To die would be nothing. But to give up Colette!

It seemed to Louis Monet that his heart would break with pain.

He was in danger of death!

And a deep anger rose in him against the father of the young girl, against Ravignon, a thick-headed and obstinate peasant who declined an officer for a son-in-law.

How could he manage to see Colette?

Ah, it would take more than a trifle to stop him.

He recalled a charming and mad arrangement they had conceived during their last walk together.

Colette had picked a bouquet of flowers and had given him half of it.

"Here, take it, and if ever you have need to see me, if anything serious should happen in your life, you have only to send me one of these flowers and I shall understand—and that very evening I shall be at the spot we are now…"

Louis Monet had smiled at this romantic tryst proposed by Colette. He never expected to have the need of meeting the young girl alone at midnight.

He had smiled then. Now he was deeply stirred.

What a strange coincidence that Colette should have almost divined the tragic turn his life had taken.

He reached the gate of the cavalry barracks.

He felt now as though he were leaving the last place of safety and that once outside, he would be exposed to the most dangerous risks of war.

He knocked with his saber upon the guardroom door.

"La Flemme!"

"Lieutenant?"

"Forward, march!"

La Flemme rubbed his eyes, muttered, "They won't let you sleep in peace," and approached the officer.

"What is it?"

"Come and I'll tell you."

Louis Monet drew his orderly rapidly away from the barracks.

The young man had recovered his self-possession.

He had calmed his nerves, overexcited a moment before. He spoke, smiling and joking, in his usual manner.

"La Flemme, open your ears and try to understand me. You are a brute."

"Yes, Lieutenant."

"You always try to do the least possible."

"Yes, Lieutenant."

"But at bottom you're a pretty decent sort. That's why I'm going to ask you a favor."

"Go ahead, Lieutenant."

"It's rather a nasty job."

"Hell! No job's nasty if it's for you."

He spoke simply but with sincerity.

The lieutenant did not wish the matter to seem important.

From his pocketbook he took a dried flower and slipped it into an envelope.

"La Flemme, I'm going to give you a commission if you will swear to forget it after you have done it."

"All right, I swear, Lieutenant."

"Hold on—it's pretty hard to fulfill and has to be handled carefully."

A broad smile spread over La Flemme's face.

"I'll bet there's a woman in it."

"You're right, La Flemme."

"You have a dame then, Lieutenant?"

Louis Monet could not help smiling.

"La Flemme, try to understand me—and keep your opinions to yourself. I haven't a 'dame,' as you say. It concerns my fiancée."

"Your fiancée? Are you going to be married?"

"Possibly—in any case, the matter is a serious one."

"Yes, Lieutenant."

"And you mustn't make any break."

"Lieutenant, I know how to handle love affairs."

"In that case, this is what you have to do: Tomorrow morning at daybreak you will saddle your horse and you will go to Cirey. There, without being seen, you must manage to give this dried flower to Mlle. Ravignon."

"To Mlle. Ravignon?"

La Flemme laughed as though pleased.

"Well, Lieutenant, I congratulate you. She's devilish pretty and not in the least stuck up—only, there's the old man."

"La Flemme!"

"The old man who'll be your father-in-law. Say, let me tell you something, Lieutenant. I can't stomach him. To begin with he don't take to you—the proof being that just now at the station—"

Louis Monet paled.

"Shut up, La Flemme! Take care!"

An automobile came down the street.

La Flemme gave one glance at it and began to laugh.

"Why, there it goes. It's M'sieur Ravignon's car. I told you I'd seen him at the station."

Louis Monet had quickly turned into a side street, to avoid being passed by the auto.

"La Flemme, you met M. Ravignon? Did you speak to him?"

"Sure, I said, 'howdy do.'"

"And then?"

"Nothing. He hardly answered me. I guess he was after stamps for his collection."

La Flemme chuckled.

"At his age! To collect stamps! He must be cracked."

La Flemme began to laugh again, but Louis Monet quickly stopped him:

"So you quite understand? You are to take this flower to Mlle. Ravignon and then return here."

"I swear to, Lieutenant."

La Flemme offered his hand, then spat on the ground to make his oath the more binding.

"Naturally the old man, nor the mother mustn't get on to it. All right—don't worry—they won't. What! Are you stopping at the club, Lieutenant?"

Louis Monet had come to a halt outside a small clubhouse, with the pretentious name of "The Elegants' Club," frequented by offi-cers and rich young men of the town.

"Yes, I'll go up for five minutes. You are free for the rest of the night, only I count on you tomorrow morning at Cirey—and, above all, succeed at any cost."

Louis Monet could not explain to his orderly the reason for his abrupt decision. He felt satisfied that La Flemme would carry out his commission, that Colette would receive the dried flower, and that he would see her the following evening at midnight.

On entering the club he was met with a torrent of questions.

"What! You!"

"Must have been recalled in a hurry!"

"Any news of the war?"

Before him stood a young man of twenty-three or twenty-four, with folded arms.

"How about the wigging?"

Louis Monet burst out laughing.

He guessed without trouble why his entrance had made a sensation. Had he not announced his week's furlough?

And Paul de Tersy's remark about the wigging referred to the reprimand Colonel Bayen was supposed to give him.

"Here I am, gentlemen, ashamed but not repentant."

He purposely exaggerated his pretended anger:

"Pretty tough, don't you think? One hasn't the right to lose ten louis at baccarat now! Upon my soul Colonel Bayen must think he is in command of schoolboys, not of dragoons!"

His words were greeted with laughter.

"What did you answer?"

"I suppose you swore to give up cards?"

Louis Monet, in pursuance of his role, drew up a chair at one of the card tables.

"Gentlemen, I made no answer. But as I consider myself free to do as I please when off duty, here is my reply—I take the bank for twenty louis; who will play with me?"

"That's right, Monet—they can't scare you."

Paul de Tersy applauded loudly. He was an inveterate gambler. He did not live in Lunéville proper, but owned a chateau not far from Cirey. He appeared at the club regularly every evening. An orphan and rich, he played with a recklessness which would have earned him some notoriety in Paris but which exposed him to criticism in the small provincial town.

The table quickly filled with players and those who did not play stood around watching the game and offering criticisms.

"Colonel Bayen is an idiot. If he had called down de Tersy one could understand it, but Louis Monet rarely plays."

Now the luck seemed to be with Monet this evening; he won bet after bet until de Tersy finally rose.

"I've had enough. I've already dropped thirty louis. Whose turn next?"

"Seems to bring you luck to be hauled over the coals by the colonel."

A business man sat down and announced:

"I'll take the bank—twenty louis."

He had scarcely finished speaking when de Tersy, who had been examining the cards, gave a sharp cry.

"Ah!"

And as the other players were about to take their places, he added:

"One moment, gentlemen!"

"What is it? What's the matter?"

De Tersy did not reply at once—he continued to examine the cards, an extraordinary smile on his lips.

"It's very queer."

"What is queer?" answered Monet, drawing near. The young man pretended not to hear; he turned his back to the officer, remarking:

"Luck is a vain word, but some know how to help it. Then we call it cleverness—"

With a grim laugh, he tore the cards while the players watched him, amazed.

"What's the matter with you, de Tersy?"

"I have lost thirty louis with marked cards."

A hand touched his shoulder and swung him round.

"What do you mean?"

De Tersy answered calmly:

"What I mean is that I have lost thirty louis playing with marked cards."

Louis Monet pressed harder:

"Do you accuse me of cheating?"

"My dear fellow, you can take it as you will. If the cap fits, wear it. These gentlemen will understand."

He gathered the torn cards and showed unmistakable markings on them.

"What do you think of that?"

Had de Tersy seen Monet's eyes he would have been very much afraid.

The lieutenant had concentrated into his look all the fury that was in his heart.

There could be no mistake. He had taken the previous bank. It was he whom de Tersy accused of cheating.

A complete silence reigned in the room.

The club members stood around, unable to deny the evidence. The cards had been marked.

That, however, did not prove the guilt of Louis Monet.

"Well, gentlemen, what do you think of it?"

At this moment Monet suddenly remembered a fact he had forgotten under the insult.

Had he the right to retaliate?

Ought he to accept or provoke a duel?

With acute suffering, he recalled the last words of Colonel Bayen.

"You are in danger of death! Any pretext may be used to kill you, either by crime, accident, or a duel. You no longer belong to yourself, you belong to France—you belong to your mission."

Louis Monet made a supreme effort to avoid taking de Tersy by the throat.

"All this is childish," he replied at length. "I am above suspicion. My only mistake was to play with Monsieur de Tersy since he clings so hard to his money."

And while his words were received in chilly silence, Louis Monet left the room and the clubhouse.

Ah! how shocking it was, this appearance of cowardice!

And yet he had done right to leave.

He recognized this.

"Had I remained a second longer, I would have struck him. A duel would have followed."

A duel! Had he escaped one of the traps which Colonel Bayen had warned him against? In that case, de Tersy was a spy, a wretch in the pay of Germany.

Louis Monet stopped.

This conclusion made him shrug his shoulders. De Tersy a spy?

It wasn't possible! De Tersy lived at Cirey and was known to the Ravignons. Colette herself treated him as a friend, often played tennis with him…

This young man, rich and idle, could not follow the wretched trade he accused him of.

"No, the quarrel had not been prearranged. How could he have known that I was to be attacked? *Nobody could have heard what Colonel Bayen said to me!* Consequently…"

A neighboring clock struck midnight.

"I'm crazy. There's no sense in walking about this way. The first thing to do is to return home and place the document in a safe place."

Mechanically he felt his pocket. The document was still there. For a moment he feared it might have been stolen.

Again the shock of his apparent cowardice made him start, and he kept repeating to himself:

"That's not worth a moment's thought. France comes first, myself afterwards."

A fine motto the unhappy officer had chosen.

5. Colette

The cavalry barracks slept; it had not yet struck four in the morning and reveille was still distant when La Flemme appeared before the sentries.

Naturally he was questioned.

"Where do you come from? What do you want? Where's your permit?"

La Flemme, staggering slightly, did not propose to be bothered.

"Where do I come from? Can't tell you. Where I'm going—that's more important, and as to my permit, you'd have to have pretty big spectacles to see it."

He then passed along, throwing behind him:

"Detailed to the cartography."

That caused a laugh.

"Go on! You're as much detailed as I am," cried one man. "You wouldn't be so cocky if you weren't the lieutenant's orderly."

"Maybe so," replied La Flemme, calmly, "but then you see I am."

He moved off, clanking his spurs and whistling a military march.

La Flemme was not forgetting his commission, but with his natural modesty, he worried a little over the method of accomplishing it.

But his anxiety soon gave way to optimism.

"Bah! After all, I understand women. I'll talk very politely to her and everything will be all right."

La Flemme crossed the courtyard and entered the stables, hailing the guard.

The man quickly climbed out of a manger where he was taking a nap against the regulations, and, expecting a punishment, he stammered:

"Present, Lieutenant!"

La Flemme burst out laughing.

"That's all right. Only me."

A few moments later he was trotting down the highroad towards Cirey thinking how he might accomplish his mission.

"For after all," he thought, "it isn't enough to get there. I've got to see the lady to give her the flower—without being seen, too—without the father or mother suspecting. That's not so easy."

It seemed to him that his chances of seeing her alone were mighty small.

"Have to prepare a plan first," he growled.

He brought his horse to a walk and lit a cigarette. Very soon he rubbed his hands.

"I have it," he cried joyfully, and imitating an officer's voice, he ordered:

"Prepare to charge! Charge!"

The same day that La Flemme was galloping towards Cirey, M. Ravignon at ten o'clock in the evening was seated at home, drinking his coffee after a good dinner and preparing to spend a quiet evening.

He was a thickset individual, about fifty, with stubby hair and mustache, broad shoulders and rough peasant manner.

He was, besides, a man of importance in Cirey, who watched over the interests of the commune with the same thoroughness he displayed towards his own.

"Father Ravignon," as he was called by the village children, did not belong to Cirey. Fifteen years before he had made his appearance there as a simple workman, offering his services for the harvest. But this simple workman knew how to save.

Two years later he bought land. This was the beginning of his fortune, which grew constantly, by fortunate speculations in the corn market, by advantageous deals with army contractors, by a series of commercial operations in which he displayed a marvelous ability—and the knowledge of a lawyer.

Rich and honored, Ravignon was considered one of the most popular men in Cirey, even before his election as mayor, a piece of good luck that had crowned his life with success.

Of very simple tastes, he preferred to live in a reconstructed farmhouse rather than build a new dwelling, and this went by the name of "The Domain."

Still, he knew how to make himself comfortable. The bathroom he had installed was the talk of the place, as were the dresses of his daughter, the exquisite and pretty Colette.

Colette herself was considered as a living enigma.

Her extreme fairness, delicacy, and elegance had won for her the nickname of "The Parisian."

Mme. Brigitte Ravignon was also alien to the race of strong, heavily built country women.

For a number of years it was not known that Ravignon was married until one day he announced in the Café des Négociants:

"Well, I think I've saved up enough pennies to bring here my wife and daughter."

This produced a small-sized scandal.

People asked why he had hitherto concealed his marriage. But when Brigitte and Colette arrived, gossip finally ceased and the incident was forgotten.

It was known, or thought to be known, that Ravignon was the son of Breton peasants. He was supposed to have married, against his parents' wishes, a maid from an inn at Rennes. Occasionally it was whispered that perhaps Colette was not his daughter.

But Ravignon, powerful and rich, simply paid no attention to these calumnies.

Although a thorough miser and absorbed in his money, yet Ravignon had one real passion. He collected postage stamps with a craze amounting almost to madness.

He was at this moment occupied in placing in his album a precious example of a rare San Domingo issue. He glanced up, annoyed, as his study door opened.

"Is that you, Brigitte?"

"Yes, master."

Brigitte was a complete contrast to Ravignon, being slight and delicate in build, with white hair and a look of constant fear in her eyes.

"What do you want?"

"I'm worried about Colette's health."

Ravignon burst out, angrily, thumping the table with his heavy fist.

"Colette! She's a little fool—that's my opinion. And she'd feel as well as I do if she wouldn't waste her time in ridiculous mooning.

Besides, it's a bit your fault, Brigitte. The child needs good advice, but instead, you encourage her in her dreams. Ah! very intelligent of you, I must say."

Once started he did not stop.

"What's the matter now? Why hasn't de Tersy been here?"

"Master, I think they've had a quarrel, so M. de Tersy must have gone back to Lunéville."

And then she added hesitatingly.

"He must have met Lieutenant Monet at Lunéville."

"Lieutenant Monet! That worthless fellow! Because he's rich he imagines he has the right to idle his time away. For an officer in peacetime has nothing to do."

Brigitte ventured timidly:

"But M. de Tersy—"

"M. de Tersy owns land. He is noble and a friend of the farmer. His estate adjoins mine and when he marries my child the boundaries will be pulled down. Ah! 'The Domain' will then be worthy of its name—wide and broad."

Brigitte again protested:

"When M. de Tersy marries your daughter. But first Colette must be willing."

"She'll agree, that I warrant."

"Then she must cease loving Lieutenant Monet."

Ravignon thumped the table again.

"I don't want to hear any more about that loafer. And if he comes here again, I'll kick him out!"

Brigitte sighed, not daring to answer.

"Good night, master."

"Good night, good night."

Ravignon took up his magnifying glass and bent over his stamps. His conscience was at peace.

Brigitte went noiselessly towards her room.

The poor woman was strangely upset.

Tears came to her eyes.

"Poor child," she murmured.

As she passed Colette's door, a shaft of light shone beneath it.

Mme. Ravignon opened the door.

"You are not asleep, Colette?"

"No, mother. It's such a beautiful evening I am watching the stars."

"And thinking of the man you love," replied Mme. Ravignon tenderly.

"Yes—that's true."

"That soldier belonged to his regiment, didn't he?"

"Yes, mother, the 32nd dragoons."

"He didn't speak of him?"

"Oh, no, mother."

"And you didn't send any message?"

"I didn't dare to."

Mme. Ravignon smiled.

That afternoon, during Ravignon's absence an incident, or rather an accident, had happened to excite the inhabitants of the farm.

A cavalryman of the 32nd dragoons who was known to be the orderly of Louis Monet had fallen from his horse just in front of the house.

He struggled to his feet, apparently half stunned and uttering unintelligible words; finally he had begged Colette and Mme. Ravignon insistently:

"Something to drink, my good ladies."

He had been taken in and made to lie down and not long afterwards he was able to leave, apparently quite recovered.

"The soldier made me think of Louis Monet," sighed Mme. Ravignon, and she added as she kissed Colette good night:

"I don't blame you, dear, for being true to the man you love and I shall never blame you for having chosen him."

The good woman then went to bed, convinced that she knew all the secret thoughts of her daughter.

What would she have said had she seen Colette, left alone, take a dried flower from her breast and fondly kiss it?

6. Loyalty

At ten in the evening of the same day, Louis Monet had the impression of waking from a strange dream.

He had been wandering about for a long time, watchful, with nerves on edge, and now suddenly he became quiet and peaceful both in mind and in body.

"Ah, upon my word, I've been imagining nonsense for the past twenty-four hours. The colonel was exaggerating. Hang the danger—I'm going to see Colette! But will she keep the appointment? Will she understand? Remembering her promise? The urgent appeal that dried flower represents? And even if she has understood, can she escape from her home?"

Ah! he did not doubt her. He remembered too well the deep sincerity in her tones when she said:

"If ever you should be in danger or be passing through a hard time, if you should ever need my tenderness and love, don't hesitate. Send me one of these flowers and I will come to you."

The lieutenant reached one of the crossroads in the woods on his way to Cirey and stopped. He tethered his horse by the bridle and began his wait. And as the moments sped, he felt that tender happiness which the approach of the loved one inspires.

After two good hours, a footfall made him start.

"It is she."

And then a great fear struck him. Suppose she had been followed. Suppose he had enticed her into danger!

He hid behind a hedge, revolver in hand.

But his alarm was unnecessary.

It was Colette—Colette, alone and walking timidly glancing right and left into the shadows.

He sprang toward her and gave a great cry of love and gratitude.

"Colette! You? Oh, how good of you to come!"

He took her two hands, scarcely daring to touch her lips.

The young girl was trembling and on the verge of collapsing.

"If you only knew," she murmured. "If you only knew how afraid I have been—when your orderly pretending to be hurt, gave me your flower. You are not ill? You are not in danger?"

Louis Monet, who had hoped to give up to love these first moments so ardently longed for, and keep silent as to his motive for coming, betrayed himself.

Ah! It was not Colette alone he saw before him, it was not only his sweetheart that he clasped in his arms.

As he had done the evening before, he now experienced a strange hallucination.

Colette, his heart, his love, she was much more, she was France!

He realized in a flash what it is that binds a man so solidly to his country.

His country was the blessed land of the hearth. His country was there where Colette lived.

Tremblingly he replied:

"Colette, I begged you to come because I had to see you, because we swore to share our joys and our sorrows, to hold our hopes and dangers in common."

It would have been a surprising speech from the lips of the brave lieutenant of dragoons had another heard it, but Colette did not misunderstand his words.

She guessed that a mystery lay hidden in them—a serious and tragic mystery which sometimes passes like a tornado over the lives of the most peaceful.

"What is it?"

"I cannot tell you."

And as Colette betrayed a movement of surprise, at his apparent lack of confidence, he continued:

"Colette, I have sworn on my honor to keep silent."

Colette realized that she had not the right to insist further.

Timidly, she asked:

"And war? Shall we have war?"

"Yes," he replied simply.

"Soon?"

"Very soon."

"And you will be among the first to go?"

"Without doubt—if I am still living."

"If you are still living? What do you mean?"

He avoided a direct reply, determined to keep his oath of silence.

"Colette, you love France?"

She answered him in the words he had himself imagined:

"France? Yes, France is she whom I love… It is you."

So she thought as he did, mingling as he had done the idea of love and of country.

"Well, Colette, for France I must face a danger, a terrible danger! And if I have sought this interview tonight, it is that I might loyally and honestly give you your liberty."

He lowered his voice:

"You can no longer be my fiancée. It would be cowardice on my part to hold you prisoner to your promise. Colette, I have consented to die!"

Colette protested ardently:

"You have consented to die? But you have consented to die for France. Do you think that makes you less dear to me? Do you think that because I risk becoming your widow I can give up my love?"

Ah, what a brave soul lay hidden in this frail and fragile young girl! What superb defiance of fatality!

"Your widow." The word was a promise, an oath of love.

"In speaking this way," she continued, "you are not only thinking of the war that may break out?"

"That is true, Colette."

"And this mission, is it important?"

"Very important, Colette."

The gentle girl hesitated. She seemed almost to guess a part of the tragic truth.

"To die is nothing," she murmured. "To do one's duty, that is what counts. Oh, if I could only help you."

She implored him:

"I beg you to be frank. Can I do nothing? Am I to be debarred from helping?"

Louis Monet felt a strange agony of mind. Ought he to reject such devotion? Had he the right, on the contrary, to expose the woman he loved?

He was afraid to make a decision.

Colette feverishly continued to beg.

"You hesitate, Louis. Don't you trust me?"

The lieutenant grew pale and trembling, at the very thought of what he had to do—what he ought to do. An echo of Colonel Bayen's words came to his memory.

"You must hide this document where nobody can find it—but where it can always be recovered. In case of death, your mission would pass to the person who survives, as I myself pass it on to you."

Alas! the meaning of these words was unmistakable.

Who would dream of looking for the mysterious and tragic document in the peaceful home of the Ravignons?

What German spy would tear it from Colette's hands? And was not Colette the faithful friend, devoted unto death to him and to France? But it meant exposing Colette to the terrible vengeance of the enemy.

Louis Monet cried:

"I won't, I won't!"

But Colette, by his side, still pleaded:

"For France."

And he gave in. He knew in a flash the glorious defeat of voluntary sacrifice.

Ah! What a strange love scene was this tragic and painful interview!

Louis Monet now took out the redoubtable yellow envelope.

"Colette, this document is of inestimable value—my first duty is to preserve it. Nobody yet knows that it is in my hands, therefore nobody can guess that I place it in yours. If any misfortune should happen to me you will receive from me the necessary instructions. Colette, will you accept this charge? Will you help me to keep it?"

Colette, quivering, had taken the envelope and hidden it in her corsage.

"I will keep this document," she said in a broken voice, "as I keep the promise of your love."

But he insisted further. There must be no possible mistake. Although it hurt to do so, he must point out the danger of such a trust.

"Colette, they would kill me to get this document, and they might kill you also. It is for France that I ask it of you."

"And it is for France that I will second you—and also because I love you."

Louis Monet would have liked to express his love and admiration, but the words would not come.

Alas! It was not the time for love.

He had to fight first, to conquer.

After would come the laurel of victory and the perfume of kisses.

A silence between them was broken by Colette:

"When shall I see you again?"

He feared the future, but he had to answer:

"Will you ever see me again?"

Another silence, the silence of the hostile forest, in whose heavy shadows it seemed that mystery lurked, waiting for the dawn.

Colette held out her hand.

"Dear, I must leave you."

Almost coldly he said goodbye.

The shadows were not only around him, they were within. He doubted whether he had done right.

But as Colette moved away, he rushed to her, clasping her in his arms.

"Colette, I love you!"

"I love you," she answered.

It was love's eternal duet.

"I shall love you always."

"Always?"

"If I die, my last thought will be of you."

"I don't want you to die."

Triumphant, their love revolted against Destiny.

Colette, with a quick movement, escaped.

"Go, go! Someone is coming!"

"Who? Nay, it isn't possible."

"I'm sure of it! Do go! We mustn't be seen together!"

"But I can't leave you alone!"

"It is not a question of me. You mustn't think of me!"

She placed her hand over the document.

"Ah," cried Monet, "what a sad parting!"

Then, yielding to her prayer, he plunged into a by-path and ran to his horse.

A few moments later he started at full gallop as though in flight.

In the meantime a young man suddenly appeared before Colette, flashing a pocket lantern into her face and bowing with a sarcastic smile.

"You! Mademoiselle Ravignon? And alone? Here in the woods! At such an hour? I can't believe it."

Paul de Tersy appeared in utter amazement.

But Colette played her part perfectly.

"Alas, it is I, and alone—and I shall be well scolded if you tell on me."

Paul de Tersy smiled again.

"I'll hold my tongue," he declared, "but if it is not indiscreet, may I ask where you have been?"

"Oh, what curiosity," she replied, adding: "You might have guessed, I think. I've been to see my friend Berthe. We've made a plan together to induce father to take me to Lunéville on Sunday to the prefect's garden party."

Paul de Tersy continued to smile, and that smile would have doubtless troubled Colette if she had seen it.

She took his arm playfully:

"Come as far as the house with me. I'll go in by the side door."

So arm in arm, like two comrades, they walked down the road.

7. A Case of Conscience

For the tenth time at least, La Flemme, on tiptoe, opened Louis Monet's bedroom door.

He grumbled to himself.

"The idea of still snoring at eleven in the morning!"

La Flemme, who would have slept until three in the afternoon if allowed, thought it his duty to wake his lieutenant.

His method of doing this was somewhat peculiar.

He began by calling:

"Lieutenant! Lieutenant!"

But the sleeping man did not wake.

Louis Monet had reached home very late the night before, and was now resting in a deep sleep.

La Flemme had an inspiration.

On the mantelpiece a vase filled with water waited for the flowers it was to contain. La Flemme, with his duster, gently knocked it to the floor.

But this had no effect.

"Good Lord! What a spree he must have been on last night!" exclaimed La Flemme.

He next threw down a clock which fell with great clatter.

Louis Monet continued to sleep.

Then La Flemme lost his temper.

"I shall have to tickle his feet if this goes on!"

But another plan suggested itself.

By the wall stood a picture which Louis Monet had not yet hung. La Flemme seized and flung it on the bed.

This time Louis Monet woke with a start. Furiously angry, he cried:

"Animal! Brute! Idiot! You'll get a week for this!"

La Flemme smiled amiably.

"I am doing the room, Lieutenant."

Louis Monet now caught sight of the broken clock and vase on the floor.

He sat up.

"Doing the room, clumsy. What's all that?"

"Debris, Lieutenant. I haven't swept yet."

Nothing ever worried La Flemme.

"Debris! You're trying to make game of me. You'll get a week for this."

"All right," replied La Flemme tranquilly. "One and one make two."

"And what's your idea of throwing pictures at my head?"

"I didn't know you were there, Lieutenant."

The lie was so prodigious, it quite disarmed Louis Monet. He burst out laughing.

"You didn't know I was there? Why, you idiot!"

"I thought you were at the quarters."

"I'm not on duty today."

"Maybe, but the lieutenant colonel wants to see you in a hurry. That's why I have wakened you, Lieutenant."

"The lieutenant colonel? What for?"

He scented a fresh mystery.

"You're not drunk? It isn't the colonel who wishes to see me?"

"No, Lieutenant! The lieutenant colonel."

"Well, get my things ready. I'll dress."

An hour later, Louis Monet, out of breath from a quick walk, presented himself at the cavalry quarters.

He felt anxious and somewhat nervous.

What was he going to hear now? What had he to fear? And above all what was he to do if the lieutenant colonel gave him an order jeopardizing his mission?

Scarcely had he appeared in the guardroom when an orderly addressed him:

"Lieutenant."

"What is it?"

"You are expected in the audience room."

"All right, orderly."

Louis Monet fancied that the man had slightly smiled as he performed his commission.

Why?

Was it generally known that the lieutenant colonel wanted to see him?

More and more uneasy Louis Monet presented himself before his chief a few moments later.

The officer was reading a newspaper which he threw aside with a movement of anger.

"Ah! there you are! Have you slept well?"

"Why—certainly—Colonel."

"You are sober again?"

Louis Monet started.

What did this greeting mean? This scornful tone and attitude?

"Sober again? I don't understand you, Colonel."

The officer rose, folding his arms and speaking with sarcastic emphasis.

"Really? You don't understand me?"

"No, Colonel."

"Do you deny being drunk yesterday and the day before?"

Louis Monet answered dryly:

"Colonel, I'm not good at guessing puzzles."

"Which means?"

"That I beg you to explain your insults."

Louis Monet spoke with such force that the colonel in his turn seemed surprised.

"Ah! You think I insult you by supposing you drunk? I thought I was offering you an excuse."

"An excuse? For what, Colonel?"

"For what you have done."

Louis Monet completely lost his head.

"Good heavens! What have I done?"

The lieutenant colonel took a step toward him.

"Lieutenant, some things are not done, and when they are done, there is only one way of making reparation. There are things which must be wiped out with blood."

"With blood?"

Louis Monet mechanically repeated the words.

Was the lieutenant colonel crazy? What was he talking about?

With the end of his riding whip the colonel picked up one of the papers from the floor.

Scornfully he handed it to Louis Monet.

"Read that, Lieutenant."

"What?"

"Head of the third column."

Louis Monet searched for the article published in a small local paper.

"Do you deny it?"

Louis Monet did not trouble to answer.

The letters danced before his eyes.

"A rather serious scandal has taken place at the 'Elegants' Club.' While playing with the honorable gentleman farmer, M. Paul de Tersy, well known in our district, an officer of the garrison, a lieutenant of the 32nd dragoons, M. L. M., sufficiently designated by stating that he belongs to the cartographic department, committed a deplorable mistake.

"Taken red-handed, convicted of using marked cards, M. L. M. furthermore declined to fight. The military authorities will doubtless take up the matter."

Louis Monet not only understood the allusion, he grasped the purpose and the spirit with which it was written.

In that moment he suffered a thousand deaths.

To be publicly dishonored and when he was not guilty. When, not only had he not cheated, but when his refusal to fight had been occasioned by his duty, which prohibited the duel.

Shaken with anger, Louis Monet flung down the paper.

"It's abominable!"

"Do you then deny it?"

"I should think I did!"

The lieutenant colonel was impressed.

"Lieutenant," he continued, somewhat less severely, "I don't understand this story—all the papers in the town mention it. Come, we are alone. Will you confide in me? Will you answer me as though I were your father? Frankly, have you done this? Yes or no?"

"What, Colonel?"

"This dishonorable action, cheated at cards?"

Louis Monet drew himself up.

"Colonel, on my word of honor, it is an outrage."

"Ah, I'm glad of that. I believe you. So it is a simple calumny. An attack by one of these reptiles who would soil our uniforms?"

Louis Monet hesitated to answer.

A calumny? Alas! it was something quite different. It was much worse than a calumny, it was a trick to push him to extremes. He realized the sinister truth; Colonel Bayen had been right, he was being tracked. They were trying to force him to fight.

But suddenly Louis Monet revolted against this suspicion. It couldn't be possible!

Nobody knew that he had been given the mission.

Nobody could be aware of it.

He hesitated to answer and the lieutenant colonel a moment ago convinced of his sincerity, noticed his distress.

"Well, you don't answer? You mean that this is a simple calumny?"

"Yes, Colonel, a simple calumny."

He had scarcely spoken the words, when the officer thundered:

"Lieutenant Monet, if this is the truth, then I am surprised that you are here!"

"Why, Colonel?"

"On reading that article you should have rushed off in search of this Monsieur de Tersy. You, an officer of dragoons! Do you not know how to deal with liars!"

The lieutenant colonel paced up and down:

"Well, are you silent? You don't stir. You grow pale!"

Louis Monet had become livid.

What could he do? What could he answer?

Accept this duel that was being urged upon him? Let himself be accused of cowardice?

In a changed voice, stammering, he answered:

"I cannot explain, Colonel but I respectfully beg to ask the permission of Colonel Bayen."

Alas! Louis Monet had to drain the cup to the dregs.

"Colonel Bayen is absent—in any case he would send you to fight."

"I cannot fight, Colonel."

"Why?"

"Because—I cannot."

A long silence ensued.

By a supreme effort of will Louis Monet remained rigid, in an attitude of disciplined respect. From the pallor of his face he seemed more dead than alive.

The lieutenant colonel stopped abruptly:

"Lieutenant, you will return to your rooms. I shall take no decision until the return of Colonel Bayen—since you appeal to his authority. But I cannot hide my surprise. Go, Monsieur. Consider yourself under arrest."

"Very good, Colonel."

Louis Monet saluted and went out.

In the street he walked like a drunken man.

The blow was terrible—the worst that an officer and a brave man could receive.

"I am doing my duty, and I let myself be treated as a coward. It is horrible."

And other thoughts came to add to his misery. Colette would read the papers. And did she not know this Paul de Tersy? The young girl, like the others, would take him for a wretched coward.

And again, what did Colonel Bayen's absence mean?

While war seemed to be more and more imminent it as unbelievable that the father of the regiment should have left town.

Might not his departure have something to do with the terrible mission he had entrusted to Louis Monet?

But another question occupied the young man. It obsessed him, it haunted him.

"There are but two hypotheses, and one of them only can be the right one... Has this shameful accusation to do with my mission or has it no connection with the yellow document that I gave to Colette?"

Louis Monet returned home under arrest in a distressing bewilderment of feelings.

La Flemme questioned him jokingly.

"Well, Lieutenant, did you get a calling down?"

But Louis Monet gave him a look which quickly silenced him.

"Leave me," he ordered, "leave me alone until I call you."

"All right, I understand."

Now at six in the evening while Louis Monet was lying on his sofa in an agony of mind he heard two gentle raps at his door.

He sprang up and cried:

"Come in!"

La Flemme put his head in.

"I told you to leave me alone."

But La Flemme's face expressed such excitement, that the lieutenant questioned him:

"What is it? What do you want?"

"Lieutenant, it's war! We are mobilizing!"

Louis Monet seized his orderly by the arms.

"War! You are sure? Is it official?"

"Yes, Lieutenant."

"La Flemme, I am under arrest, and I must go out—at any cost! Go and find the lieutenant colonel, if you have to force your way in. Say to him: 'By everything you hold sacred, Lieutenant Louis Monet asks a day's leave.'"

Ten minutes later La Flemme ran at full speed towards the cavalry quarters, muttering:

"Good God!—It's enough to send a man crazy. What's got into the lieutenant? If only the lieutenant colonel will see me."

Meanwhile Louis Monet paced up and down his room like a wild animal in a cage.

He repeated to himself Colonel Bayen's last words.

"Immediately mobilization is official, you will go to the strategic bridge of Vezouse. You will go there at any cost, and in spite of whatever orders you may receive from your superiors."

And, terrified at the thought of what he might have to dare, Louis Monet sighed:

"If only the lieutenant colonel gives me permission."

8. France Comes First

Twenty minutes later a heavy footstep shook the stairs and a door banged violently.

La Flemme, in spite of his lazy tendencies, had hurried. He returned out of breath and perspiring.

"Well?"

"Well, there's a fine mix-up," panted La Flemme.

"Everybody's up in the air—organizing, packing. It's no joke, I can tell you."

Louis Monet ground his teeth impatiently.

"I don't care about that. What did the lieutenant colonel say?"

"The lieutenant colonel? Nothing—but he swore like a truck driver—and then he wrote something on a card."

"For me?"

"I guess so—it wasn't for the pope."

La Flemme unbuttoned his dolman and took out a visiting card in an envelope with some lines written upon it.

Louis Monet shook with anxiety.

His fate was about to be decided. What had his chief said? He could scarcely make out the words, but finally he deciphered the order.

The lieutenant colonel had simply written this:

"If you want leave for the purpose of fighting, I grant it. If it is for any other motive, I refuse permission."

The following words were underscored:

"Mobilization is official. In the absence of Colonel Bayen, I prefer to be minus an officer than to have a coward in my regiment."

Louis Monet collapsed on the sofa as though he had been shot.

"It's horrible!" he muttered.

Mobilization was official.

War was about to begin—a war of revenge—a war to the death between Germany and France, the eternal enemies.

And he was under arrest on parole!

His honor obliged him to keep to his rooms to wait for the orders of his chief.

At the same time he knew that he ought to set out for the strategic bridge of Vezouse without a moment's waste of time to begin the work he had been entrusted with, upon which might depend the fate of the campaign.

"If I break my parole, I shall be dishonored," he muttered, "and if I remain faithful to it and a prisoner here, I shall fail in my mission."

And then suddenly, he saw his duty clearly.

Of what value was this absurd thing called conventional honor?

To fail in honor because he broke his parole in such circumstances! Absurd! He called La Flemme.

The orderly, who had withdrawn, worried by the lieutenant's manner, presented himself.

"Well, what's to be done?"

Louis Monet, without a tremor in his voice, gave him his orders:

"La Flemme, go to the cavalry quarters, see that my equipment is in order, then return here and wait for me. Wait as long as it is necessary; I may need you."

"Begging your pardon, Lieutenant, but what are you up to? You have a queer look."

Louis Monet did not answer this indiscreet question. He added:

"Give me my revolver."

"Your service revolver, Lieutenant? It is in quarters."

"Give me my Browning."

"All right, here it is."

La Flemme handed it to the officer, but his manner was so odd that Louis Monet questioned him:

"What's the matter with you?"

"Why, Lieutenant, I thought—that you were under arrest—so—and now I see you getting ready to go out—that won't do!"

Louis Monet gave him such a look that the orderly felt he had gone too far.

"I've made a break, eh?"

The officer put his hand on his shoulder.

"Look here, never talk carelessly. You don't know and you cannot know. One thing you may be sure of: I am going to do my duty."

And leaving La Flemme completely bewildered, Louis Monet went out.

In truth, the officer had a strange repugnance for the part he was to play.

Like all Frenchmen he disliked any work connected with espionage.

And what was this work to be?

What was he to do when he found himself upon the bridge?

"You are to watch," said Colonel Bayen, "and you are to kill without hesitation, anyone who approaches in a suspicious manner."

Louis Monet could not help a shudder in recalling this strange command.

He knew the Vezouse bridge very well. It had been built by the engineers, and it was said had a close connection with special mobilization plans.

Was it only on account of its strategic value that he was to guard it?

Louis Monet thought:

"One might suppose that Colonel Bayen sent me there for the sole purpose of letting me kill a German spy."

Another thought struck him.

Colonel Bayen was absent.

He was not at Lunéville.

Where was he?

On the Vezouse bridge, of course!

And this hypothesis seemed very likely.

Foreseeing mobilization, it was not improbable that Colonel Bayen himself had gone to take a look at the bridge.

Monet had still several miles to go. He hurried on, jumping the hedges and ditches.

How charming the country looked in the failing light.

Who would guess the approaching horror, which doubtless would cover the country with blood?

War! It was certain, almost declared.

Monet quivered with joy.

Something expanded within him—the pride of youth, pride of

his profession, the joy of duty to accomplish.

He laughed at his former scruples.

He complained of having to do spy work as if any work was vile which served the country!

Suddenly he came to a halt. A cry escaped his lips:

"Good God! Too late!"

What was happening?

The peace of the evening had been broken by a report, followed by faint explosions.

Louis Monet instinctively guessed:

"The bridge! The bridge!"

Forgetting his weariness and the advice of Colonel Bayen to be prudent, he rushed headlong like a madman.

"Ah, the scoundrels! German espionage was capable of everything. Only a few hours ago mobilization had been decided upon and already hostilities had begun."

When he reached the top of the hill and came in view of Vezouse a cry escaped him.

He had not been deceived.

A mine had blown up the strategic bridge.

Debris and a thick dust filled the air, together with the acrid smell of gunpowder.

Not a living soul was to be seen.

The lieutenant shook his fist in impotent rage against the cowardly and invisible enemy.

At ten o'clock La Flemme was beginning to be seriously alarmed when a rap on the door announced the return of Louis Monet.

"You, Lieutenant," cried La Flemme as he let him in.

Louis Monet was pale and exhausted. His torn clothes and muddy boots gave evidence of his long search along the banks on the Vezouse for the scoundrelly author of the catastrophe. He dropped on to his sofa and then for the first time remarked the pallor of La Flemme's face.

"What's the matter," he cried, "what has happened?"

"Lieutenant, have you heard the news?"

"Good Lord, no! What is it?"

"Colonel Bayen has been murdered."

"Colonel Bayen!"

"His clothes were found covered with blood and with a bullet hole through them. He had been shot through the heart."

Overwhelmed, Louis Monet bowed his head.

Presently, however, a new feeling asserted itself.

Colonel Bayen had fallen. Very well. His death had been foreseen. The soldier for a long time had made his sacrifice. And was not he there, his substitute, ready to continue the work, ready to avenge him?

But at this moment, he met La Flemme's eyes and read in them further news.

Louis Monet felt instinctively that he had something horrible to learn.

"Well, what else is there?"

"Lieutenant, I daren't tell you."

"Why not? Speak!"

La Flemme stood against the door of the room as though to bar the way to his officer.

"Lieutenant, to begin with, I must ask you to have confidence in me—that I have no hesitation—that I know it isn't true, and above all, that there is nothing I wouldn't do for you."

La Flemme stammered out his protestations of devotion.

Louis Monet, not understanding, repeated:

"Speak!"

Then La Flemme in a low tone explained the horrible thing.

"You see, Lieutenant, it's this way. When the death of the colonel was known, why it made a big stir. Well I was about to return here when the lieutenant colonel ordered me to wait for him."

"And then?"

"The lieutenant colonel came here."

Louis Monet shrugged his shoulders. What did a broken parole matter? He was indeed above the opinion of the lieutenant colonel. The drama of his secret mission, of which he was henceforth to carry the burden alone, made him indifferent to smaller matters.

"Well, he came here and didn't find me—what then?"

"Then—then—"

Louis Monet seized him by the arm and shook him violently:

"Go ahead! What else?"

"Afterwards something extraordinary happened. When the

lieutenant colonel and I arrived here, do you know what we found? Your uniform—No. 2—on the floor and your revolver on the sofa! Yes, your service revolver—the one you asked for before going out and which I thought was at the quarters."

Louis stared in amazement.

The lieutenant did not yet understand what his orderly was driving at.

He could not gather his wits together. He spoke almost calmly:

"Well, what does that prove?"

The orderly declared briefly:

"Seems that a shot had been fired from your revolver—and besides, your uniform was covered with mud like the mud on the banks of the Vezouse—and it's on the banks of the Vezouse that the colonel's effects were found—it's supposed that his body must have been thrown into the water—so—"

This time Louis Monet understood.

"It can't be possible," he cried, shaking with anger. "They don't believe that!"

La Flemme continued:

"The lieutenant colonel then began questioning me—and then he sent for the captain and they talked together for ever so long. In the end, Lieutenant, they believe—I have to tell you—they believe that it was you who killed the colonel—and you are to be arrested!"

"Arrested!"

To the amazement of La Flemme, Louis Monet burst out laughing.

Arrest him! What nonsense!

The thing was too ridiculous! Arrest him for murder!

Why his innocence would be easy to prove.

Besides, La Flemme was mistaken. He could not have understood what had happened.

If they had wanted to arrest him, they would have left a guard at the entrance—they would have laid a trap.

But La Flemme went on:

"You are to be arrested, Lieutenant, or rather, you are already under arrest. So am I. Five men are hidden on the stairs—four to prevent your escape, the fifth to give warning at the quarters. I am not allowed to go out, either."

La Flemme, once started, gave all the details, and as Louis Monet listened, bit by bit it dawned on him that he was wrong to shrug his shoulders at the absurd accusation brought against him.

His innocence could easily be proved, but how long might it take to establish it?

And now when from one end of the country to the other there would be a fever of mobilization, could he expect to get quick justice?

And then he grew pale as the truth dawned on him, clear and precise without the consolation of any doubt.

In a flash he saw the whole terrible intrigue which had unfolded during the past days.

Himself menaced, and in fear of not accomplishing his mission, Colonel Bayen had confided his tragic secret to him, had charged him with safeguarding the official document.

And then the German espionage had got to work.

The adventure at the Elegants' Club had been arranged to dishonor him.

To prevent his presence at the Vezouse bridge, the papers had been made to publish his cowardice, and he had been placed under arrest.

Then Colonel Bayen had fallen, a victim to his duty. And as the authorities required a guilty man, he had been chosen for the purpose.

Ah! the monstrous power of German espionage!

It was known that he was hastening to the Vezouse bridge and it had been blown up before his arrival.

It was known that he had left his rooms and during his absence they had left there a uniform similar to his and covered with mud—and his revolver with one shot missing.

The plan was so simple, so marvelous, and so tragic in its consequences.

Naturally the military authorities could not be mistaken.

He would be arrested, locked up.

And at the very moment when seconds were worth years! When he a to recover the famous document and its instructions upon which the issue of the campaign depended.

Quick action was necessary; he must find some way of tricking the German espionage.

Louis Monet leaned on the table, his head in his hands, and reflected:

"To begin with, I must get back the mysterious document and to do that I must dodge the German spies... If I should die my mission would be lost."

And who were these spies who seemed to be so perfectly informed?

How could they have organized the adventure of the Elegants' Club twenty minutes after Colonel Bayen had spoken during the noise of the galloping horses?

Once more the name of de Tersy came to his lips.

Many things seemed to point to him, but many others to his innocence.

Besides, how could de Tersy be in the confidence of the German espionage?

With a gesture of indifference and rage, he muttered:

"No matter who the man is, I must get back the document for which Colonel Bayen died."

He turned to La Flemme.

"Listen, terrible things are happening, La Flemme, which I cannot explain to you. Have you confidence in me?"

"Yes, Lieutenant."

"And are you willing to die for France?"

"That goes without saying, Lieutenant."

"Very well, then make haste—"

Louis Monet drew the orderly across the small apartment, repeating the phrase he had made his motto:

"France comes first! Myself afterwards... All for the country—for the war of revenge."

9. A Mysterious Photograph

"Where are they? Do you see them?"

"They are just below, Lieutenant."

"Who commands them?"

"I can't see very well, but I think it's the captain of the 3rd squadron."

"Very well. Step back and listen."

Five minutes went by and the plight of the unfortunate lieutenant seemed worse than ever.

Louis Monet had not been deceived when he thought he heard the sound of a patrol in the street. As La Flemme had said, one of the soldiers left on guard had hastened to give the alarm that the supposed murderer of Colonel Bayen had returned. Immediately a mounted guard had been sent and stationed outside the building.

"Lieutenant, they are knocking."

"Are they all coming in?"

"No, two remain outside."

"All right—we'll manage in spite of them."

The young man, at this moment, seemed ready for the most desperate measures.

He had no scruples left.

Since the German espionage was trying to crush him in such a terrible manner, he would accept the challenge—even with joy—calm, now that the struggle was inevitable.

"La Flemme, listen well to me."

The orderly was visibly trembling.

"They are coming up, Lieutenant. You can hear their feet on the stairs."

Louis Monet shrugged his shoulders.

"We have still five minutes, it will take that time to break in the door."

Did the lieutenant intend to revolt against military authority?

"La Flemme," continued Monet, "I can't explain to you what is happening. The situation is very simple—either you believe in me or you think me a scoundrel."

"I believe," interrupted La Flemme, "what next?"

"Next, I'm going to ask you to go to the quarters—yes—by and by—try to find out what the orders are—where the regiment is going—if anything further has been heard about Colonel Bayen."

"Right! And afterwards?"

"Afterwards—you will rejoin me."

"The devil! Where!"

"I'll wait for you in the sand quarry just outside Lunéville on the Épinal road—you know it?"

"Yes—but—"

"But what?"

La Flemme scratched his head, embarrassed: "Why, Lieutenant—without offense—I think you'll be put in handcuffs."

"No, they won't handcuff me."

Loud knocking was now heard, but the lieutenant paid no attention to it.

"I'm going to clear out through the window," he explained.

He leaned out watching the movements of the two men placed on guard.

Evidently they had received orders to watch the cellar windows and did not raise their heads.

"Not a word, not a sound, La Flemme," whispered Louis Monet. "They will let you go free, you have only to pretend that I have not returned to the apartment. They will doubtless think that I guessed the presence of the soldiers and escaped by the roof. So, goodbye!"

Louis Monet was admirably calm, although the thing he planned to do was very dangerous.

Standing on the windowsill, he reached out and seized a gutter pipe which overhung his apartment.

From there, his plan of flight was simple. Clinging to the pipe, hanging in midair with the agility of an acrobat, he advanced to the roof of the neighboring house, fortunately on a slightly lower level.

This house was surrounded by a large garden. For the convenience of workmen, iron steps had been placed in the wall, and by their aid Louis Monet rapidly descended into the garden. Jumping over the railing, he found himself safely in the street.

But while he made off quickly, turning occasionally to make sure that he was not followed, he felt no sense of joy in his freedom.

On the contrary, his face clouded over.

"Where should he go?"

Suddenly he recalled what Colonel Bayen had said:

"If anything happens to me, go and see the second curate of the church of Saint-Jacques. Here is a line asking him to explain his recent visit to me."

What could this unknown priest tell him? What new mystery a waited him?

"Alas," sighed the lieutenant, "my difficulties are now really beginning."

And he might have added: "With the menace of greater danger."

And as he hurried through the streets of Lunéville he recalled the mysterious warning of the unfortunate Colonel Bayen.

"You are in danger of death! German espionage is all-powerful and all-daring."

Henceforth Monet could not doubt that he was at grips with the formidable Prussian organization.

Furthermore, it was beyond question that the German spies were aware he had been delegated to the redoubtable mission formerly in the hands of Colonel Bayen. "But what I can't understand," he thought, "is how they learned it."

He distinctly remembered every detail of his interview with Colonel Bayen. The words of his chief could not have been overheard, for they could not have reached another ear but his own.

And yet twenty minutes later at the Elegants' Club, he had been a victim of an attempted duel.

"It's incomprehensible," repeated Louis Monet. "How could our conversation have been overheard? Who could have known it?"

Paul de Tersy? He dismissed the idea for lack of evidence. Besides, Paul de Tersy could not have overheard his conversation with Colonel Bayen.

After a time Monet reached the small square where the house of Abbé Jandron stood. He had many times admired the garden belonging to it.

He came to a stop, surprised.

The windows were lighted up, the priest had not gone to bed.

"Ah! that's extraordinary!" thought the officer.

"What can he be doing at such an hour?"

Then he shrugged his shoulders with a laugh. He would be finding mysteries everywhere now!

He rang the bell.

It was Abbé Jandron himself who opened the door.

"Abbé, I ought to—"

But the abbé cut short his excuses.

"Well," he asked nervously. "Have you any news? Is anything known yet?"

Louis Monet was taken aback.

What was the abbé talking about?

"Pardon, but—"

The abbé cut him short again:

"Come in! Come in! You must give me details—did the district attorney send you—or the lieutenant colonel?"

Louis Monet felt completely stunned.

What did this priest know? What was he about to tell him?

Louis Monet, who had followed the priest into a study, drew out his card and the note from Colonel Bayen.

"Abbé, I think there is some mistake. You seem to be expecting somebody. I am really here by chance. Will you read that note, written by Colonel Bayen a few days ago!"

With trembling hand, the abbé tore open the envelope. He seemed equally stunned:

"So you weren't sent by the district attorney nor by the lieutenant colonel?"

"No," replied Louis Monet, "I came from my own chief, Abbé."

"And you want to know the details of my visit to Colonel Bayen?"

"Exactly, Abbé."

"You do not know the consequences? You haven't heard the end of the adventure?"

Louis Monet felt his heart beat faster.

What was the priest about to confide to him?

"It's a very serious matter, Abbé, and I beg you to tell me."

"Very serious, yes, Lieutenant."

He invited his guest to sit down and then recounted the extraordinary visit he had been induced to make to Colonel Bayen.

And while he explained the greeting he had received from the officer, Louis Monet grew more and more terrified.

"What you have told me is terribly mysterious, Abbé. The woman who sent you to the colonel is undoubtedly an accomplice of the murderer, who yielded to a religious scruple and desired to have the colonel make his peace with God. In fact, that is what the colonel himself thought. I remember quite well what he said. 'I shall not be killed without a warning. They had the irony to send me a confessor.'"

"And this woman must be found at any cost. We must know who she is."

"I know who the woman is," replied the abbé.

"What!"

"Listen to me. I had completely forgotten this incident, Lieutenant, and had set it down to a stupid joke. When today at half-past five, I learned of Colonel Bayen's murder, you may guess my feelings. It seemed to me that the murder had a direct connection with my adventure.

"The police should have been notified!... I rushed to the district attorney's office—he was out. I asked where he could be found—I was sent to Colonel Bayen's home where he had begun an investigation."

"And then?"

The priest hesitated. He had grown very pale.

"Oh, then—what happened was unbelievable. When I reached Colonel Bayen's quarters, I found the district attorney engaged with the lieutenant colonel. Naturally the house was in the greatest disorder. A servant showed me into Colonel Bayen's bedroom, and there—"

"There?"

"There in a secret drawer which had been opened by the authorities, I saw a photograph, and beside it a picture cut from a local paper. The photograph was that of a young woman quite unknown to me—the picture was that of a woman of certain age undoubtedly taken at some fête, and this woman I recognized. She was the same woman who had sent me to see Colonel Bayen!

Louis Monet appeared stupefied.

And yet he did not guess what was troubling the priest.

"But, Abbé, does not that explain everything? This woman must have been a friend of Colonel Bayen's, and her action the result of Christian zeal… Perhaps the death of the colonel and this incident may be mere coincidence."

The Abbé Jandron put his hand on the lieutenant's arm.

"Listen to me—you do not know all. Amazed at the sight of the picture, I questioned the servant who had shown me into the room. I asked him if he knew, by chance, why Colonel Bayen had hidden the illustration in the secret drawer, and if he knew the name of the woman it represented."

"Well?"

"Well, Lieutenant, the servant answered: 'Oh, very well, Abbé. Those photographs are the colonel's wife. The one taken when she was young, the other later. It seems she died twenty years ago and was buried in the Boche's country.'"

Louis Monet was dumbfounded at the priest's extraordinary recital.

He had heard, of course, all the garrison gossip.

He knew that Colonel Bayen had lost his young and tenderly loved wife in Berlin.

It was, therefore, not the fact that the colonel was a widower which stupefied him, but the incoherence of the abbé's adventure.

Beyond doubt the priest could not have received a visit from Mme. Bayen, since Mme. Bayen had been dead for twenty years.

The servant's testimony was materially impossible.

The photograph of the young woman might indeed be that of Mme. Bayen, but the illustration representing a middle-aged woman could not be the same person, since Mme. Bayen had already been dead for twenty years, and had died young.

"Abbé, there is a mistake on the part of the servant and on your part also. You have been the victim of a resemblance."

The priest shook his head.

"No, Lieutenant, no! I am sure of what I say. The portrait of this dead woman is the portrait of my visitor. And yet, I know that must be impossible."

After a few moments, Louis Monet questioned him:

"Have you told all this to the district attorney?"

"Naturally."

"What did he think of it?"

"I don't know. He seemed persuaded, as you are, that it was a case of chance resemblance. But I was able to convince him to the contrary."

"Then, what did he decide to do? To look for this woman?"

"Exactly."

The priest rose and opened a drawer in his desk which was locked.

"The district attorney wishes to clear up the matter and has had some reproductions of the portrait made. Tomorrow detectives will be on the lookout for her. I brought a copy of the portrait away with me. I shall show it to my parishioners in case someone among them may know the original."

An intense curiosity had taken hold of Louis Monet. He attached no importance to the abbé's words, but who was this woman—undoubtedly an accomplice of the murderers?

"You have the copy here, Abbé?"

"Yes, Lieutenant, this is it."

Louis Monet no sooner saw the photograph when he staggered back pale as a sheet, and he would have fallen had he not clutched the window curtains.

It was a photograph of Mme. Brigitte Ravignon, the mother of Colette!

10. Horrible Certainty

The trumpets sounded a joyful march, and behind the music, the regiment kept time—superb—as though going to a fête.

Louis Monet, who had lain hidden in the quarry for twenty-four hours waiting the return of La Flemme, seemed to be going through a horrible nightmare as he watched the dragoons march by.

How often had he heard this music during maneuvers!

Mechanically he numbered them:

"Fourth squadron—second platoon—first platoon—third squadron—third platoon—first platoon—second squadron—"

And there on the flank of the column was his place! And there he ought to be, mounted on Caboche, with drawn saber, so happy to be alive, to be on the march!

Where was the regiment going?

It was going to fight.

The unhappy lieutenant gave a deep sigh. Ah! the painful irony of things!

After having dreamt for so long of revenge! After having dreamt of this departure with an exasperated desire of battle, of the charge, of victory!

And the very day the dragoons march to the frontier, to be alone in a quarry, like a wretch, a coward who hides, a deserter, a spy!

The regiment had passed by!

Some laggards were hastening at a gallop to rejoin the ranks. Then the heavy carriages thundered along the road, the ambulances, a forge, bread wagons—and when the last of them had gone, when the road was empty again and nothing remained but a cloud of dust, Louis Monet, struck to the heart, fell to the ground, his face in his hands, and shed scalding tears.

He had taken leave of Abbé Jandron with such suddenness, muttering words without sense, that the priest had been completely taken aback. But the rapid walk to the quarry and the pure evening air had calmed his nerves. He was able to collect his thoughts and study the problem that lay before him.

In the first place the abbé had recognized in the photograph the woman who came to see him. And he himself had identified this woman with Colette's mother.

Now the woman could not have been the wife of Colonel Bayen, since his wife was dead twenty years ago in Berlin.

Had the servant purposely misled Abbé Jandron or not?

After thinking it over Louis Monet decided it had been done on purpose.

"The servant evidently said it was a portrait of the late Colonel Bayen's wife to throw the abbé off the scent. Therefore the servant was a spy."

But how did the colonel happen to own a portrait of Colette's mother? And why did he tell the priest that he did not know what woman could have sent him?

Louis Monet had read too many of the dark stories of espionage not to know how these sinister intrigues are managed.

Of course! Colonel Bayen, a widower, had loved Brigitte and had made her his mistress.

Brigitte Ravignon, bit by bit, had learned his secret and discovered the existence of the yellow document and had then sworn to get hold of it.

Then who was Brigitte? Unquestionably a spy. Colonel Bayen, entrapped in an intrigue of which he did not realize the gravity, had cut out of a paper the picture of Brigitte Ravignon—who being the wife of the mayor of Cirey, was almost a celebrity.

The colonel had hidden this photograph until one day his orderly had caught him looking at it. He had then given a quick and false explanation:

"'This is my wife, my poor wife.'"

But at this point Louis Monet perceived the contradiction.

Just now he had decided that the servant was a spy who had purposely lied. And now he found him innocent.

Ah! It was impossible to guess the answer to these mysterious intrigues. And it was still harder to know exactly what part Brigitte Ravignon was taking in them.

And Colette? What part was she playing? Was she an innocent

victim? Was she a redoubtable accomplice whose duty it was to betray with smiles and oaths of love? Colette was a friend of the scoundrelly Paul de Tersy. Was she his accomplice too?

Lieutenant Monet felt a great pain and a great fear. Alas! to whom had he confided the precious document which contained so terrible a secret? To Colette. And it was Colette, the daughter of a spy, who held the document upon which the very safety of France might hang!

If Colette should betray him, the document would be forever lost.

"And all that would be left for me would be to kill myself," he added.

To die! No, not yet.

He had not the right.

To die would be to desert.

"My mission comes first," he thought.

His impulse was to rush to Cirey and learn the truth.

But ought he not to wait for La Flemme?

Surely the help of this devoted friend would be of service to him.

But why didn't La Flemme come? What did his prolonged absence mean?

He may have been killed by spies.

The night wore by and the first streaks of daylight appeared, the time when desperate resolutions are taken.

Louis Monet, at the end of his strength, decided:

"If La Flemme is not here in an hour, whatever happens I shall go to the Ravignon's."

He had fever. He wanted to fight.

Now, at the precise moment when the hour came to an end, he heard footsteps approaching.

"They may be the police!"

And then he gave a cry of rage in thinking that he should be there, dreading the arrival of the police like a criminal!

He now hid himself in one of the dips of the ground.

A figure suddenly appeared.

Monet sprang up.

"La Flemme! La Flemme!"

It was, in truth, the orderly.

As he drew close, Louis Monet had another alarm.

La Flemme was in a pitiful state.

His face was streaked with blood, his clothes were torn, his muddy boots and one spur missing bore witness to a fight.

"Where have you been?—What has happened to you?"

La Flemme dropped onto the ground like a log.

"Where have I been? In a rotten bad place!"

La Flemme explained:

"After you left, they got a line on me—accused me of helping you off—eight guys tried to haul me to prison, but I made them feel the weight of my fists and the toe of my boot. Say, Lieutenant, it's a deuced queer game you're making me play! Now I've batted my superiors and I'm also a deserter. I hope you won't let them shoot me."

La Flemme was joking.

He had, of course, guessed that Louis Monet had serious reasons for his actions—and that was why he had not hesitated to keep the appointment at any cost.

Louis Monet stood up:

"Come, La Flemme."

"Right away, Lieutenant? I'm ready for bed. It's nearly two o'clock and daylight isn't far off—only, where the devil shall we turn in? It wouldn't be healthy for us to be seen."

"Go to bed, La Flemme? That's not the question. We are going to Cirey."

"To Cirey? But the horses?"

"We are going on foot."

"And the police?"

"We'll keep out of their way."

"But the Boches? Just now I heard that things were getting warm."

"The Boches! Ah, I'd like to meet them! Come along, La Flemme!"

La Flemme grumbled:

"About time you changed my name—don't fit any longer... All last night I was on the go—just came from a scrap—and now it's starting all over again—the less of La Flemme the better."

Louis Monet did not even hear these well justified recriminations.

His heart and his duty called him to Cirey—to Colette—to his destiny.

11. A Dying Confession

They had been walking for an hour when suddenly Monet stopped, calling:

"La Flemme!"

"Lieutenant."

"Did you hear that?"

"What, Lieutenant?"

"Why, a shot!"

"A shot? Lieutenant, I don't want to appear a fool, but I think you're going crazy—there's nothing to be heard except the frogs."

"Come on! Come on!"

More and more nervous, Louis Monet kept his ears open and fancied he discovered indistinct noises in the peace of the night, like the clamor of a crowd greatly excited.

Three distinct times he thought he caught the distant echoes of firing.

There may be fighting at the frontier.

And the lieutenant, pondering over the mystery of the military operations which might be already beginning, possibly had begun, tried to guess the formidable tactics of the gigantic struggle which was to set France and Germany against one another.

Germany wanted war. It was therefore certain that she had prepared her offensive, and upon the breaking of diplomatic relations, she would try to invade France.

Louis Monet said to himself:

"They may be fighting already a few miles from here! Besides, if the 32nd dragoons have gone, it is because enemy patrols have been signaled."

And he feared that the peaceful little village of Cirey might be already in the midst of the struggle.

But he tried to reassure himself.

"No! No! That is not so. I certainly heard the firing of guns, but are the Germans already in France? They would not have dared.

Real fighting could not take place for a fortnight. Every book on tactics would agree to that, especially as Germany would not dare begin the offensive in that quarter."

Now, as he recalled his theories, learned in school during peace, he found himself, with the suddenness of a catastrophe, plunged into the horror.

It happened very quickly.

The two men, at the time, were in a wood about three miles from Cirey.

Suddenly overhead they heard a formidable noise, strange, unknown.

It seemed as though an enormous automobile was going at full speed through the air.

A second passed, two seconds—centuries.

And then, suddenly, in the tops of the trees something red glowed.

An oak, struck by an invisible object, fell.

The ground trembled. Clouds of dust arose and stones hurtled, mingled with pieces of steel tearing the trunks of the trees.

"La Flemme?"

"Lieutenant?"

"All right?"

"Yes, and you?"

"All right."

The two men stood up—for the wind of the shell had thrown them violently to the ground.

Less than ten yards away a deep hole had been dug in the ground. An odor of powder caught them by the throat.

La Flemme laughed calmly:

"Well, Lieutenant, I must have been asleep—they are certainly fighting, since the shells begin to drop."

Louis Monet did not reply.

With clenched teeth and fists he watched the sky where falling stars were beginning to trace their lines of fire.

A few seconds more and then a formidable and fantastic noise filled the valley and the wood; the unloosed rage of a hundred guns firing together.

The French batteries were replying to the German batteries.

"It's getting warm," exclaimed La Flemme.

The orderly was obliged to shout to make himself heard.

Louis Monet put his hand on his shoulder.

"Battle! At last."

And while shells struck down trees and the distant glow of fires lit the sky, Louis Monet cried:

"Forward!"

The officer at this moment felt a new spirit born within him.

The sounds of battle awoke in his heart tragedy, suffering, and the valor of a Frenchman defending his country.

It seemed to Louis Monet that the Prussians were defaming the invaded territory.

If shells were falling in the wood, it meant that they were fighting at Cirey.

And if they were fighting at Cirey, it meant that the enemy had crossed the frontier.

"Forward! Forward! We must drive them out!"

Louis Monet scarcely knew what he was saying.

The noise of battle intoxicated him like wine.

He drew his sword, rushing forward toward the contending armies.

La Flemme ran to him.

"And your mission? And Mlle. Colette?"

Louis Monet stopped abruptly.

"The yellow document! Colette! That is true."

He must leave to others the glorious death—the intoxication of charging at the head of his squadron—the soldier's work.

Destiny put him aside crying:

"Not yet."

"You will be doing more than fighting," Colonel Bayen had said, "you will save the country! Your duty is to perform the mission I give you."

And while he plunged forward, no longer towards the battle, but towards the shadowy struggle of espionage, Louis Monet thought:

"I must serve with all my strength! I must serve above all when service is cruel… You are right, La Flemme. We shall fight later on! The first thing is to recover the yellow document."

After walking some distance further they came into the

highroad.

"This is the way, Lieutenant."

Louis Monet shook his head.

"We must stick to the woods."

And as they turned into a by-path, Louis Monet asked himself:

"What am I going to find? Does Colette know that de Tersy is a scoundrel? Will she return me the yellow document? Is Colette still there?"

Added to the noise of the cannonade they now heard the crackling of machine gun fire.

"They are fighting in Cirey, perhaps before Colette's house," he judged.

And then, suddenly, as Monet and La Flemme came out of the wood, they saw a windmill in flames, like a gigantic torch, lighting up the whole horizon.

Five hundred yards away stood the white house of Colette. The windows were aglow with light.

Ah, probably the mayor and his family were preparing for flight.

"Quick! Quick! Or we shall be too late!"

He forgot all precautions. One idea dominated him.

Colette was there. She must return the yellow document. Once in his hands he might be free to go and fight.

They were both running now.

But they had not gone a hundred yards when they stopped and looked at each other, questioning whether they had heard aright.

It sounded like the despairing call of a voice about to cease forever.

"Help! Help!"

A wounded man must be close by—perhaps some stray bullet had taken its toll of human life!

They sprang forward. Monet was the first to see a figure, apparently in final convulsions lying at the foot of a tree.

As he bent over the indistinct form, a cry of horror escaped him—a cry of hate—of fury.

"De Tersy!"

The irony of destiny that it should be Louis Monet who came to the aid of Paul de Tersy!

The wounded man lay with closed eyes and white face, apparently inert.

Was he dead?

Or did he half-consciously recognize who was bending over him.

Monet questioned him with trembling voice:

"Can you hear me? Where are you hurt?"

De Tersy opened his eyes.

His face became terrified.

"Monet! You!"

"Yes. Don't be afraid. Are you in pain?"

"In terrible pain—I am dying."

He spoke in gasps, probably choked by some internal hemorrhage.

La Flemme remarked:

"I don't see any wound—there's no blood on his clothes."

De Tersy made an effort to lift himself up. He looked imploringly at Louis Monet.

"Help me—I shall breathe easier."

Louis Monet did as he was asked.

Later, perhaps, Louis Monet would reproach himself for having acted so quickly, on the spur of the moment.

La Flemme repeated:

"But, Lieutenant, where is he wounded?"

Paul de Tersy, with white lips, gasped painfully.

"Can we lift you?" suggested Louis Monet. "Where are you wounded?"

The wounded man stared before him as though he dared not look at the officer."

"De Tersy, answer me! Are you suffering?"

He leaned over the dying man, whose lips moved. The words he spoke were strange, stupefying:

"I'm lost—can't be helped—no importance—but—don't want to die—without telling you—what I have done—I'm a scoundrel—"

"The document—the yellow document?—" questioned Louis Monet breathlessly.

"Yes—ask your forgiveness—the deuce—I was hard up—bust—so I had to have Colette's dot—and she didn't love me—but her father was willing—Oh! Oh!—you understand?"

Louis Monet replied:

"Yes—all that doesn't matter—the document?"

Paul de Tersy seemed not to hear him.

With dilated eyes, he continued:

"So—you see—I had to compromise you—make you a man that nobody would marry!—And that's why I made use of the marked cards—oh! They served their purpose—I was sure after that that Colette would not have you. Well—I'm dying—"

"The document? The yellow document," repeated Louis Monet for the third time.

Paul de Tersy did not answer.

La Flemme bent over and roared:

"The document?"

Paul de Tersy seemed to rouse from his stupor.

"The document? What document?"

He did not appear to understand. He added:

"Oh, don't make me talk—I am in pain."

But Louis Monet felt pitiless towards this dying wretch.

"Your dishonoring me doesn't matter—if you wanted Colette's money, that doesn't matter, either! But you have betrayed France! You have done so by order of Germany. You have tried to prevent me from recovering the yellow document—you are the accomplice of Brigitte Ravignon—you tried to steal the yellow document. Has Colette given it to you? Ah! answer me if you want my forgiveness."

Paul de Tersy replied clearly:

"I don't understand you! I don't know what document you are speaking of. I saw Colette three days ago—but I have not seen her since."

And in his delirium probably, he repeated:

"Forgive me, Monet. I have dishonored you—I needed money— oh, to be a gambler! That is terrible!"

He was silent for a moment.

His face took on a comforted look.

"I don't understand," murmured La Flemme. With a movement, Louis Monet silenced him. The wounded man spoke further:

"Colette!—Colette loves you! You must tell her that—I had the courage to say everything I have said.—Tell her you are not a thief!"

He articulated the last words with infinite labor. Then a spasm seized him—he half raised himself—his eyes took on a look of horror almost superhuman. Then suddenly he fell back motionless.

"Dead," murmured the officer.

But at this moment La Flemme gave a cry of despair.

"Back, Lieutenant—quickly! The Prussians!"

Less than fifty yards away some shadowy figures appeared, followed by the sharp crackle of rifle fire.

La Flemme and Monet found themselves the target for two companies of the enemy.

12. Silent Words

Twenty minutes later, out of breath and exhausted, Louis Monet dropped behind a hedge. It took him a few moments to grasp the meaning of what had happened.

As La Flemme cried "Go back!" he had the sharp impression of terrible danger.

Not only did they run the chance of being shot by the advancing Prussians, but the awful peril of being surrounded and made prisoners.

From every side Teuton uniforms could be vaguely seen. Louis Monet did not hesitate. As he could do nothing further for de Tersy, he cried in his turn:

"Back! La Flemme!"

Bullets whistled about their ears.

At this instant Monet tried a final ruse.

He cried to La Flemme:

"Separate! You go to the right. We'll meet later on!"

The orderly understood.

The idea was to confuse their pursuers.

Monet reached the woods and was soon hidden in the underbrush.

What had become of La Flemme? Doubtless he too, had ben able to cover his tracks.

The lieutenant sighed deeply.

Fate seemed to be pursuing him, for now he had lost the only companion in whom he dared confide.

As for de Tersy he had made a clear confession. Ruined by gambling, he had wanted to marry Colette and get hold of old Ravignon's money.

This exculpated de Tersy from the charge of being a German spy—a criminal but not a traitor to his country.

The lieutenant started suddenly:

"But if this is the case, then I have been mistaken in a number of other ways. There has been no plot against me. German spies have not been tracking me down."

After a moment's thought, he shrugged his shoulders. If the club adventure could be cleared of any connection with spy work, another action was certainly the work of treason.

Colonel Bayen had been murdered. He had been murdered under conditions which made it certain that Brigitte Ravignon had foreseen his death.

Suddenly Louis Monet listened.

A carriage was coming towards him. He heard distinctly the horse's hoofs and the creaking of the wheels.

Where could he hide? Two walls, too high to be climbed hemmed him in on either side; nothing but a narrow ditch between them and the sidewalk. Into this he dropped, lying flat on the ground. The carriage came round a turn of the road and advanced. When it had gone a few yards past him, he raised his head.

Did he really see what he thought he saw? Was he not the victim of hallucination?

The carriage was driven by a German soldier—he noted the long cloak and the spiked helmet. But it was not the soldier he stared at.

In a flash Louis Monet thought he could distinguish the two occupants of the carriage.

Yet he must have been mistaken!

"Paul de Tersy," he murmured, "was it really Paul de Tersy I saw? And near him, that woman, who appeared to be bound? Could it have been Mme. Ravignon?"

He asked himself if he was going mad.

Paul de Tersy alive—only slightly pale, when he had seen him dead a few moments before!

And Mme. Ravignon, a prisoner, bound?

Ah! That wasn't possible. Mme. Ravignon was a spy, belonging to the German espionage. She could scarcely be bound and in a carriage driven by a soldier of the Kaiser!

The vision was so incomprehensible that Louis Monet dismissed it from his thoughts.

"I was mistaken," he said to himself.

With a movement of rage he continued on his way.

Ah! to know! To pierce the mystery of this great net of espionage in which he was struggling! Who were the scoundrels to be unmasked? Above all, to learn the truth concerning Colette. With beating heart and heavy of spirit, Louis Monet now ran along the street towards the Ravignon's house. Of course he would find there proof that he had been mistaken! He would hear Mme. Ravignon's voice! He would find the house occupied!

When Louis Monet reached the house, he found it silent and abandoned.

The doors had been broken in. The windows were without panes. One of the walls was blackened by fire.

Then, in spite of the danger, Louis Monet went in and searched from garret to cellar.

Everywhere he found traces of the struggle, objects overturned and the sinister proof of an abominable tragedy.

Why should German soldiers pillage the home of a spy?

And what had become of its inhabitants?

Was it really Brigitte Ravignon he had seen in the carriage? Was she a prisoner for not having done her work well enough?

And Colette?

Frantic with anxiety, Louis Monet crossed the garden which extended back of the house.

As he passed a small building used as a pigeon loft, he stopped in bewilderment—to find its one window brilliantly lighted.

He approached and with difficulty stifled a cry which rose to his lips.

A man's figure was silhouetted clearly against the lighted room.

What was he doing, and who was he?

He recognized the man at once. It was Ravignon, the mayor of Cirey, and his occupation was more than strange. He held two oil lamps near his face and he was speaking—that is to say he was moving his lips, but no sound came from them.

Louis Monet was about to hail him, but checked himself.

"Is he making signals?" he asked himself.

But Ravignon was absolutely motionless except for his lips which moved incessantly.

For a moment Louis Monet thought of the possibility of some scientific mechanism, of a secret telephone.

This supposition he dismissed, as no telephone existed which could transmit silent words.

The officer now cast suspicious eyes around him. The night was pitch dark. It was not possible to see three yards ahead in the garden. The idea came to him to rush into the building and confront the mayor of Cirey.

He was just on the point of doing so when raising his eyes again he noticed that Ravignon had shifted his attitude. He had put down his lamps and held a pair of glasses with which he studied the horizon with evident attention.

Louis Monet turned. And this time he guessed at least part of the truth.

Some distance away in the direction of the village he saw a lighted window, and it was this window that Ravignon was examining.

Louis Monet hesitated no longer.

"I must find out," he murmured.

Using the utmost precaution he left the garden and ran towards the lighted window.

In less than ten minutes the officer reached Cirey, and immediately understood the horrible danger which confronted him.

Cirey was taken. German soldiers were bivouacking in every street.

"If I am seen I shall inevitably be made prisoner," he felt.

He wore his officer's uniform. His identity was beyond question. But he did not hesitate.

From the shadow of a street corner he sprang over a hedge and landed in a garden. From there he climbed the railing into the next garden and so gradually advanced towards his object, the lighted window from which the signals were given. The risk was enormous and at every moment he expected to be shot down by a sentry.

At length he reached a circle of lights which proved to be the campfires of several German soldiers. He dodged to one side without being caught and finally arrived at his destination.

Behind the lighted window he saw a sight which was equally incomprehensible.

A Prussian officer stood in the same position as Ravignon with two lighted lamps held by his face, and he, too, was speaking mutely. By his side lay a field glass through which he must have watched the mayor of Cirey.

Louis Monet, amazed beyond measure, stood below the window, not knowing what to think.

"They are talking silently! Can they be—?"

Turning his eyes away for an instant, he saw the wall of the only amusement hall in Cirey. It was a modest movie theater.

Ah! Suddenly he divined the truth.

A few months ago the papers had printed an amusing anecdote.

A number of mutes had been taken to the theater to see a movie performance. During one of the most pathetic films they had burst into wild laughter. This was occasioned by the fact that they had been able to read the lips of the actors who were making jokes among themselves and speaking words which had no connection with the story of the film.

It was not impossible that these two men, spies, had achieved the same faculty.

Louis Monet swore with rage.

"The devil! Ravignon is betraying us. He is the spy!"

There could be no doubt of that.

Their method of communication was safe and sure.

Ah! Now he had direct proof of the mayor's guilt.

And, alas! He had the explanation of the mystery which had given him so much anxiety.

He had asked himself how it could have been possible to overhear the conversation which took place between Colonel Bayen and himself.

It had not been necessary to overhear their words.

Ravignon had read them on the lips of the colonel.

In fact, the very precautions taken by the unfortunate officer had been the means of the catastrophe.

Had he not held the interview by the window so that the noise of the wagons might cover his words?

And Ravignon had been in Lunéville that very evening when Colonel Bayen had given Louis Monet the yellow document.

The lieutenant had passed him in the town and La Flemme had seen him at the station.

Yes, Ravignon knew he had taken possession of the yellow

document.

Then what part had Brigitte Ravignon played?

"That, I cannot guess!" thought Louis Monet. "There is no proof of her guilt. Indeed, may she not have sent the priest as a warning, having got wind of her husband's intention to murder Colonel Bayen?"

As Louis Monet put this question to himself, he recalled the carriage he had passed a few moments earlier. He had wondered why Brigitte Ravignon, whom he suspected of being a spy, should be a prisoner of the Germans.

But, on the contrary, it was quite simple if Brigitte was an honest woman, if she had tried to save Colonel Bayen.

Again, he thought he had seen de Tersy in the carriage. Might not de Tersy have lied in making his so-called confession?

Suppose he were a spy?

In that case, it was natural for him to have feigned death, knowing he had nothing to fear from the approaching Germans.

Ought he not to have guessed the infamous trap?

Everything now became clear.

Ravignon, reading the colonel's secret by his lips; Ravignon warning de Tersy at the club; and then de Tersy playing the part of a dying man. Ah! de Tersy had succeeded marvelously.

And Colette? What had Colette done? What had become of her?

Ah! he no longer doubted. Colette was certainly innocent.

Had she escaped with the yellow document at the moment the Prussians entered the village?

Had she fled later, upon finding her father a spy?

Or was she ignorant of it all?

Or again—and Monet could not entirely drive away the thought—was she her father's accomplice?

The officer had no hesitation as to his duty.

He must return to Ravignon's house, force the mayor to confess, if necessary through fear of death.

Louis Monet sprang out of the garden.

But in his anger he neglected to take the most elementary precautions.

The noise he made called forth an immediate challenge:

"*Werda?*"

At the same time figures sprang up on all sides. He was surrounded.

At last he was face to face with the enemy.

He cried:

"*Vive la France.*"

An oath and a bayonet thrust answered him.

He jumped to one side.

The German soldiers were afraid to fire on account of wounding their own man. They rushed upon Monet.

Louis Monet did not wait for them to arrive.

He seized the German by the throat and strangled him.

The man struggled, then fell backwards to the ground, inert.

The officer continued his flight. Where could he go?

To try the gardens would inevitably mean to be caught.

He climbed a railing and found himself in a street.

Behind him the Germans were in full pursuit.

He ran forward at top speed and then turned sharply into the first lane he came to.

Twenty yards further on he came to a halt.

The lane was a blind alley.

It was hemmed in by tall houses on either side and an impassable wall at the foot.

13. Her Father

At the moment when Louis Monet had caught the mayor of Cirey in mute conversation with a Prussian officer, he had guessed many things.

He had the conviction that the redoubtable spy who had occasioned him such terrible misfortunes was the father of Colette, also that Brigitte Ravignon was innocent.

He had the certainty that he had really seen Paul de Tersy and Mme. Ravignon in the carriage.

But to learn the whole truth he would have had to be present during certain fantastic happenings which took place beyond his vision.

Paul de Tersy, whom La Flemme and Monet had left for dead, was so much alive that the moment the two men were in full flight, he jumped quickly to his feet, shouting in the purest German:

"Hi there! you brutes! hurry up! Catch the fugitives and kill them!"

He then passed through the lines and hurried to Ravignon's house.

But how was he able to pass the Prussian lines with such ease?

By reason of a small red card upon which was written, "Special Detective of the War Police," a roundabout way of saying "spy"!

Five minutes later de Tersy reached the mayor's house. There he found Farmer Ravignon busy superintending the work of some uhlans.

The orders he gave were surprising:

"Brutes! Who sent me such a rotten lot of soldiers? Aren't you even able to pillage properly? I tell you to break down the doors— the windows—destroy the furniture—fire the house!"

The young man was astounded:

"Are you crazy? What on earth are you doing?"

Ravignon answered dryly:

"I'm whitewashing myself. By the way, I want you—come

along."

After giving a few more orders, he took the young man to the cellar.

"I don't care to be killed yet and here we are safe from shells. Well, what is new?"

Ravignon had no longer the appearance of a peasant. He spoke with authority, and as a man accustomed to command.

On the contrary, de Tersy lowered his voice, hat in hand, and no longer resembled the elegant young man who drove his cars at such speed through the country.

"Monsieur Ravignon, one question first. What did you mean by whitewashing yourself?"

At the question Ravignon gave a loud laugh.

"You are young, de Tersy!"

He explained:

"Why I'm destroying my things to whitewash myself in the eyes of my dear citizens of Cirey. If my house should be exempt from the general destruction, suspicion would be raised in the minds of the French authorities."

The scoundrel laughed again at his ingenious precaution. Then suddenly his eyes lighted.

"But that is not the question. I need you, de Tersy. Somebody has to be taken away."

"Your daughter?"

"Bah! What a fool you are! My daughter doesn't bother me—it's my wife."

The wretch crossed the cellar and opened a heavy door. He then threw the light of his dark lantern on the ground.

"There she is!"

Paul de Tersy could not restrain a movement of surprise.

Bound and gagged, Brigitte Ravignon lay on the floor.

"You seem surprised," exclaimed Ravignon. "But that's the way it is. When you came under my orders as a spy I warned you against this cursed woman. I told you she could not be given a moment's liberty. She loves the French too well. Ah! I think she will get over that—for lack of an object. God punish England and protect our arms—there won't be many French left, if I guess right.

"Now then, de Tersy, to work!"

"What am I to do?"

"You are to take this woman away."

"Where?"

"To the Vezouse."

And as de Tersy started back, alarmed, the mayor added:

"Don't be so childishly stupid. I tell you the woman annoys me, therefore I suppress her—it's as clear as daylight! You are to take her to the river above the locks, fill her skirt with stones and send her to the next world. And I warn you, beware of her! On no account take out her gag. She is a woman of indomitable energy. She would be capable of crying out and attracting attention, which would be uncomfortable for both of us—for both of us. You understand?"

"Yes," said de Tersy.

"Then off you go—and hurry."

A moment later they threw the unfortunate Mme. Ravignon into a waiting carriage, driven by a German soldier, and started along the road where soon afterwards they had been seen by Louis Monet.

After Paul de Tersy had gone with the woman he was to murder Ravignon betook himself to his pigeon loft and there got into immediate communication with the head of the invading army.

Firmin Ravignon naturally little thought that he was being watched by Louis Monet and gave way to the height of joy and good humor, when, five minutes later he left the pigeon loft, or rather descended by a ladder to the cellar below.

"Tra, la! la!" he sang. "Things are certainly getting better and better."

Then, becoming more serious, he said in a strange tone:

"Eh! Big stakes are on the table now! My word! I think I shall end a millionaire—with the secret I hold—and by marrying her, as I hope to, her fortune will be mine. The combination is decidedly a good one! It took a long time to succeed, but it's succeeding at last."

The scoundrel stopped suddenly. Upon entering the cellar, he called:

"Colette! Colette! Are you there?"

"Father! It is you?"

"Yes," replied Ravignon in a paternal tone. "It is I, my poor child. Ah! What a day! But don't worry! Your mother is safe and we two are going to escape."

"Father, tell me first—the battle—did we win?"

Ravignon answered with a chuckle which Colette did not notice: "Yes, 'we' were victorious."

And while Colette trembled with joy, the ignoble coward added:

"Cirey is taken, but that is of no importance. Come, we must hurry."

An hour later, a fantastic scene, a horrible drama, began, and Colette wondered if she were not losing her reason.

Ah! the shocking adventure, the unbelievable nightmare she was to live through, the unhappy girl!

Accompanied by Ravignon, she was obliged to go through the familiar village of Cirey where German soldiers were getting drunk according to their usual custom.

Colette was instantly surprised that her father showed no anxiety.

He held in his hand a small red card which he showed ostentatiously and which seemed to be honored everywhere.

What was it?

Colette questioned:

"Father, is that a passport you have; have they given it to you as a magistrate?"

"A passport," he laughed. "It's something much better." Then he added: "Be careful, Colette... Call me 'Monsieur.' There are more surprises in store for you."

In the principal square of Cirey a superb automobile was stationed before the city hall. Two chauffeurs, whose uniforms bore the imperial arms, were on the seat. Ravignon whispered a few words to them, then opened the door.

"Kindly step in, Mademoiselle!"

Tremblingly Colette took a seat in the sumptuous car.

At this moment a fusillade began.

"Oh, father," Colette cried instinctively.

Ravignon gave her a terrible look.

"Keep quiet, now!"

Then he laughed suddenly.

His manner became so good natured and cheerful that Colette for a moment felt reassured.

Alas! the poor child would have wept her heart out had she known the significance of the shots—had she known that in a neighboring street Louis Monet was fleeing like a wild beast pursued by exasperated German soldiers.

Fortunately Colette was ignorant of that.

She seemed to be living in a fantastic dream, from which doubtless she would wake in a moment and smile at the pleasant and tragic incidents she fancied were actualities.

The automobile speeding through the night, the German chauffeurs with the imperial arms, obeying her father, Firmin Ravignon, the French mayor of the French commune of Cirey.

The automobile, after a quick run of twenty minutes, stopped and turned into the grounds of a villa which Colette, who rarely made extended excursions, did not recognize.

Immediately two footmen in knee breeches sprang down the front steps and opened the door.

"Kindly step down," murmured Ravignon.

Upon the steps, Prussian officers, the cursed soldiers she hated, were standing in groups.

One of them, very decorated, stepped forward and inquired:

"To whom have I the honor of speaking?"

And Ravignon answered in such manner that Colette thought she would faint.

"Kindly announce to his majesty his personal counselor, Professor Krampft, who wishes to speak to him upon an urgent matter."

She could not believe her ears.

Ravignon, calling himself Professor Krampft, giving himself the title of personal counselor!

While she stood voiceless and ready to fall, the much decorated young man spoke to Ravignon with infinite respect.

"Your excellency is expected. His majesty has given orders to admit your excellency without delay."

Krampft, or rather Ravignon, smiled and nodded.

"Very well."

The officer asked:

"Is mademoiselle to accompany you?"

"Certainly."

Colette felt everything turning round.

An audience? She was being taken to an audience—and her father had the title of excellency? And he spoke authoritatively to those dogs of Prussians! The frightened girl would have liked to scream. She was not given time. Ravignon, or Krampft, took her by the arm.

Father and daughter followed the officer into a large drawing room. There, chamberlains hurried forward.

"Is his majesty in the small drawing room?" asked the young officer.

Upon getting an affirmative answer, he opened a door and announced:

"His excellency, Herr Professor Krampft, personal counselor to his majesty."

Now, more than ever, Colette fancied she was going mad.

In the room a man was standing dressed in a colonel's uniform, the very sight of whom made Colette shrink with disgust.

Oh! She recognized him without trouble. This hated individual, this criminal, this coward, who intended to be the death of so many men for the good pleasure of his imperial will.

Indeed his features were celebrated.

That low and sloping forehead, that Jewish nose, those puffed lips that stuck out, and swollen ears, the shortened arm, that sickly, angry person filled with pride—all proclaimed the name of the man. "William II," Colette murmured in spite of herself."

"The Kaiser! The emperor of Germany—the enemy!"

Now the emperor, with folded arms, cold and calm, smiled at Ravignon.

"Howdy do, Krampft, howdy do, Fantômas."

"Sire, I am happy to salute you. It is twenty years since I had the honor of seeing you! Twenty years that I have been your servant—twenty years I suffer at being away from your majesty!"

But Ravignon-Krampft, for the mayor of Cirey was no other than Professor Krampft, the "Fantômas of Berlin," now one of the emperor's most powerful spies, was surprised.

William II did not answer immediately.

He seemed to be thinking.

Suddenly he exclaimed:

"You exaggerate, Krampft."

Then, pointing to Colette:

"Who is that child?"

Krampft retired three steps.

Oh! what an actor he was!

What an expression of kindness and of enthusiasm he assumed.

Ravignon had turned to Colette bowing:

"My child may this day be the happiest of your life! May this minute be the most glorious of your existence! And may your majesty find now the merited reward of a generous heart in the joy your majesty will be witness to."

He retired three paces more and cried:

"Colette, you are not my daughter as you suppose! Colette, kneel at the feet of your father. Sire, here is your child. Colette is your bastard."

Colette, whiter than death, shrank back with horror. What could those abominable words mean? She did not understand! She did not want to understand!

Krampft explained:

"Colette, one day the emperor of Germany, your father, loved. You were born of this love. The emperor might have suppressed you, but he wished you to live! He wanted you to be happy. Ah! Colette, you whom I have treated as a daughter and whom I must call 'your highness' now, throw yourself at the feet of your real father! You are his child, his bastard, love him, adore him—like the good German that you are!"

Horrible words! Tragic words which wrung the heart of the young girl. She tried to speak but could not, she gasped for air. A mist spread before her eyes and she fell at full length on the floor—unconscious.

The abominable Krampft sprang forward.

"Sire, her joy was too much for her."

William II had not moved a muscle when Colette fell.

He spoke simply:

"Decidedly you exaggerate, Krampft!"

Before the personal adviser could answer, the Kaiser rang and motioned to the chamberlain who sprang forward.

Krampft certainly did not expect what happened next.

A cry of rage escaped him.

A door had opened allowing two persons to enter. At sight of them, Krampft stepped back in dumb amazement.

"Brigitte," he murmured. "De Tersy!"

Suddenly the Kaiser advanced to him.

"You are mistaken, Krampft. You have given them their wrong names."

The Kaiser pointed to Brigitte Ravignon.

"Your wife, you say. Nonsense! Mme. Bayen, the wife of the French colonel."

Then he went to Paul de Tersy, taking him affectionately by the arm:

"And my son!" added the Kaiser, "the bastard of William II. The child I put in your care!"

Krampft remained speechless, then he stammered: "Sire! Sire! A lie! Can your majesty think—Colette—it is Colette—"

"That's enough," replied the Kaiser.

He rang again.

Undoubtedly orders had been given already. Soldiers and officers entered.

William II pointed to Krampft.

"The firing squad for him. He has lived long enough."

And he added, jokingly:

"That shows the danger of exaggerating, Krampft."

Then the sinister individual pointed to Colette:

"She is to go, where you know—and let it be done quickly."

Colette was carried out, insensible.

Krampft was dragged and hauled away, a miserable wretch shaking with agony.

The Kaiser surveyed his purple face and staring eyes:

"Very odd, very odd," he murmured.

When they had left the room, he resumed his impassable mien.

"Kindly explain, Mme. Bayen, why you are here? These people interrupted us. I await the end of your story."

Mme. Bayen—Brigitte Ravignon—was she really the wife of the murdered colonel?—continued her narrative which had been cut short by the arrival of Krampft and Colette.

"Sire," murmured the poor woman, "I will tell you the rest, and I hope to move your majesty to pity. I was then put in the carriage and your son, this cursed bastard whom I hate, tried to murder me! Oh! Sire, for a long time I had known the terrible truth, for a long time I had understood Krampft's plan.

"It is true you had formerly a natural child, which you put in Krampft's charge after making the unfortunate mother disappear. Krampft was to steal the child as you took my poor little Colette from me.

"Time went by. Colette grew up. De Tersy became one of your spies and Krampft prepared his design: to make you recognize Colette as your own daughter and marry her to de Tersy.

"Then, holding the proofs, Krampft was in a position to threaten de Tersy, ignorant of being your son. And so he could cheat your majesty and blackmail de Tersy, whose hands would be tied."

The Kaiser nodded.

He understood the infernal plan of the wretched Krampft. It was simplicity itself.

Substitute one child for another—deceive the emperor of Germany—get money from him under threat of exposing the whole affair.

"Madame," said the Kaiser slowly, "Krampft will get the punishment he deserves. Six bullets in his head. Continue your story—you were in the carriage, you say?"

"And I was about to be murdered, Sire—but I succeeded in tearing with my teeth the gag they had placed in my mouth, swallowing the pieces. I was then able to speak to your son, to tell him the secret of his birth. 'I know you are the bastard of William II, I know that the emperor is not far away. Do not kill me. Let us go and see him. Show him your shortened left arm and I who am the mother of Colette, will tell him the truth.'"

"Which I know already. I've had Krampft watched. But, tell me, de Tersy believed you?"

"Of course, father!" cried the infamous young man. "I was already your spy, what happiness to learn that I was your son!"

The emperor continued to smile:

"Mme. Bayen," he murmured, "you see that even the most complicated adventures end well. The truth always comes to light. But there are two things that need some explanation."

The Kaiser's eyes were cold and cruel.

"Why the devil did you send that idiotic priest to your husband? It nearly upset everything."

Mme. Bayen shuddered at the question.

"I am a Christian, Sire. Foreseeing the coming war and realizing the danger my husband would run, I wanted to incite him to make his peace with God."

"Granted. But here is another thing: How the devil did this fool of a Krampft get you to pass as his wife for such a long time? Frankly, I expected you to kill yourself. I was amazed to get his reports that you were still alive."

"I am a Christian, Sire! That explains all. A Christian does not commit suicide."

Then, suddenly at the end of her strength, the unhappy woman flung herself on her knees.

"Sire, have pity and grant me my liberty—above all, grant me the life of Colette! How can the poor child have deserved your anger? We will disappear! We will live wherever you wish!"

Mme. Bayen did not see the Kaiser shrug his shoulders.

"Sire, I have given you your son—you cannot refuse me the life of my daughter."

"Do you think so, really? Then you must be mad," replied the Kaiser, calmly.

He rang once more. Two officers entered.

William II pointed to the woman at his feet.

"She is a madwoman. A dangerous lunatic. I think a wagonload of insane persons is starting for Berlin. Send her with them and take especial care that she does not escape."

The unhappy woman was dragged away.

14. Flight

When Louis Monet found himself cornered in the blind alley and realized that escape was impossible, a great calm came over him.

And while he listened to the harsh cries of the soldiers searching for him, a smile came to his lips at the thought that his capture would be of no advantage, since he did not possess the yellow document.

Besides, was his capture inevitable? Was there no way of eluding the Prussian soldiers?

Louis Monet spoke German perfectly. He could overhear the noncoms questioning the soldiers after the fusillade which Colette had heard.

They had heard a suspicious noise in the garden, they had found an individual who had strangled one of their men and made his escape.

"You brutes! What became of him?"

"He is there, Sergeant. He is cornered."

"Very well, then go and get him."

"Certainly, Sergeant."

"Is he armed?"

"No, sir, if he had been, he'd have used any weapon he had just now."

"All right, tell him to throw up his hands. If he refuses, shoot him."

Louis Monet overheard these orders and although they announced his death, he could not help laughing at them.

Throw up his hands! Surrender! Ah! these Prussians didn't know him.

He drew his saber.

At any rate he would strike a blow before he fell, riddled with bullets.

"Line up there, you brutes! Six men here to cut off escape, the others forward! I will follow."

A smile crossed the lieutenant's lips.

This simple order expressed all the difference between the French and the German races.

When a French officer gives a command, he places himself in front of his men. He is the first to be exposed to danger.

How different with the barbarians! How prudent that noncom!

In a moment the sound of heavy footfalls was heard.

Louis Monet took a last look around. The blind alley was straight for about twenty yards; it then made an abrupt elbow. Louis Monet thought:

"I can't stay where I am. I shall be a clear mark for them. I shall be killed before I can strike... On the other hand, if I stand at the turn I can spring out upon them."

He advanced a few paces and then an exclamation of amazement escaped him. Quickly he knelt down and examined the street.

"Saved! I'm saved!" he cried.

And indeed his discovery was most providential.

A manhole!

It would be necessary only to lift the lid, descend into the sewer and make his escape through it.

The German soldiers would not find out the ruse for some time. Probably they would search the houses first, and this would give him time to evade them.

Ten minutes would be enough to find another manhole on the outskirts of the village and so make his escape across country.

Louis Monet struggled to lift the heavy lid. He tore his nails and made his hands bleed.

It would not budge.

He was about to give it up when a sudden thought came to him.

The workmen use a lever for the purpose. His saber might serve as such.

He put it through the ring and pressed with all his strength. A sharp crack followed and the saber lay broken in two.

"Curse it!" swore the lieutenant.

And then another thought entered his mind.

How was it that a small village like Cirey had a system of drains almost metropolitan?

Did the manhole really lead to a drain?

He recalled the fact that owing to the proximity of a waterfall, the village was lighted by electricity. What he had taken for the entrance to a drain was simply the lid of one of the small holes used by electricians for connecting the cables. Furthermore, for fear of dampness, these holes were generally sealed with cement. He felt the edges of the lid and sure enough they were firmly cemented down. A cry of anger escaped him.

Not only was this means of escape cut off, but he had destroyed his only weapon as well!

"I'm done for. There's nothing left but to surrender."

Surrender? Nonsense.

He would face the enemy and die the death of a soldier.

And now beyond the elbow Louis Monet saw lights dancing on the wall.

The prudent soldier, fearing an attack in the dark, had brought along some lanterns.

With a bound, Louis Monet sprang back.

"Die? I haven't the right to die. I must accomplish my mission."

In a flash he flung himself into the gutter, one arm stretched out on the sidewalk, the other half bent under him. And with legs apart he remained rigid.

What was he thinking of? What was he attempting to do?

The Prussians turning the corner of the alley, appeared in close formation, stretching from one side of the alley to the other.

In the middle of these lines of men and rifles, two soldiers marched, carrying powerful automobile lamps which lighted up the scene.

The sergeant cried:

"Surrender! Hands up!"

A soldier exclaimed:

"The alley is empty!"

Another shouted:

"There! On the ground—in the gutter!"

Louis Monet felt the light of the lamps were being directed on him. He remained without movement.

And what he was waiting for inevitably happened.

"He is dead!" shouted some voices.

The sergeant howled:

"Advance, you brutes!"

Then the men rushed forward in a disorderly mob.

Louis Monet was the center of a dozen soldiers who thought they were surrounding a dead body.

It was the moment the energetic officer awaited. With tense muscles, he suddenly sprang up:

"Vive la France!"

He sent the two lamps flying with a couple of blows from his broken saber.

Alarmed by this unexpected resuscitation and blinded by the sudden jump from light to darkness, the German soldiers retreated in disorder, calling for help.

And Louis Monet, with splendid courage, was ready to take advantage of this panic so cleverly brought about.

His broken saber did rough and terrible execution.

Three times the officer drove it to the hilt into living flesh. Shouts and yells followed:

"Help! Help!"

The men left in ambush at the entrance of the alley ran forward in scattered formation. This was what Louis Monet also had hoped for.

The lieutenant, with one shoulder bruised by the butt of a gun, ran towards the second lot.

In the purest German and with absolute self-possession, imitating the voice of the sergeant, he ordered:

"Forward, you brutes!—there are ten of them over there."

The soldiers in the darkness of the night were deceived. Someone flying from the danger zone had ordered them forward. It must be their chief.

And Louis Monet passed.

Leaving the alley and running at top speed he rushed down a street endeavoring to distance those who would inevitably soon be at his heels.

But he was not yet out of danger.

The streets were patrolled. At any moment he might be challenged by a sentry.

Louis Monet then did a wise thing. He dropped into a walk.

But where could he go? Where could he hide? He might be able to escape detection in some dark corner during the night. That would be to merely postpone the evil hour.

"I must find the means to go about freely," he murmured. "I must get out of this invaded territory and continue the search for Colette."

Alas! What he suggested seemed impossible to realize. He thought.

"I am in uniform. At the first streak of dawn my dress will give me away."

And this thought decided him.

The first thing to do was to find a change of clothes.

But where could he find them.

Cirey seemed to have been entirely evacuated by the French.

Before the invading horde, the inhabitants must have fled, and if any, more courageous, had thought of remaining, the bodies he had seen on the street left him in no doubt of the fate reserved for them.

The lieutenant went forward. Frequently he had to turn sharply aside to avoid groups of uhlans walking about.

Ah, if only he could get out of Cirey and gain the open country!

But he was too well convinced that the precautions taken by the Germans made such a plan impossible. Undoubtedly the village had a cordon of troops around it.

What was to be done?

He came to a decision:

"Can't help it. I must take the risk."

He supposed that the army of occupation had naturally requisitioned the houses—that in each would be found a billet of officers or men. But there was a chance that not all of them had been taken.

"May my lucky star protect me," he murmured.

He decided to chance knocking at a door.

He reasoned thus:

"The soldiers will pick out the most comfortable houses, so I'd better try some tumbledown shack."

Some distance further he came to a halt.

He noticed in the moonlight a low building which seemed modest and peaceful. Its shutters were tightly closed.

He rang the bell. It made such a racket he feared the whole village would be alarmed.

He was wrong. Nobody appeared to hear it. He rang again with the same result. Then a sudden thought struck him:

"What a fool I am to ring! Why not break in the door? Either the house is occupied by French people or it is occupied by Germans, and in the latter case, it would be to my advantage to surprise them while asleep."

He drew near the door like a thief.

The footsteps of a passing patrol were distinctly audible.

15. Fatality

There was not a moment to lose if Louis Monet really wanted to succeed in his extraordinary undertaking.

The patrol might be perhaps at the end of the street, so he had about five minutes ahead of him to work in.

"The devil take it if I can't break in that door in the time," he murmured.

A quick survey of the lock brought forth a growl:

"Luck doesn't seem to be coming my way."

And in truth he had good reason.

The lock was one of those safety ones and the screws which held it were put in from the inside.

"Not the least hope of forcing it," he muttered. As for the door, it was solid and strong and made of good oak.

"The best thing I can do is to go elsewhere," he decided.

The house was slightly back from the road. He ran quickly to the sidewalk with the intention of trying another house.

However, before venturing further, he took the precaution of glancing up and down the street.

And lucky for him he did so.

The patrol had come to a halt on his right.

Now, this stoppage was made for the purpose of rejoining another patrol coming from the left.

Louis Monet muttered:

"It's becoming simpler and simpler. I can neither go to the right nor to the left and if I remain where I am I shall be caught inevitably."

He had only a few seconds to decide in.

His situation was quite as critical as it had been in the alley.

He was about to resign himself to his destiny as a new thought struck him:

"What about my mission? If I can't open the door, why not try the windows?"

The lower ones were protected by wooden shutters only. The usual iron bars were absent.

Louis Monet summoned all his strength and attacked the one nearest at hand.

The shutters yielded so easily that he nearly fell backwards. He was now face to face with the window.

It would have been a simple matter to break it to pieces with one blow of his saber hilt, but the noise of falling glass would certainly be heard by the patrol.

Louis Monet now gave a fresh proof of his quick wit.

He removed a ring from his finger and using the diamond it contained, he began to cut the glass.

The broken piece fell inside with slight noise, having slid down the drawn curtains.

Louis Monet now put his hand through and unfastened the hasp, then sprang in and closed the window again.

It was time!

The steps of the patrol passed by a moment later and he gave a sigh of relief.

When parting the curtains, he had caught a glimpse of the interior, enough to identify the room as being a dining room.

"The outside danger has passed," he declared, "but what shall I find here?"

On tiptoe and taking infinite precautions, he felt his way along the wall, looking for the door. When he had found it a fresh anxiety arose. Would it creak when he opened it? Would he not awaken his improvised hosts? And who were they? French people or German soldiers?

Just as he expected, the door emitted a wail, all the more prolonged for the slowness with which he opened it.

"Charming music," he murmured. "I shall be challenged without doubt."

But the house remained silent and peaceful. After a brief reflection, he decided:

"By Jove! I can't be wrong. These people must be devilish tired to sleep so heavily. Now I fancy the French who remain at Cirey won't be in any mood to sleep, consequently I shall probably find myself face to face with Prussian officers."

He advanced further until he reached a staircase. His hand touched the banisters and he determined to go up.

Under his weight, the stairs creaked strangely.

"It's amazing," he thought. "I don't seem to wake a soul."

He was still more surprised on reaching the first landing not to hear a sound of any sort.

"Must be the house of the Sleeping Beauty," he said to himself.

Feeling his way along the walls, he ended by reaching another door.

This must lead to one of the sleeping rooms.

By opening it he would be burning his bridges. Without a moment's hesitation Louis Monet turned the handle and entered the room.

Again nobody.

"My word, the house is empty," exclaimed the lieutenant.

But as he said it something very much alive struck him in the chest, climbed over his shoulders and fled away.

With an oath he sprang to one side. Again his luck was against him. For he bumped into some piece of furniture apparently covered with fragile ornaments.

With a clatter and bang this fell to the ground.

Then in spite of himself, Louis Monet burst out laughing.

"This time I've done it."

But after the racket had ceased the house again became silent as before.

Had he had the luck to enter an empty house?

Was it possible that a single house had escaped being requisitioned by the Prussians?

Louis Monet calmly lit a match.

The first thing he noticed was a large bed which was empty and unmade. A night table stood by its side and upon this was a candle.

"Must be the palace of a thousand and one nights," he exclaimed almost joyously.

He lit the candle and examined the room. Near the door he noticed the crockery he had thrown down. After a brief survey he concluded:

"A spare room. Let's try elsewhere."

Taking his candle he went into the passage. There he discovered what had struck him as he entered. An enormous cat, with back up and flaming eyes, sat watching his every movement. Louis Monet did not stop to pet it.

Another door faced him. This he opened suddenly and then he started back in fear, cold from the unpleasant impression he had received.

The room in disorder, showed only too characteristic details.

Near the bed were two large brass candlesticks with half-burned candles in them.

Upon the chairs petals of flowers were scattered, evidently dropped from bouquets.

"Ah," he cried, "one would say a funeral had taken place here. Perhaps the Germans have respected the house through superstitious fear!"

Some papers lay on a table. These Louis Monet glanced over. They explained why the invading army had been given orders not to occupy the house.

They contained a doctor's certificate to the effect that the patient had died of typhoid fever.

Upon making this discovery Louis Monet could hardly refrain from a gesture of alarm.

As a matter of fact what was he doing in the house?

He had come to find clothes.

Would he not be obliged to put on the dead man's clothes, and possibly die of typhoid?

"Can't help it," he declared after a moment's thought. "To die one way or another isn't of great importance. Besides the period of incubation is long enough to allow me to fulfill my mission and find Colette."

So, in spite of the sinister surroundings, the young man opened a wardrobe.

He smiled at what he saw there.

"That will make a capital disguise," he said to himself.

The clothes hanging up belonged to a priest. Chance had brought him to a priest's house.

Louis Monet hesitated no longer.

Hastily he took off his uniform and donned the clerical garb.

To be sure the robe was a trifle too narrow in the shoulders and a bit too long, but it could be buttoned.

"Now, I have only to take off my boots and trousers and my disguise will be complete."

Indeed he was about to finish his toilette when suddenly in the silence of the night a loud ring at the bell startled him.

Who could it be? Some relative of the dead person or the patrol? Louis Monet thought:

"Bah! If I couldn't break in the door how can they? I'll just keep quiet and they'll soon get tired of ringing and go away."

But a second and then a third ring followed.

Louis Monet, standing by the window, was now able to overhear the conversation below.

"Colonel, there is nobody here!"

"Ring again, idiot!"

A Prussian officer and his orderly stood at the door.

From one side came the sound of horses' hoofs.

They were doubtless the mounts of these obstinate visitors.

"Let them ring. I shan't stir," Louis Monet decided.

"Ring again, Karl! Can't you see there is a light at the window! Someone has probably heard us and is dressing to come down."

Louis Monet cursed.

How imprudent of him to keep the candle lighted.

"After all, there are only two of them," he thought. "I'll let them in and if they are too curious I'll knock them down with the first object that comes to my hand. I'm worth two Germans at any rate!"

The lieutenant had forgotten his strange costume. Beneath the long priest's robe his boots and spurs stuck out.

Fortunately he had never worn a mustache.

"I'll risk it," he decided.

He clattered downstairs and unbolted the door.

"What do you want, officer?"

The Prussian politely took off his cap.

"Abbé, I would like to have a word with you."

There was no way of avoiding the request.

"Please come in, sir."

Candle in hand, Monet led the way to the dining room.

"Abbé," explained the colonel, who was easily recognized as being a staff officer, "I must apologize for disturbing you at such an hour, but events—"

"Ah, yes, events," said Monet in a solemn voice.

The officer quickly turned to him.

"Then you know? Someone has told you?"

"No, no, I know nothing—I simply referred to the war."

The two men had entered the dining room.

"Kindly sit down."

"Thanks, Abbé."

Louis Monet himself was about to sit on the table, but remembered in time that such an attitude would not be becoming in a priest. He chose a chair instead.

"Abbé," continued the Prussian. "I am here upon a matter which concerns your holy ministry."

"Very good," replied Louis Monet.

At this moment the lieutenant made a discovery.

"Good Lord," he thought, "I mustn't turn my head, I have no tonsure!"

"Abbé, I must begin by asking you an indiscreet question."

"Pray do, officer."

Louis Monet began to grow weary. He was not accustomed to sitting still. Mechanically he crossed his legs. But no sooner had he done so than he felt a pang of alarm. He discovered that he still wore his boots and spurs! He uncrossed his legs in haste and tucked them under his chair, thinking:

"How the deuce can I take off my spurs without being seen? I can no longer move hand or foot."

The Prussian officer continued:

"The question is this: Are you a true believer? Are you ready to face danger and annoyance to perform your duties as priest?"

"Sir, a priest does not hesitate. Martyrdom has its charms for him."

This answer seemed to relieve the colonel.

"In that case," he declared, "my mission is very much simplified, for you are the priest I was in search of. Besides you can make your mind easy. The danger you run is only apparent. I give you my word of honor that no harm will come to you."

The gravity of the colonel, and the strangeness of his words caused some anxiety to Louis Monet.

"What am I to do?"

The Prussian rose.

"Abbé, I will explain in a few words. A woman is about to be shot—or rather that is not quite it—a woman is to be suppressed. The method used makes little difference. This woman, for special reasons, has been granted an interview of three minutes with a confessor. I am here to ask you if you will be that confessor."

Louis Monet grew dizzy.

A woman was going to be executed. He was asked to go to her!

"Sir," he replied, "I have not the right to refuse, but I must warn you that I do not speak German."

"The woman in question is French."

Louis Monet exclaimed angrily:

"A French woman you are going to kill?"

"Yes, Monsieur," said the colonel coldly.

"Very well, come along!"

Louis Monet quite forgot his role of priest for the moment.

A woman was going to be assassinated.

It was not the priest but the soldier who would go to her—not to confess her but to defend her to the death.

Louis Monet went forward a step, clanking his spurs with bravado. Fortunately the Prussian colonel seemed rather upset.

"Wait, I haven't told you all yet, Abbé."

"What else is there?"

The colonel explained in a hesitating voice:

"The matter is rather unusual—I scarcely know how to explain it—you see, it's this way: This woman is—and this is her crime—a very interesting personage, so his majesty the emperor has given orders to have her suppressed…"

"The Kaiser!" shouted Louis Monet.

"Yes, Monsieur. And therefore the woman cannot continue to live. Even her death must not be known. In a word, Abbé, it is necessary that you should not recollect the place where you are to see her."

The false abbé demanded:

"Explain, I beg you. What conditions are imposed upon me?"

"You must permit us to blindfold you first of all."

"Very well, you may blindfold me."

"Then you must swallow a drug."

"A drug? What do you mean?"

"Oh, a quite harmless drug—a light soporific. This will ensure a lapse of time before you could talk of what had happened. And this time we need."

All this seemed far from clear and the colonel was right in supposing that a priest might hesitate to agree.

But the Prussian was not dealing with a priest but with a soldier whose heart was filled with anger.

What an abominable crime was this studied and calculated murder spoken of in such cold blood!

"Well, it can't be helped," thought Louis Monet. "If I have to die I shall die, but no one shall say that I shrank from a like adventure."

Louis Monet accepted without hesitation.

"I do not feel that I have the right to refuse what appears to be my duty. You may blindfold me. I will drink what you wish me to drink, but I will answer the call of this penitent."

"Are you ready to follow me?"

"Whenever you wish, officer."

Louis Monet stepped back, and in doing so his spurs clanked. He quickly added:

"Just a moment, to change my cassock. I dressed rather hurriedly when you rang."

"Certainly Abbé, certainly."

The Prussian officer bowed.

"And allow me to compliment you. For a priest, you are braver than a soldier."

Louis Monet had to bite his lips to hold back a retort.

The compliments of such a blackguard were worse than the greatest insults.

16. She

Having removed his spurs, but kept on his boots, for he could find no others in the priest's wardrobe, Louis Monet returned to the dining room.

The few moments he was alone had given him a chance to reflect.

Was he really doing his duty in plunging into this adventure, the consequences of which might be disastrous?

Colonel Bayen had said:

"You must think of your mission before everything. You no longer belong to yourself. You are not free to do what seems good to you. You must first save France!"

But a second's thought convinced him that his duty was actually to go with the colonel.

As to this woman, it suddenly came to him that she might be no other than Mme. Brigitte Ravignon.

He had seen her with de Tersy, bound and a prisoner.

He guessed that she was in possession of terrible secrets, perhaps that of the yellow document.

His duty then would be to do his utmost to discover them.

The Prussian officer met him with a smile.

"You have not taken long at your toilette, Abbé, a further cause for congratulation. As a matter of fact, had you refused to come, my instructions were to bring you anyway, by force if necessary. Again, I say, you need be under no apprehension. No harm will happen to you."

"That is understood, Monsieur," replied Monet.

"Then allow me to blindfold you."

"Now?"

"Yes. You must not have the least indication of where you are going."

But while the Prussian officer bound his eyes with a heavy silk scarf, Louis Monet had a sudden fear.

Was he not being caught in the most transparent of traps?

This story of the woman about to be murdered seemed most unlikely. Might it not have been invented to lead him, undefended, to a violent death?

The Prussian officer having tied the bandage took the lieutenant amiably by the arm.

"Allow me to guide you, Abbé, as you will be blind for a short while."

Then he added in an off-hand tone:

"By the way, I forgot to mention, having complete confidence in your word of honor, that upon the slightest move on your part to uncover your eyes I have orders to blow out your brains."

"Very well, Officer. I shall do nothing that would interfere with my ministration to my penitent."

The colonel became more and more amiable. He warned Monet of each obstacle.

"Take care, Abbé. Raise your foot, there is a step. Now, lean on me. Here we are at the carriage."

A few moments later he took his place in the carriage. He easily recognized it as being an old landau for hire which had doubtless been requisitioned when the Germans took possession of Cirey.

The horses started off at a round trot, turning rapidly to right and left, then apparently going in a circle.

After five minutes Louis Monet gave up all hope of following the direction taken.

The Prussian officer began questioning the supposed abbé. Apparently he belonged to the formidable German espionage organization.

Was the spirit of France good? Did he expect to be victorious? Himself, he was convinced that it would be over in a few days—and besides, if France were absorbed by Germany it would be for her own good. "We would give her our culture—we would teach her commerce and industry—in a word, we would help her to become civilized."

Louis Monet could hardly hold himself in. He declared with fury:

"Sir, I consider that France is civilized—and that Germany is a land of barbarians. Excuse me for speaking so frankly, but doubtless you forget that you are talking to a Frenchman."

The colonel growled out a few words, then asked:

"You have not brought what is necessary to administer the sacrament?"

"No, because I did not have the accessories in the house. Besides, I cannot believe that this woman is to be executed—I hope I may be allowed to intercede for her."

"You are mistaken, Abbé. The decisions of the Kaiser are irrevocable."

"The decisions of justice are still more irrevocable," replied Louis Monet. "Murder has to be paid for, cowardice expiated."

But he quickly realized that he must observe a more prudent attitude if he did not want to expose himself to fresh danger.

"Allow me to pray, Monsieur," he said.

After about an hour's ride in the carriage Monet had the impression that they had turned into a graveled road, probably an avenue leading to a house.

"We have arrived. I will help you to get out, Abbé."

Louis Monet, leaning on the arm of his guide, stepped onto a path.

"Follow me," ordered the officer. "Put your hand on my shoulder and walk without fear."

After a few steps, he spoke again.

"Lift your feet, there are four steps to go up."

With nerves on edge and his curiosity excited to the highest pitch, Monet made an observation which rather surprised him.

It seemed that they were entering, not an inhabited house, but a building under construction.

He noticed the cool air that comes from stones freshly put in place and cemented. Also an odor of plaster and chalk. The humidity was evident.

"I am being taken to a cellar," he thought.

But a moment later he found himself walking on a thick carpet.

"Please sit down, Abbé. A moment of patience."

He bowed without speaking.

Where was he? What was happening?

Was he alone in the room with the Prussian officer or were there others watching him?

He could hear nothing. The silence was absolute.

After a few moments Monet felt a strange physical impression.

Very brave, he had never known fear! He was now to know the throes of that atrocious feeling which tortures and breaks down the spirit.

"Ah! I was mad to come here! I've fallen into a trap. This Prussian officer undoubtedly belongs to the spy service and I run the risk of meeting Ravignon or de Tersy. If either of these men catch sight of me, it's all up."

At this moment a new voice broke the silence.

"Send away the masons. The priest is here."

He did not understand the meaning of these extraordinary words.

Steps approached him. Another voice spoke:

"Abbé, your guide told you the conditions under which you can see your penitent?"

"Yes."

"So you will not refuse to take this drug?"

"I will not refuse, Monsieur."

"You have been told, and I repeat, that it is quite harmless. It is merely a soporific which will induce a peaceful sleep. This will guarantee us your discretion and will not hurt you."

Louis Monet bowed again.

One thing struck him. The perfect way these cursed Prussians spoke French.

And what a formidable machine it was that regulated the words and actions of these individuals who would not stop at the murder of a woman if the Kaiser so ordered!

The Prussian officer who had accompanied him now spoke.

"If you will hold out your hand, Abbé, I will give you the drug. Afterwards, I beg you to follow me immediately. The effect of the drug is very rapid, in twenty minutes you will be asleep."

Monet held out his hand and taking the glass put it to his lips, saying:

"Drink without fear? Would you do so in my place?"

And then, in one gulp he swallowed the contents of the glass.

A burst of laughter greeted his sally.

"Well answered, Abbé! You are certainly a brave man! We admit that in your place we would not be quite easy—but, after all, it is war."

"No," replied Monet coldly. "It is outlawry. I am ready to follow you."

He was taken by the arm and led away.

He was obliged to go up steps and down others. Vainly he tried to get some knowledge of his surroundings.

At length a door opened and he was pushed forward.

"Abbé, you may remove your bandage now. Monet tore it off and found himself in the middle of a sumptuously furnished room. Bookshelves armchairs, a sofa, and numerous card tables filled the space.

But what he noticed most particularly was the wall opposite. An enormous breach had been made in it, recently filled in with bricks, of which several seemed not even to be sealed.

What did it mean?

Was this the work the masons were doing when ordered away?

Surrounding him were three officers. They had revolvers in their hands with triggers cocked ready to fire.

Louis Monet thought:

"Well, I couldn't get out of here alive if I tried to!"

One of the officers he recognized with a start.

It was the same individual who had signaled Ravignon.

"Abbé," said one of his jailers, in a menacing and sarcastic voice. "You are now about to learn a State secret. Look!"

He then went to the wall and removed several of the bricks.

Monet could now contemplate the most frightful and abominable of visions.

In the wall where she was to be buried alive was a woman whom Monet recognized at the first glance.

Colette!

Colette in the hands of the Prussians!

Colette who was to be murdered in such a cruel way.

Louis Monet was about to spring forward and tear away the stones, but suddenly he paused.

Colette raised her eyes and saw him.

An expression of joy, of stupor came into her face as she recognized beneath the priest's robe—Monet!

And Monet could read in her clear eyes where he had so often sought for tokens of love, an order absolute and formal which he did not understand but which he must obey.

"Not a word, not a movement. Do not recognize me. Do not try to save me!"

These were the things her eyes said.

"God God!" stammered the lieutenant.

Then instinctively playing his part, he joined his hands.

"My poor child."

Behind him, unmoved, stood the three officers.

And then Colette spoke.

And what a torture it was to hear her!

"Father, I have brought you here to place in your hands a sacred mission, a mission which alone can allow me to die in peace."

"Speak, my child."

Louis Monet no longer knew what he said. He moved and spoke automatically, and found the words instinctively that a priest would have used in his place.

Colette went on:

"Father, I begged permission to see you, saying that I wished to confess. But it is not a confession that I want to make—it is a mission I would entrust to you. Father, I beg you to listen with all your soul to the prayer of one about to die."

Louis Monet guessed that these words had a secret meaning.

"Father, I had a fiancé whom I adored with all my heart. I would have given my life a thousand times for him. Father, I want you to find him."

"What is his name?"

Colette looked him in the eyes.

"My fiancé is Louis Monet—he is an officer in the 32nd dragoons. I want you to tell him that he will be in my thoughts until I die—that I have been worthy of his love, and that I order him to do his duty as I have done mine."

Colette's voice trembled. She repeated:

"As I have done mine."

Louis Monet understood the importance of these words.

Undoubtedly the young girl wanted to reassure him about the yellow document.

She continued:

"Tell him not to worry over me—not to weep—that I even forbid him to think of me until the war is over. Let him fight! Let him accomplish his mission—as an officer."

What courage the young girl must have had to keep her composure. How patriotic to bid him not try to save her but perform his duty without a tear.

Louis Monet, with tortured heart, bowed his head sadly.

He could not utter a word.

Colette went on:

"And when he swears to be faithful to my orders, you will give him this ring—which he will wear in memory of me."

An officer stepped forward and handed a ring to Monet.

This ring Colette had given to her savage murderers before being shut in her living tomb.

"I will wear this ring," murmured Louis Monet in an anguished voice.

Then suddenly he swung round, unable to longer restrain himself.

"You can't kill this woman! You wear a soldier's uniform! You are not cowards!"

One of the officers replied:

"Abbé, there are things you don't know—this girl is the bastard of William II. She must die!" Louis Monet staggered back, struck to the heart, while Colette gave a choking sob.

The bastard of William II.

Could it be possible?

At first Louis Monet would not believe it, but Colette's tears finally convinced him.

Alas! Why didn't the unfortunate officer know that Colette herself was mistaken, having fainted at the moment when Krampft admitted his lie?

"Why didn't he know that it needed the monstrous imagination of Krampft—of Ravignon—to attempt to make Colette pass for a child of the abominable master of Germany?

"The emperor's bastard!" he cried. "I don't believe that! If it were so why would the Kaiser have her murdered?"

"State secret," said the officer simply.

"Then why this torture? Why the horror of this death, slow and cruel? It isn't true! She is not the Kaiser's daughter!"

"State secret," replied the officer again.

"State secret!" Monet cried, forgetting all prudence. "Then I'll make this state secret known throughout the world! And the whole world will punish your infamous master."

"No Abbé. You will say nothing," answered an officer calmly. "Tell me, haven't you a strange sensation in your hands—a heaviness of head? Are you not very thirsty?"

Louis Monet grew pale.

Yes, that was quite true. He had noted the symptoms. He shouted:

"You have poisoned me!"

"No, make your mind easy. Come, Abbé, I will explain—only I do not want the woman to hear."

"I don't want to leave her!"

"Oh, you will see her again, I give you my word. I've only a couple of words to say to you."

Louis Monet glanced at Colette. Her eyes said obey and he obeyed.

17. Towards Forgetfulness

"Sit down, Abbé."

The officer had taken Louis Monet into an adjoining room furnished with soft carpets, and tapestries on the walls. One could speak here without fear of being overheard.

The officer lit an excellent cigar.

"I'm sure you think you have been poisoned, Abbé, in spite of my assurances to the contrary; won't you believe me?"

"I don't know what to think. I believe you capable of anything."

The officer bowed ironically.

Possibly he took it as a compliment.

"Capable of anything? You exaggerate. But capable of many things. Besides, you will soon know."

The officer took several puffs at his cigar.

"Abbé, you have just heard that the girl who is to die is the Kaiser's bastard. That is a serious matter—but there is something still more serious. By the way, how do you feel?"

"I feel an extraordinary torpor, my head is heavy and my eyes smart. I have occasional dizziness."

The Prussian nodded at each symptom.

"Very good—that's it exactly."

He gave a short laugh, blew some smoke into the air and continued:

"You might easily guess that we would take precautions against the possibility of your spreading abroad this troublesome business—French ideas are so stupid, as in fact are those of the world."

Louis Monet now felt a violent headache.

"I don't understand you."

"You will, Abbé. In a word, we were anxious to give this girl the consolation of an interview with you and at the same time make it impossible for you to spread the story; so we had to discover a method of depriving you of any recollection of what had taken place. You understand?"

"No!" shouted Monet. "Explain! If you have poisoned me, say so!"

"That wasn't necessary. We have no hesitation in killing when it is necessary, but not otherwise. You have not taken poison, Abbé."

"Then you intend to keep me prisoner?"

The officer shook his head.

"A prisoner might escape someday. We thought of something else."

"For pity's sake, what?"

"A very simple plan."

The German gloated over the evident anguish of his victim.

"We made you drink a mixture of laudanum, belladonna, and curare."

"Yes, and this soporific—if that's all it is?"

"It is something more, Abbé. Its effects vary. May I explain them to you?"

"Go on! Go on!"

Monet would have risen, but his legs gave way under him.

"This draft will first produce a deep sleep which will last four or five hours."

"And when I wake?"

"Ah, you will then, Abbé, understand the ingenuity we have used in mixing this drink. When you wake you will have completely forgotten everything that happened from the moment you drank the potion until the moment you open your eyes."

Louis Monet felt himself to be the plaything of some hideous nightmare. He would forget everything that had happened. He would forget that he had seen Colette, that she was William II's bastard. He would forget the horrible death of the heroic child, and perhaps that she had ordered him to fulfill his mission before everything.

"It isn't possible!" he cried.

"I beg your pardon," replied the officer, "it is most possible. For instance, when you wake you will remember that I went to your house to get you to come to a dying woman—and that is precisely what you may have to testify to someday. Therefore it is useful that you remember it. For the rest, your discretion is absolutely guaranteed by the power of the drug."

"Then since I am to forget everything, why not tell me more?"

"Ask me what you want to know?"

"Well, tell me why you invented all this?"

The Prussian seemed at a loss.

"I don't understand."

"I mean, you are not the sort to have pity on a woman. Why did you play this abominable trick? Why tell the girl that you were bringing her a priest and then make it impossible for me to acquit myself of her last wishes?"

The Prussian laughed.

"Why didn't we simply refuse her request? I will tell you. The woman holds an important secret, so we offered her a bargain: To allow her an interview with a priest in exchange for her secret. Furthermore, if she should then refuse we informed her that she would be walled up alive, but if she kept her promise we would simply blow out her brains."

Louis Monet felt as though he suffered a thousand deaths.

Colette's secret could be no other than that of the document.

Would she yield to the torture or would she betray it? No, Colette would not speak; she had merely pretended to agree to the bargain.

Then what had become of the yellow document? The officer rose:

"Well, have you nothing else to ask? Are you asleep already?"

Monet had suddenly closed his eyes and his head fell forward on his chest.

"That's splendid," laughed the officer.

He now put his hand on Monet's shoulder and shook him violently.

"Come, wake up!"

But Monet seemed dead asleep.

"That's all right! The drug has done its work. This chap will have a great sleep and nothing can wake him up! The next thing is to get rid of him."

The officer was mistaken.

Monet was not asleep. In fact, he was wide awake.

The idea had come to him to try the only ruse left.

He must take some notes before the drug made him insensible.

These he could use when he woke up again?

But how to take them?

His one chance lay in hastening his departure. Probably they would send him back to Cirey. He thought:

"Ah! Let me but find the yellow document and end this horrible mission and then I shall be free to lay down the burden of my life."

Colette was lost.

She would sacrifice herself for her duty to France. He, too, would do his duty and then seek death in serving his country against the Germans.

The officer interrupted his thoughts by calling:

"Karl! Ulrich! Put this man in the carriage that is waiting. The coachman has the necessary instructions."

Louis Monet felt himself lifted, limp and lifeless, by two servants who placed him on the cushions of the landau. A voice asked:

"Are you going with him?"

"No, that isn't necessary. He will sleep until five or six tomorrow evening."

He was to go alone! So much the better.

He would be better enabled to fight against sleep.

The door of the landau was shut and bolted. In a moment the carriage started.

Louis Monet cautiously opened his eyes.

Would it be possible to recognize the road they were taking? In that case he might return in the hope of rescuing Colette. But he found himself in total darkness.

As an extra precaution the wooden shutters protecting the window glass had been closed.

Louis Monet once more plunged into despair.

"I have neither pencil nor pen nor even a pin to scratch notes on my cuff," he said to himself. "Besides, if that were even possible, the danger would be too great for they might be discovered."

And then suddenly an idea came to him.

He still wore the diamond ring he had used to cut the window pane in the priest's house.

Why not use it again to cut a few words on the carriage window?

The lieutenant understood shorthand which made the task simpler. He began tracing:

"Colette innocent—Colette daughter of Kaiser—Colette walled up alive," and he added: "Yellow document must be saved. I have Colette's ring on my finger."

But as he finished the last words a fresh anxiety took hold of him.

These notes would be of no avail because he would not remember that he had made them.

"At least I had better lower the glass so nobody else can see them."

The effort to do this made him stagger.

He lost his balance and a jolt of the carriage flung him violently against the opposite door; his arm struck a ledge of the window and opened a vein in his wrist.

The blood spurted out and Monet fell back on the seat and lost consciousness.

Was the officer beaten at last? Was German espionage to triumph?

Colonel Bayen—a hero—had been murdered. Mme. Bayen had been thrown among mad folks and was being carried to Berlin. Colette, the gentle Colette, when fairly resigned to a horrible death, would preserve silence. The brave La Flemme had not been sparing of his efforts and devotion.

And Louis Monet himself—would he ever find the yellow document for which he had already sacrificed more than his life—his love?

Second Part: Towards Victory

1. The Head of the Service

While the unfortunate Louis Monet was being taken bleeding and unconscious towards an unknown destiny, a strange scene was being enacted in the villa which the emperor of Germany had made his headquarters. The Kaiser stood in a sumptuous room, one elbow on the mantelpiece, smoking a large cigar and commenting to his bastard son with joyful confidence on the first results of the campaign.

"This war is quite simple and will be soon over. Austria will supply me with her enormous siege guns. Liège will not resist. Namur may give me more trouble—in any case a week is enough for the invasion of Belgium—the French will wait for me on the Alsace frontier. Now the mobile wing of my armies is moving by the north. You follow me, de Tersy?"

The bastard did not seem quite at his ease. He wondered what William II was driving at.

He was terrified of saying the wrong thing and bringing upon himself one of those crushing replies for which the Kaiser was famous.

"Sire, not one of your words is lost."

William II smiled:

"Call me 'father'—nobody hears us."

William II continued:

"So France, invaded in the north, will make but slight resistance. Then I shall attack perfidious England and—"

The emperor had just said: "Nobody hears us."

He was mistaken.

It was true that the room contained nobody but the Kaiser and his bastard. And yet not one of the emperor's words was lost, not one of his nefarious projects but was known.

Somebody was listening and smiling too, ironical and mocking. This individual muttered:

"He is a monomaniac."

After a moment, he added:

"He is a fool."

Where was this inquisitive eavesdropper who dared to criticize the politics of William II?

The Kaiser went on:

"Nothing can stay my plans, nothing can oppose my will. What I have decided upon will be done. Krampft will be shot, Colette will disappear also! Mme. Bayen will no longer be dangerous shut up with the insane. You see, my son, nobody can resist me."

Paul de Tersy bowed.

The unknown person answered the Kaiser's last words, in a low, fierce whisper:

"I can, Sire."

At the other end of the room the thick wall concealed a hiding place made for the purpose of espionage and also to safeguard the person of the Kaiser.

It was from there that the individual had dared to bid defiance to the master of Germany.

Who was this personage?

Tall, slight, well built, with close-cropped light hair, he wore a beard and mustache so perfectly trimmed that one might doubt whether they were real. His eyes were hidden under blue glasses and his coat was long and tightly buttoned, giving him the appearance of a Protestant clergyman. His hands were gloved.

Who was he?

A servant of the Kaiser or some French patriot ready to revenge the invaded territory? Whoever he might be he continued to listen to the conversation, growling from time to time.

"What idiots!"

Then, as the Kaiser repeated:

"Success is certain. This war will be a series of uninterrupted victories," the unknown calmly declared:

"And what about the yellow document?"

Thereupon, this individual slowly and carefully left his hiding place. He pressed a secret spring, the wall opened, and he found himself in a hall.

He muttered, it may have been ironically:

"And yet the emperor's will must be obeyed!"

He then took a few steps towards a room from which voices were heard:

But if the emperor's will should lead to the downfall of Germany? "Ah, well, we must save our masters—in spite of themselves!"

He entered the room where a dozen persons were gathered, who rose at his approach, bowing respectfully.

"Howdy do, gentlemen. These are my orders. You Ulrich and you Karl will remain on duty at the door of the room his majesty is occupying. Two others will watch the person who is now in conversation with his majesty. You will also get rifles and cartridges from my personal baggage—my servant will give them to you. These will be used for the execution you know of. Another thing— is the bandage ready that I ordered?"

"Yes, chief."

"You will see that it is used to bind him."

"Yes, chief."

"Has the ditch been dug?"

"It has been dug, chief."

"In that case the execution can take place?"

"Certainly, chief."

"Very good. Choose six soldiers. I'll go and see our man and I will give you the signal."

This strange master, who was treated with such respect, moved towards the door.

"It is understood that nobody is to be allowed near—that is your work, gentlemen."

"It shall be done, chief."

Chief—of what service?

A German could have answered that question.

There is in Germany a service that is not spoken of without a shudder.

Its title is simple: Secret Service. By that is meant, Espionage Service.

The head of the service is simply the chief spy of Prussia, the man who organizes the worst abominations, the direst cruelties, who recoils before nothing if a diplomatic or military advantage is to be gained. Like master, like man. The Kaiser had evidently a worthy executioner of his vilest designs.

But this made it all the more strange that the master spy should think and express himself as he had done.

After giving his orders to the men who were no other than spies in his pay, the chief made his way to the cellar.

Undoubtedly the building had long been prepared to shelter William II when the campaign against France should begin. The peasants of the neighborhood had never guessed that this unfinished house, still surrounded by scaffolding, was in reality fully equipped within for the special uses it was to be put to. Even the cellars had their secret construction.

They were dungeons.

Before one of them, two soldiers mounted guard.

"Is the man here?" asked the chief.

The two soldiers bowed.

"Open."

A moment later the sinister individual entered the cell.

"Hello, Krampft!"

A burst of laughter answered him.

"Krampft?"

"You seem in a good mood, Krampft."

"Pardon, there's a mistake—have to look elsewhere for your Krampft. I'm all alone—Ravignon!"

The chief grew pale and recoiled a step.

"Look here, you needn't disguise your voice, Ravignon. It is I, Rauerdt, who is speaking. No use pretending, eh! I know that Krampft and Ravignon are one and the same person."

"You are mistaken, Monsieur."

"I'm mistaken, am I?"

The chief turned angrily:

"Light up, there!"

A brilliant electric light suddenly illuminated the cellar.

Before Rauerdt stood an unknown man dressed in the uniform of a French dragoon, who looked at him with surprise and mockery in his eyes.

"Who are you?" asked Rauerdt.

"Why, I'm Ravignon. Seems to surprise you but it's so—ah, you're looking at my clothes. I'll tell you how it is—you see uniforms have come into fashion since the mobilization."

The dragoon burst into laughter.

Rauerdt, pale with rage, stepped forward:

"Who are you?"

"Monsieur Ravignon."

"No use lying to me. I happen to be the master spy of Germany. l know Krampft—Ravignon—consequently—"

"Delighted to meet you," interrupted the dragoon. "Now, I'll present myself. It's true I'm not Ravignon. As for Krampft, I don't know who he is. My name is La Flemme, orderly of Lieutenant Monet. Does that suit you?"

La Flemme calmly sat down on the wooden bench.

Rauerdt wondered if he could be dreaming. Two hours earlier he had seen Krampft—Ravignon—arrested in the emperor's study and brought to this cell and now—

"How did you get here?" he asked sharply. "And where is Krampft?"

"You're inquisitive, aren't you?"

La Flemme jumped up, clanking his spurs.

"Well, I'll tell you how it is. You see, I was looking for my lieutenant—a landau passes—naturally I chase it—my lieutenant was inside! Then out pops some of your soldiers from a hedge—they pinch me—thirty they were against me."

"And then?"

"Then they brought me here."

"But Ravignon?"

"Why, Ravignon was here."

"Ravignon *was* here, but he isn't here now?"

"So it seems—well, then they shoved me into this cell. But just as I came in I passed M'sieur Ravignon. Then I don't exactly know what happened. 'Don't stir,' he says to me, 'I'll save your lieutenant.' Then he said something else in German to my guard and then he lit out. Since then I've been waiting here. So I'm glad to see you and have a chat."

Rauerdt, pale with anger, jerked out:

"You shall die." Then turned and gave another order.

"Bring here the firing squad."

If La Flemme did not understand what had happened, Rauerdt understood only too well.

Krampft had simply seized the chance of escape when another prisoner was brought in. This was easy, as in the surprise of his arrest the other spies had not been notified.

The two men who had brought in La Flemme knew Krampft as being one of them and naturally let him go.

Rauerdt went to La Flemme.

"You are to die. But if you tell me where the yellow document is, I will let you go free."

La Flemme shrugged his shoulders.

"I don't know where it is, and if I did I wouldn't tell you."

The door of the cell opened. Rauerdt pointed to La Flemme:

"Take him away."

"Are you really going to kill me?"

And, as nobody answered, he added:

"Guess you're mad because my lieutenant slipped through your fingers. After all, you can put a dozen bullets into me. My pals of the 32nd will return them with interest."

With that he burst into loud laughter.

Oh, truly death had no terror for him. He would meet it with perfect calmness, an absolute and complete contempt.

He placed himself in the center of the squad and shouted:

"Forward! March!"

Twenty yards behind the patrol Rauerdt and one of his spies were talking.

"The will of the emperor must be done," said Rauerdt. "For instance, Krampft was condemned to death—and he is far away—that makes one. As for Colette, de Monet and Brigitte Ravignon, you will help me."

Rauerdt's companion appeared to quite understand; he nodded his head. Then, as the patrol came to a halt by the side of an open grave, the spy asked:

"But who is this fellow?"

"I don't know," admitted Rauerdt.

"Has he spoken?"

"He says he knows nothing."

The soldiers lined up opposite the dragoon.

The spy questioned Rauerdt.

"And we are to treat him?"

"Like the other one."

"Very good, chief."

The spy advanced to the condemned man.

"One moment. He must be blindfolded."

Three minutes later a shout was heard.

"*Vive la France!*"

And this shout was drowned in a salvo of shots.

Rauerdt calmly smoked a cigarette.

"See to his burial," he said to the spy.

"Very good, chief."

Rauerdt swung round and started in the direction of the imperial villa.

"Krampft is far away—this one is—shot. Now, for the other!"

Arrived at the house, Rauerdt quickly hid himself in one of those extraordinary passages in the walls and made his way to the second story.

Suddenly he stopped. Through a peephole in the wood, he saw an officer whom he knew.

This man, under the guise of a shopkeeper, had kept an important agency at Nancy for the purpose of urging French soldiers to desert.

The officer was surrounded by masons all belonging to the espionage service.

But what interested Rauerdt was an enormous breach in the wall through which he could discern the delicate features of Colette.

"Krampft condemned to death—Colette buried alive," he muttered. "The emperor's will must be done, but it's lucky I am here."

Had he any pity—for the girl?

Assuredly not.

He must have simply said to himself that once Colette was dead, all chance of recovering the yellow document would be gone.

The officer addressed Colette with cold indifference.

"Come, you must be reasonable. Tell me, where is the yellow document?"

Colette replied firmly:

"No, I shall not speak."

"But we have kept our part of the bargain. We brought you the priest. We gave him the ring. Therefore, we have your word—"

Colette interrupted, vehemently:

"I gave you no promise. You said, 'we will bring you a priest and you can give him any commission you like. Afterwards you must choose—either torture or you must speak.'"

"Well?"

"Well, I choose the torture. I shall not speak."

"You are crazy."

"I am a Frenchwoman."

"You will die."

"No matter. My country will be saved."

"Your secret will perish with you."

"It will not perish."

"But you were not able to confide it to the priest?"

"I have nothing to say."

"Nothing can frighten you?"

"Nothing."

"And that is your last word?"

"My last word will be *'Vive la France.'*"

"Very well, so much the worse for you. You will be walled in alive. You will suffer for maybe four or five days. I shall allow enough air to pass in so that you can breathe. You will die from hunger and of fear."

He asked again:

"Will you speak?"

Colette remained silent.

"Put in the first row of bricks," he ordered. When this had been done, the officer again asked:

"Will you speak?"

Colette made no reply.

"Close the breach."

At length only a narrow crack remained.

"For the last time, will you speak?"

"Vive la France!" was the heroic reply.

The last brick was put in place.

Rauerdt looked on with apparent anger and contempt.

"How intelligent," he murmured, as he rapidly made his way along the passage. "Will you speak?—No?—Then I shall kill you!"

The master spy laughed.

"The emperor's will must be done, no doubt of that, but there is also no doubt that I must find the yellow document."

A moment later Rauerdt came downstairs and satisfied himself that his spies were at their posts, and on guard.

"This campaign begins interestingly for me," he said. "My role promises to be as important as was Stieber's in 1870. Unfortunately I haven't a Bismarck to second me.

"But I have what they hadn't in 1870—an emperor's bastard to help me."

Rauerdt reached the hall door. He seemed to hesitate a moment, then pronounced these strange words:

"Well, at any cost I must make my executed man talk."

And he gave a loud laugh.

2. It Is a Lover

The shutters—never open—allowed a soft light to enter the large, well-furnished room, in the middle of which stood a woman.

Half naked, a short skirt displaying her ankles, and a low-cut corsage her superb shoulders, she was playing the castanets and dancing with passion and abandon truly Spanish.

Then suddenly one of her little slippers flew to the ceiling and she stood motionless, panting, stretching out her arms in a gesture of weariness.

"*Caramba!*" she cried. "*Santa Madona.* I haven't an ounce of steam left!"

What a strange creature was this dancer. She passed from one emotion to another without pause.

Noisy, the moment before, she suddenly became silent. And then with a quick bound she sprang to a cheval glass, picking up a powder box on the way, and began powdering her shoulders.

"*Caramba!* It's warm!"

A man's voice answered with a drawl:

"That's so—and it's good fun."

"I'm thirsty," exclaimed the dancer.

"You generally are. Whisky and soda?"

"No. Some water, vinegar and sugar."

"Carlotta, you treat me like a pumpkin!"

"You are not polite, my dear."

"Bah! That's not necessary between us—and besides, call me 'my lord.'"

The woman burst into laughter.

"My lord, you are delightful."

"So are you, Carlotta."

"You are gallant, your highness."

"Come and sit down. You won't dance any more?"

"No, I'm going to sing."

The woman picked up a guitar and began tuning it.

"Leave that alone. Remember it's Sunday. You'll scandalize the neighborhood."

"Then I'll go to sleep."

"Yes, I think you'd better."

From the depths of a sofa piled with soft cushions a masculine figure emerged. It was Paul de Tersy. William II's bastard was strangely dressed. He wore sky blue pajamas with collar open, showing he had been suddenly awakened from a prolonged siesta by the singing and dancing of his mistress.

"Now," he added, "get some rest."

He seated himself on the edge of the sofa beside Carlotta, who peacefully drank her strange mixture.

"You haven't been yourself since you came to Berlin three days ago," he remarked.

"Why, my lord?"

"You are all up in the air."

"I have good reason to be."

De Tersy rose and lighted a cigarette at a perfumed lamp that stood in one corner.

"Your destiny is a strange one," he continued. "You were a lion tamer in a menagerie, which suited your instinct, too. I pass by, see you—"

"Fall in love."

"You please me—and you become a dancer in Lunéville."

"Dio Santo! What a bore that was!"

"Then war broke out—"

"And you became the emperor's son."

"I send for you, and here you are in Berlin in this furnished apartment. Well, this is the right kind of life. Money, a good time, and prospects! Upon my word, being a bastard is a fine job."

Carlotta suddenly flung herself at full length beside her lover.

This girl, "discovered" by de Tersy, was very pretty like most young Spaniards.

A brown skin, large eyes and red lips, she was in the flower of her beauty.

"The right kind of a life, yes," she replied. "But one must be careful and not be beguiled into a fancied security. We both love money, my dear. So let us try to get a fortune. By the way, are you quite sure you are the emperor's bastard?"

De Tersy burst out laughing.

"That is the least of my worries," he replied. "The emperor thinks I am and that is the essential thing."

"Perhaps. What do the princes say to it?"

"They have neglected to tell me, my dear."

"And when you spoke of me?"

"I haven't spoken of you."

"But when you brought me here?"

"Oh! I left that to a confidential friend, a sort of spy who seems interested in me."

"What is his name?"

"I hardly remember—oh, yes—Rauerdt."

De Tersy had evidently not the least idea of the importance of the chief spy he treated so cavalierly.

Carlotta, with a woman's curiosity, questioned further:

"What did you say to him?"

"Oh, that I had a friend—meaning you—that was bored—that you had better be brought here—and—here you are!"

"*Caramba!* You're an idiot!"

Carlotta sprang up suddenly and confronted her lover, her arms folded, and an angry look in her eyes.

"Well, what's the matter with you?" he asked.

"Don't you know the Kaiser won't stand fooling with women? Haven't you read in the papers—"

"I never read the papers."

"That the crown prince himself—"

De Tersy rose in his turn.

"Oh, shut up," he said. Then putting his hand on Carlotta's shoulder, he spoke coldly:

"My dear, since you think you can advise me upon a subject I carefully avoid speaking of, I will be plain with you. It's true that I was imprudent to bring my mistress here. My august and respectable father allows no nonsense over women. You are quite right. That is why I don't propose to risk getting in his bad books on your account. Which means that you will please be careful, hide yourself, avoid making our liaison public—in a word, keep out of sight."

"*Caramba!* You have nerve!"

"Say, rather, I am sharp. I like you, you like me, and everything is all right. Only, the day that you cause me any annoyance, I fire you—understand?"

Carlotta had doubtless understood these menacing words, but she was careful not to show it.

Humming an air, she began another dance in front of the glass.

De Tersy shrugged his shoulders.

"And now I'll say good night. *Noblesse oblige.*—I must remember that I am the Kaiser's bastard. I have engagements to keep. Until tomorrow—"

Twenty minutes later, in correct attire, de Tersy left the apartment, frowning as he went downstairs.

If the truth were told, he felt slightly uneasy.

Had he not made a mistake in bringing this woman here?

When he reached the street where the German crowd was buying up editions of the newspapers which gave the first news of the war, he threw off his anxiety.

"Bah! We shall see. To begin with, nobody knows that Carlotta is here!"

In the meantime Carlotta herself was thinking deeply.

"He's a fool, *Santa Madona!* He doesn't love me, I only satisfy him. He might leave me at any time. But there's a fortune to be had, if I can only seize it."

With half-closed eyes she viewed herself in the glass.

"I'm foolish to be worried! I'm beautiful. After this one, another! The former mistress of the Kaiser's bastard! *Caramba!* that is almost a patent of nobility!"

Carlotta stretched herself on a sofa, hoping to take a nap.

But she wasn't sleepy. Then she yawned—

"I'm bored!"

Her fine nostrils twitched.

"What an ugly town this Berlin is! Always smells of cabbage!"

She yawned again. Then an idea came to her.

"I'll try my luck with the cards."

She cut and dealt a hand.

Suddenly she paused and listened.

"Ah! Who can have rung the bell?"

The maid who opened the hall door found herself in the presence of an unknown and well-dressed man, who questioned her in the purest French.

"Madame Carlotta?"

"She lives here, Monsieur, but I don't know if Madame—"

The visitor pushed his way into the hall.

"Go back to the kitchen."

The young servant stared at him.

"To the kitchen?" she repeated.

"Right away!" replied the strange visitor. "Well, what are you waiting for?"

Suddenly he took out a fifty-mark bill and handed it to her.

"Take this—I haven't come to annoy your mistress. She'll be glad to see me."

Fifty marks have powers of persuasion, even m the eyes of a good Spaniard.

The maid retreated a few steps.

Then the visitor advanced and opened the drawing room door.

"You are beautiful, Madame," he began.

The servant burst into laughter.

"Divine Jesus—it's a lover!"

The visitor had addressed these words to Carlotta, bowing.

"You are beautiful, Madame—so beautiful that you compelled me to follow you and force your door. I beg you not to punish me by a cruel look from your eyes."

Upon hearing these strange words Carlotta wondered if she were not dreaming.

Who was this man addressing compliments to her? What did he want? Where had he met her? Anxious and yet pleased, Carlotta answered:

"But I don't know you, Monsieur—I don't know how you dare—"

"I do not know how I have dared myself, Madame! I think that loving you must drive a man mad—that is my excuse—I saw you—I wanted to see you again and here I am. I would have given anyone a fortune in exchange for your address. That was not needed. I heard the sound of your voice from the street—so I came up. The magnet attracts iron as your beauty attracted my heart."

"Señor, you amaze me."

"Señorita, you intoxicate me!"

The man fell at Carlotta's feet. He trembled.

Was he really what he seemed, a lover?

Carlotta, who was rather simple, was half inclined to believe him, although the whole affair was so amazing.

Not knowing what to say and not daring to play the role of a woman insulted by undesired advances, she temporized:

"Señor, you came at a bad time—the cards were 'unfavorable.'"

"It isn't possible they can be against me!"

The stranger rose, took the pack, then flung them on the table, announcing:

"Nine and ten of hearts! The triumph of love, Señorita."

Then, with an enigmatic smile, he drew out his pocketbook and took from it a handful of banknotes.

"Señorita, I would like to keep these lucky cards as a souvenir."

So saying he placed the cards in his pocketbook, leaving the banknotes in exchange.

"Señorita, I have a request to make."

"What is it, Señor?"

"Grant me permission to tell you that I love you."

Carlotta jumped up, laughing.

Why, you've been telling me nothing else for the last quarter of an hour!"

"Possibly, Señorita, but I would like to say it more clearly. Your evening is free. Let us dine together. Tonight you must give me that rose you wear in your hair."

"Caramba! You don't mean that!"

"Get ready, Madame."

"Señor, it's madness!"

"Love, Señorita."

"But I have a lover."

"He is not coming to see you this evening."

"I cannot compromise myself."

"We will go to my house."

"And run the chance of being seen!"

"A carriage is waiting for us."

"Señor, I am not free."

"Señorita, the swallows fly whither they will."

Carlotta was puzzled. This lover who so daringly intruded into her apartment and invited her to dinner and who—an argument not to be scorned—bought two cards with a handful of notes, seemed very much in love, but slightly disturbing at the same time.

"I don't know you," answered Carlotta.

"Let me introduce myself."

The stranger took a step nearer her and with the outrageous cheek of a rich German exclaimed:

"Ten thousand francs for your evening."

"My smiles are worth a fortune."

"In that case, twenty thousand."

"My good will is not to be bought."

"The finest flowers in my conservatory?"

"Very well! Wait for me."

Carlotta had suddenly made up her mind.

She was devoured with curiosity.

What did this man want? Who was he?

The best thing would be to see it through rather than remain in uncertainty.

If the individual were merely a lover, it might be worth while cultivating his acquaintance.

If his attentions hid other motives, she must learn what they were.

In a few moments she was ready.

In spite of her simple origin, Carlotta had the instinct of women accustomed to the strangest situations. Her dress that evening was a triumph of diplomacy.

Without being too striking, it was elegant and gave her the appearance of a woman of taste out on a spree.

"Where are you taking me?" she asked.

"You will see, Señorita."

"What folly you are leading me into!"

"What kindness you are showing me!"

A private carriage was waiting outside.

Carlotta, who did not know Berlin, could not guess the street they were taking. After a short drive they stopped by the steps of a sumptuous-looking mansion.

"Señorita, we have arrived."

Carlotta got a good look at her lover. He was about forty, black hair turning gray, his mustache and beard carefully trimmed.

Undoubtedly he was rich. His dress indicated as much and his house confirmed it.

His manner was so fervent that Carlotta thought:

"I was right to come. He is really a lover."

But as she entered the hall, hung with old tapestries, she had a strange impression.

About a dozen men dressed in black, evidently not servants though common-looking, rose on the entrance of the pair.

Carlotta's cavalier spoke sharply:

"I am not to be disturbed—secret service. I shall dine alone."

She was surely mistaken.

Why did her host announce that he would dine alone?

She turned to him instinctively and a half-stifled cry escaped her.

His face had completely changed.

From dark he had become fair. He wore neither mustaches nor beard. Eyeglasses were on his nose. Carlotta was afraid. She would have liked to run away. The man now took her by the arm.

"Come on, don't be afraid."

The man's manner had also changed. He spoke sharply, commandingly, and with the characteristic intonation of the German.

"Ah! Mamma Mia! Who are you?"

"Come in here," replied the man.

He opened a door, pushing Carlotta before him, then closed and locked it.

The room had a sinister look. It was long and narrow, a cell without furniture. A bench ran round the bare walls.

"Sit down. I want to talk to you."

Carlotta collapsed rather than sat—more dead than alive—upon the bench.

"It's cowardly! It's criminal!" she cried. "Who are you? What is your name?"

The man rolled a cigarette. With a slight smile, he answered:

"Rauerdt."

"The spy Rauerdt?"

"Spy is scarcely the word; say rather, the head of the secret service of German espionage."

And as Carlotta, shaking with anger, was about to protest, Rauerdt suddenly ordered:

"That will do! Keep quiet! Listen to me. I am your master."

Carlotta sat dumbly, horribly afraid of this man.

"But—I have done nothing!"

"That is not the question."

The master spy of Germany calmly smoked his cigarette, walking up and down the narrow cell.

Presently he asked:

"Are you calmer now? Will you listen to me?"

"Speak! Speak!"

Anything seemed better than the agony of this silence!

"To begin with your lover, Paul de Tersy, is an imbecile. He took me for a simple spy. I am the master of all the spies in Germany. I tell you this for your own information. Now, I wish you no harm, but you must obey me. You are going to enter my service. You understand?"

"No."

"I wish you to become a spy."

"Never."

"I must know, hour by hour, minute by minute, what Paul de Tersy is doing. You will tell me."

"You needn't expect that."

"Later on, I shall have other work for you. If you want an explanation I will give it to you. There are serious questions to be solved just now. I cannot use a woman in the ordinary service. I made inquiries and think you will do."

Carlotta drew herself up, brave in spite of her fear.

"I will not obey you."

Rauerdt did not seem to hear her. He continued in the same cold, impassive voice:

"As I must make sure of your discretion, that you will not betray, I am taking a few precautions. I shall dictate you a letter—a letter in which you appear to be conspiring with an accomplice to assassinate the Kaiser. The day you commit an imprudence, for instance, repeat this interview to anyone, this letter will be used."

"I refuse! I refuse! I shall write nothing!"

"I may add," continued Rauerdt that you shall be recompensed for your work, and the secret service pays well."

"I don't want to be a spy! I shall write nothing. I would rather die."

"That is the only way in which you can resist me—to die. There is no other way."

The head of the secret service pulled down from the wall a wooden shelf which served as a table.

"Here is the model of the letter. You will be brought paper and ink by and by. You have only to copy it. You are intelligent. You will quite understand that after having written it you will have to obey me willingly."

Then, as though ignoring the horror and fear of the unfortunate woman, Rauerdt went to the door of the cell.

"You see this small window? When you finish your letter, you will slip it through the opening."

He paused and fixed a sharp look on the Spanish woman.

"Then, and only then, you will be given food—until then you will get nothing. You have the choice of dying of hunger or giving in. I hope you will decide quickly, it would be stupid to resist. Good evening, Madame!"

Carlotta saw her torturer disappear without having the strength to protest.

But the door of her cell had scarcely closed than a sudden fury took hold of her. She flung herself against it; fists, nails, knees and feet she used in the assault. She merely hurt herself without even shaking the heavy door, and, at length, fell back exhausted and conquered. She could scarcely believe in the horror of her position.

Mad thoughts flashed through her mind.

Such crimes could not be committed.

They called for vengeance. She would complain to the Spanish embassy! She would escape!

Alas! She quickly realized how impossible that would be. Who would believe her?

And then, little by little, other thoughts came to her.

After all, what mattered it what she did so long as it paid her?

She would run no danger and she had been promised remuneration.

She crossed and looked at the model of the letter. Then with a gesture of disgust, she exclaimed:

"I shall not yield."

At this moment Rauerdt was dining alone m a huge room.

The head of the secret service had a good appetite. He went through his meal quickly and with an air of contentment.

"An excellent thing to get hold of this woman," he thought. "She'll be useful. Ah! the emperor little dreams of the game that is beginning. If he should lose, he would take it out of me! I must foresee everything."

An agent now brought in a number of documents. Rauerdt looked them over while finishing his dinner.

"Any other orders, chief?"

"Yes!" replied Rauerdt. "Bring the man who was shot into my office."

"Very good, chief."

Rauerdt dismissed his subordinate with a nod, and attacked a dish of fruit.

Another agent presented himself:

"Here is the document you expected, chief."

Rauerdt cast his eyes over the paper.

It was the letter Carlotta had written.

Rauerdt did not seem surprised.

"Ah, this woman and I will get on together. She yielded without much trouble—she's of no account." A master spy always despises those he employs.

3. Master and Valet

"Will you answer, yes or no?"

"No."

"You defy me then?"

"Looks like it."

"One day I shall lose patience with you."

"That is quite possible."

"And then I shall get rid of you without the least difficulty."

"I don't doubt it."

"I may order you to be shot."

"For the second time? By the third time I shall get accustomed to it."

"You are playing a dangerous game."

"What then? My life is insured."

"You are mad to joke with me."

"And do you think it is intelligent to try and scare me?"

These dry, rapid and menacing replies were taken and given without the least appearance that either adversary would admit defeat. Who were these two men, the one threatening, the other answering with a careless laugh?

Behind a desk littered with papers sat Rauerdt who, dinner over, had gone into his office. He was the one who threatened, and the other was—La Flemme.

But had not La Flemme been executed by order of the enigmatical Rauerdt?

Had La Flemme been asked himself, he would have jokingly replied that he had fallen when the shots were fired, but he would have added that he had not been wounded.

What had happened?

Something very simple, though very mysterious. When Rauerdt had entered the cell where La Flemme was confined, he naturally expected to find there Krampft.

Pale with rage at the substitution, Rauerdt had not countermanded the execution.

The firing squad, seeing La Flemme fall, had certainly believed him to be killed.

Rauerdt, alone, could have undeceived them. He knew they had used blank cartridges—had he not furnished them himself? And if La Flemme had fallen it was on account of the chloroform with which his gag had been saturated.

But how did Rauerdt come to plan such a deception? While La Flemme knew how it had been done, he certainly did not know why he had been spared.

And this explanation Rauerdt had given to nobody.

He had saved La Flemme in the same manner he had decided to save Krampft. He believed that La Flemme had knowledge relative to the yellow document. Therefore every day he cross-questioned the orderly and without any result.

This time Rauerdt broke off abruptly.

"Very well. I give you until tomorrow to think it over."

"Oh, it's always the same story. Every evening you say. 'Tomorrow you will be killed.' Your conversation never varies."

La Flemme shrugged his shoulders and followed his jailers who had come to take him back to his cell.

And then the master spy gave way to a sudden fit of anger.

"Does this man know anything, or does he not? Ah! If I were the emperor I would not hesitate. I'd condemn him to death—like Krampft—like Monet—like Colette."

Rauerdt jeered. He repeated the word he had used at the frontier. "What a fool!"

The head of the secret service shrugged his shoulders.

"I mustn't waste time, I have work to do."

He glanced over the voluminous reports on his desk. One of them caught his attention.

"Why, this is in his majesty's own handwriting."

Rauerdt studied it carefully.

"It is a detailed account of the decisions he has taken—why does he write me all this? Does he want to find out if I am ignorant of them or does he want to acquaint me with them?"

Rauerdt's reflections were cut short by a knock at the door.

"Come in!" he cried.

A secretary entered and gave him a large envelope.

"Have you any orders to give, chief?"

"Wait."

Rauerdt tore open the envelope and drew out a sheet of paper which contained only a cross in the middle made with a blue pencil.

"No. I have no orders to give. You may go."

Rauerdt rang and ordered his carriage. Twenty minutes later he presented himself at the Potsdam palace and was shown into the Kaiser's study.

William II took no notice of his visitor. Dressed in a colonel's uniform of the White Guards, he was seated at his desk, writing. After a long pause, he suddenly flung down his pen and sat back in his chair.

"Well, Rauerdt!"

"Your majesty sent for me?"

"To discuss certain urgent measures with you. You have read my report?"

"Yes, Sire."

"Then you are cognizant of the events I wish to speak of—a cigar, Rauerdt?"

"I thank your majesty."

"It is still a question of the yellow document. What do you think? Have I done right?"

He enumerated his facts with raised fingers.

"Krampft is dead—a good thing too. He knew of the existence of the document and he was quite capable of betraying me. Colette is dead also. Women are always talkative, but the dead cannot speak. You can imagine how reluctant I was to deal so severely with her, but it was a State duty."

William II paused.

Did he expect to take in his master spy by this pretended pity?

"I have also been obliged to lock up Mme. Bayen. She had information concerning the document. Now, one person mixed in this affair has escaped me—the French lieutenant, Monet. I don't know what has become of him. Now, my dear Rauerdt, answer me frankly—have I acted wisely?"

Rauerdt bowed.

"Your majesty is always right."

"That is the answer of a courtier."

"It is the answer of a devoted servant."

"Who does not want to compromise himself."

"Who knows that your majesty does not act without giving due consideration to events which your majesty alone knows."

The emperor burst out laughing.

"Come, yes or no, have I done right? That is all I ask you."

"I have already answered your majesty."

"Come, Rauerdt, be frank—talk to me as to a friend."

"Sire, as a friend, I would say that a friend always approves of the actions of those dear to him."

"Then I order you to give me your opinion."

"In that case, your majesty, I would say that the yellow document is of colossal importance and that your majesty cannot give up the search for it."

"Well, and then?"

"Then your majesty will see that it is necessary to make these persons speak: Colette, Monet, Krampft, Mme. Bayen."

"What's that you say? Krampft and Colette cannot speak, they are dead."

Rauerdt seemed to hesitate, then suddenly came to a decision.

"Your majesty must forgive me contradicting you. I do not think that Krampft is dead."

"What!"

Rauerdt hurriedly explained what he knew of Krampft's escape.

The emperor grew pale and seemed angry:

"With Krampft alive, the yellow document may fall into the hands of the French. It must be recovered."

"Sire," replied Rauerdt calmly. "With Krampft alive we are certain of success. He can be bought."

"We must find out where he is."

"Your majesty will learn that. Krampft will certainly approach your majesty."

"But why didn't you advise me? Why keep silence? If I had known that Krampft had escaped, I would have made other arrangements. Don't you know that?"

"Sire, I know it so well that I have anticipated your majesty's wishes."

"In what way?"

"Your majesty will punish me if I have done wrong. I decided that Krampft was necessary, so I saved him. He is to be bought and he is to be feared. I have the honor to announce that Colette is under lock and key in one of my cells. Her neighbor in the next cell is Lieutenant Monet. When Krampft appears, I suggest that your majesty turn these two prisoners over to him."

William II stood in utter amazement at these words which he could not understand.

"Colette alive—Monet a prisoner— And you want to turn them over to Krampft!"

"Yes, Sire."

"Explain yourself!"

"Sire, Krampft living, is a danger to your majesty. This man knows of the existence of the yellow document. He has also enjoyed your favor. Krampft must now either wish to rehabilitate himself in your eyes or be revenged for his misfortune."

"Well, Rauerdt?"

"There are two methods of dealing with him. Either recapture and kill him or pretend to be his dupe. To kill him would be dangerous—and would not recover the yellow document. So we must pretend to be his dupe. That is why I suggest that your majesty deliver these two prisoners to him—Colette and Monet."

"Very well, but how are they still alive?"

"I saved them, Sire."

"You saved Colette?"

"Yes, Sire. I took her secretly from her tomb."

"And Lieutenant Monet?"

"He was rescued from death when he lay unconscious in a landau, disguised as a priest."

"You are a sorcerer!" exclaimed the emperor. "How did you know he was in the landau?"

Rauerdt bowed.

"I had to know it to be of service to your majesty."

"Very good, Rauerdt. I thank you."

The emperor paced up and down.

"Then the struggle concerning this cursed document is not

ended!"

"It is beginning, Sire."

"We shall never find it."

"I beg your majesty's pardon."

"What do you suggest, then?"

"It is very simple. To begin with, at any cost we must prevent Krampft taking his revenge. And the best way to do this is to pretend a great confidence in him. I suggest turning over the two prisoners to him, asking him to make them speak."

"And suppose they won't speak?"

"Then I shall take a hand."

"In what way?"

"I ask for your majesty's confidence."

"Very good, and then?"

"Then I beg your majesty to undertake a difficult task."

"What one?"

"I want your majesty to interview Mme. Bayen personally."

"You don't mean that!"

"Sire, I am sure Mme. Bayen would tell you all she knows about the yellow document."

The emperor shrugged his shoulders.

Rauerdt slyly insinuated:

"I may recall to your majesty that Mme. Bayen feels a maternal affection for Colette."

"Have you anything else to say, Rauerdt?"

"Nothing, Sire—yes—but I scarcely like to—"

"Go on!"

"I would like to ask your majesty what you have decided in regard to Paul de Tersy, friend of the spy Krampft."

William II drew himself up:

"What do you mean to insinuate?"

"Whatever your majesty pleases to understand."

"You don't trust de Tersy? He is my son—my bastard!"

"Sire, I neither trust nor distrust him. I watch and judge his acts."

After five minutes of deep thought, William II broke the silence:

"You are right. I shall take measures. I am very pleased with you."

Then with a sudden laugh:

"Besides, you have done well to be frank with me. If I sent for you tonight, it is because an hour ago I was asked for an audience—by whom do you think?"

"I don't know, Sire."

"Read this card, my friend."

"Krampft! That proves, Sire, that I was not mistaken. This man comes with an offer."

"I will buy him."

And with a wave of his hand, the Kaiser dismissed Rauerdt.

As the master spy left the palace, he seemed plunged in thought. He muttered to himself:

"The struggle is beginning. On the one hand Krampft, who stops at nothing and who wants my place, on the other myself, whom the emperor suspects. As judge: his majesty, a bungler, a fool! Besides that, a war, and besides that this yellow document which must be found."

It was late.

The linden trees gave out the perfume of their flowers.

Rauerdt took a deep breath. He seemed to be storing up energy.

Suddenly he muttered these mysterious words:

"Krampft has a weakness for de Tersy. But de Tersy is in my hands through Carlotta. Besides, I have a power, a terrible power— the ring! I didn't mention the ring to the emperor, and was wise not to. That is my last card."

What was Rauerdt alluding to?

And of whom was he thinking, when he added:

"But there is that man—that extraordinary individual! Yes, I forgot him and he alarms me!"

4. Pardon

Three days later, on a spring morning, Rauerdt stood on his steps and watched the groom saddling his horse.

"The saddle is turning," he remarked, "and who told you to lengthen the stirrup leathers? Shorten them a couple of holes."

A moment later Rauerdt was riding toward the outskirts of Berlin, with a smile of triumph on his lips.

"Everything is going well," he thought. "His majesty will take my advice about his bastard. Well, we shall soon hear what he has to say."

Rauerdt put his horse into a gallop, then suddenly pulled him down to a walk again.

"After all, I needn't hurry. I'm ahead of time."

His face clouded over a trifle.

"Lucky I told the emperor about Krampft the other day. It would have been a bad business if I had tried to hide it.

"Oh! I was forgetting that letter—that anonymous letter—what the devil does it mean?"

Rauerdt's face became livid.

What new thought had come to disturb him? He reached the first paths of the Thiergarten and made for the less frequented part of this largest of Berlin's parks.

By this time he was very much out of humor. What did that letter mean? Especially the extraordinary signature attached to it. It had reached him three days previously and had caused him the most intense surprise.

"Do you care to recover," it ran, "a document of importance which is neither red nor blue, nor white, nor violet, nor orange? If such is your wish, reflect and decide to agree to the proposition that will be made to you by

"THE MONSTER."

At first Rauerdt thought it was some joke, but on further reflection, he decided it was something quite different. There was no doubt that it referred to the yellow document. That being so, could he afford to ignore any clew, however improbable?

And there had followed other letters from the same correspondent and always anonymously signed "The Monster."

He was told to be on his guard—to beware of the emperor, of Krampft, of de Tersy—especially was he urged to help "The Monster."

What man was it who had chosen this extraordinary pseudonym?

Rauerdt wondered if he would ever meet his strange correspondent. He put his horse at a trot and decided suddenly:

"After all, there's no use worrying over it. The future will clear it up. As for this 'Monster,' I undertake to bring him to reason if ever he appears."

The master spy brought his horse to a walk again and lit a cigarette.

And then suddenly something happened. Less than a yard in front of him, a man abruptly appeared from a bypath, where he had remained hidden, and seized his horse by the bridle.

Rauerdt lifted his riding crop, fearing an assault. But immediately his arm dropped again, and leaning forward, he stared at the man.

"Who are you?" he asked.

"You recognized me. Yes, it is really I."

"The monster! You are the monster!"

Rauerdt felt a mixture of horror and pity for the individual who had barred his way.

The man's face was corroded, burnt. The cheeks were merely bleeding and terrible wounds, the nose was eaten to the bone, and the lips torn off, partially uncovering the teeth. He was truly a monster!

"You had better get off your horse, master spy," the man said calmly.

Something in the way the words were spoken doubtless impressed Rauerdt, for he dismounted without protest, passing the bridle over his arm.

"What do you want with me? Who are you? Did you write to me?"

"Yes, Monsieur Rauerdt."

"In that case, explain quickly."

"Don't worry! I have no desire to keep you."

"Monsieur Rauerdt, you know very well the subject I wrote about, so I needn't go into that."

"You know who I am, but I don't know you."

"That I shall tell you, without mentioning my name. That wouldn't interest you and would convey nothing to you, unless it were an old police affair."

"A police affair!"

Rauerdt could not recall ever having seen the man's hideous face before.

"Speak, I'm in a hurry," he urged.

"Well, I am not. If you go you won't hear some interesting things which I have to tell you."

"Tell them, then!"

"When it suits me."

The monster noticed at this moment that Rauerdt had put his hand in his pocket. He burst out laughing.

"You are thinking of your revolver—that is stupid. I'm not threatening you and besides, I may as well tell you that you can't frighten me. I am here to serve you, so—"

Rauerdt interrupted him:

"Listen to me. Yes or no, will you explain or shall I call and have you arrested?"

"Call," replied the monster.

Rauerdt was silent.

There was not a soul in this deserted part of the park. Calling would be of no use—there was nobody to hear.

"Explain yourself."

"Very well, master spy. I am simply a convict. That surprises you! You don't understand why I tell you this, you who are the friend of the chief of police? Well, I'll explain. I am a convict who wants to be rehabilitated. That's all.

"Naturally, it will not surprise you, Monsieur Rauerdt, when I say that I am an escaped convict. If I apply to you it is to avoid being retaken.

"Not wanting to be caught, I had the ingenious idea of disfiguring myself with vitriol. If I now ask for a pardon, it is because I think myself able to buy it. I want your absolute promise that I shall not be bothered in the future—that I shall be paid enough to enable me to live comfortably, and in exchange I will see that you recover the document that is neither red, blue, nor violet."

"The yellow document!"

"Exactly. Do you agree?"

"You have the document?"

"Do you think I'm crazy?" cried the monster. "One doesn't keep such things in one's pocket when one interviews the master spy of Germany."

"You know where it can be found?"

"I know a means of getting it, but upon one condition."

"What?"

"You must give me a piece of information."

"What information do you want?"

"The whereabouts of Paul de Tersy."

"What do you want with that young man?"

"Nothing."

"Well, then?"

The monster shrugged his shoulders.

"Do you think I'm going to tell you everything? Monsieur Rauerdt, take it or leave it—I demand two things, the address of Paul de Tersy and the promise I was speaking of. In exchange I will recover the yellow document for you. It's quite simple, accept my offer or refuse it!"

Rauerdt was more troubled than he cared to admit to himself, and this trouble increased as his interlocutor continued:

"Another thing: you are not to warn M. de Tersy of my visit! That would be unfortunate for you! It would show that you had been tricked and M. de Tersy would not fail to tell the emperor— or perhaps his good friend Krampft!"

This was exactly what Rauerdt thought.

"Nor do not try to give me a false address. Sooner or later I should revenge myself with all the energy of which a man who has vitrioled himself is capable."

Rauerdt could not repress a shudder.

"Finally, I warn you that I make this proposition today, but I shall not make it tomorrow. Time passes. You must decide now."

Rauerdt bit his lips till the blood came.

How could he resist this extraordinary person? A struggle with him would be dangerous, for undoubtedly he was armed.

Rauerdt felt secretly afraid. He grew pale.

"Well, I am waiting!—and if my information is correct, somebody will be waiting for you. So hurry up."

Then Rauerdt hesitated no longer.

*   *   *   *   *   *

While this strange and fantastic scene was taking place in a remote corner of the Thiergarten, between Rauerdt and the unknown, some distance away other extraordinary events were in progress. In a villa of quite good appearance with the simple inscription, "Asylum," over its door, the woman who was once Colonel Bayen's wife, had been held prisoner for several days.

The heroic woman was indeed condemned to a frightful life.

Seized by the orders of William II, she had been thrown into one of the trains returning to the capital after having conveyed troops to the front.

Shut up among the insane and with little hope of pity, she had at first thought of suicide. And then she had overcome her despair and seemed resigned to her lot.

Was it the hope of touching the heart of the royal executioner, or the desire to learn Colette's fate that helped her to live?

Possibly the nurses may have guessed the reason when they saw a strange light in her eyes, the light of determination to accomplish a duty and to resist to the end.

On this particular morning Brigitte Bayen was struck with amazement upon opening her eyes.

The gloomy room had been decorated and made cheerful during her sleep.

Superb bouquets of roses stood on the furniture. The unhappy woman rang the bell and questioned the nurse:

"Where do these flowers come from?"

She scarcely expected an answer: All her questions hitherto had been met by a sullen silence.

But this time the nurse replied amiably:

"They came from the Potsdam Palace, for Madame, with this letter."

Brigitte tore open the envelope and read the contents with fresh surprise and deep anxiety.

"Madame, I suffer, I am sorry, and I hope! All this I wish to tell you, and I shall come to you this morning to ask your pardon.

"WILLIAM."

William, the Kaiser, the sanguinary demon, had sent her these flowers, had dared to write to her, to announce his visit!

With a gesture of rage, Brigitte flung the flowers on the ground and trampled them underfoot.

The emperor wanted to see her. Very well, she would receive him. He wanted to speak to her. She would answer him.

"I will ask him for the life of Colette," she murmured, "if I am still in time."

But little did Brigitte Bayen guess what part the comedian William II dared to play before her. When the emperor bowed gallantly before his prisoner, she exclaimed in a dull voice:

"What does your majesty want with me?"

"Madame, I have come to plead with you, to beg you not to be ruthless."

"You ask that of me!"

"Yes, Madame."

"Why?"

"Because I suffer terribly. I have not come here to add to your sorrow, the thought of which fills me with anguish. I am here to ask your forgiveness."

"My forgiveness? That I cannot grant. My country would forbid me. You are the emperor-felon who at this moment is violating Belgium—the villain who unloosed this war, the monster who is sowing ruin and death everywhere. I cannot forgive you. I hate you."

"Madame, these reproaches are directed against the emperor—but it is not the emperor who asks forgiveness."

"Who is it, then?"

"The man, Madame. An unhappy man."

But, indeed, William II was badly taken in if he thought his little comedy would disarm the hate of his victim.

Brigitte Bayen stopped him with sarcasm in her voice.

"You dare to say that, Sire. You would dare anything! But your majesty will understand that I hate the man equally with the emperor. It is he who holds me prisoner—who had my husband murdered—who may have killed my daughter Colette."

While listening to her, William II seemed to be laboring under a great stress of emotion.

"You are my prisoner, that is true. But is it my fault? I feel convinced that you know something of the terrible secret of the yellow document. Could I set you at liberty under the circumstances? As to Colette, Madame, she is alive. She is like you, a prisoner, so is Monet, so must be all those concerned in the secret."

With a marvelous appearance of sincerity, William II added:

"If you suffer, Madame, so do I. I am not free to treat you as I would like. I have my duty as emperor."

And then, the Kaiser turned quickly as though to hide his sobs and bowing, hurried away, calling as he went:

"I am overcome, Madame—but you will see me again. I want your forgiveness and I shall win it."

*   *   *   *   *   *

While Rauerdt did not recover his good humor after his strange interview in the park, he had succeeded in pulling himself together and deciding upon a course of action.

He was walking his horse in one of the main thoroughfares of the Thiergarten, when suddenly he started.

Among the acclamations of the crowd, four or five horsemen were galloping toward him, and in the midst of them rode the king.

Rauerdt hurried to meet them.

The emperor hailed him while yet some distance away.

"A pleasant ride, my good friend."

"Sire, I await your majesty with impatience!"

"To find out if my visit was successful, I'll warrant? Well, don't worry, your desires will be fulfilled."

William II put his horse into a trot and signed for the master spy to accompany him.

"To begin with, the war! I have excellent news. We are advancing into Belgium. Nothing can resist us! I have just ordered the menu for my first dinner in Paris two weeks hence."

William II burst into laughter.

"As to my visit, I fancy it was entirely successful. Oh, naturally I didn't mention the subject. It was just a little sentimental comedy."

"Your majesty is a clever diplomat."

"Maybe, Rauerdt; in any case, I did my best. I behaved like a repentant schoolboy. It means everything to gain the confidence of this woman; the rest will go of itself."

William II seemed to be absorbed in his thoughts. Abruptly he asked:

"One thing bothers me, Rauerdt. What shall I answer if she exacts the liberty of Colette, or even of Monet?"

Rauerdt smiled strangely:

"You must agree, Sire."

"What!"

"Colette and Monet by that time will have confessed all they know."

"You are right," replied the Kaiser.

He pulled up his horse to allow his escort to join him and inquired:

"Have you any news, my dear friend?"

Rauerdt hesitated for an instant.

What ought he to reply?

Should he speak of the strange meeting with the monster?

An ironical smile came to his lips.

"Sire, there is nothing new in the fact that I am trying to serve you. I have done nothing else this morning."

5. Through Fear

Paul de Tersy was a strange fellow. He might be called a perfect example of the working out of the laws of heredity.

Son of William II, the imperial thief, he showed the low instincts of greed, hate, and cowardice.

Did he really love William II as he pretended to do?

Certainly not.

Upon learning the secret of his birth, he had rapidly calculated the advantages it would bring him.

He imagined that, in a sense, he would become the equal of the Kaiser's legitimate children, who had scandalized the entire world by the extravagance of their conduct.

He looked forward to every variety of pleasure and the highest honors.

Indeed, for a moment, he had hoped to be given the command of one of the armies rushing to the invasion of France.

Alas! It was not long before he was undeceived.

Upon this evening the bastard of William II was in very bad humor. Luck seemed to be turning against him.

The young man was pacing up and down in a modest room—the best to be had in the small village—muttering to himself.

"My father is charming but he is a great nuisance. What the devil is he up to now?... After all, I am his son!"

Paul de Tersy's anger was perfectly comprehensible. He had suddenly received orders to leave Berlin and betake himself to an out-of-the-way village, there to meet one of the head spies—Doctor Karl. He was told to remain there until further orders.

De Tersy had the good sense to obey. He had taken the journey and met the German doctor and now he awaited further events. He wondered if his affair with Carlotta was responsible for his disgrace.

"What a life!" he exclaimed. "Nothing to do, nothing to see! Wait I and for what?"

As a matter of fact, he had greater reason for his anxiety.

Had his birth been fully established?

And what would the Kaiser do if any doubt arose in his mind as to de Tersy being really his son?

"He would simply get rid of me," thought the young man.

It was a habit of William II to get rid of those who bothered him.

Had he not already condemned to death servants who deserved a better fate?

"Krampft didn't last long," he murmured with pale face.

Although he felt no great affection for Krampft, he had the admiration of a slave for his master.

Krampft had employed him for espionage purposes and paid him well for his services.

"The deuce! I won't think of what happened to him," he exclaimed. "I must distract my mind." He opened the door and shouted:

"Wolff! Come up!"

The unkempt head of a German soldier appeared.

Who was this orderly?

De Tersy had doubts about this man, the sole escort and guide he had been given. In all probability and in spite of his stupid appearance, he might be a spy.

"Your excellency called?"

"What time is it?"

De Tersy had insisted upon being called "excellency."

The soldier answer:

"I don't know the exact time, excellency, but when the letter arrived it was half-past five."

"What's that? A letter?"

"The letter I placed on your excellency's table."

De Tersy turned quickly.

A letter lay on a small table in a corner of the room.

"Why didn't you tell me, brute? Be off with you!"

He picked up the envelope and turned it over, his face expressing utter bewilderment.

"I must be going crazy! That writing—I recognize it—and yet—"

He tore open the envelope and looked for the signature.

It was Krampft, really Krampft who had written it.

And Krampft had been condemned to death by the Kaiser.

If he were alive it would mean that he had revolted against his master.

A correspondence with him would then be terribly dangerous.

"I must read what he has to say."

Krampft had simply written:

"I am alive, which I hope you will be glad of, my dear de Tersy. I am alive because a fool, whose name I will tell you later, saw fit to save me.

"My dear de Tersy, you, as well as I, depend upon a redoubtable master who can quite easily condemn to death or raise to the highest honors. I call him 'your majesty,' you call him 'father.' Believe me, we are both of small matter to him. It is to our interest, therefore, to avoid depending upon a caprice which can crush us down or make us the happiest men in the world.

"So I am writing to suggest an alliance which will place us in a position of becoming the masters of our master.

"Do you understand me?

"Now, nothing is simpler than my project. I have already told you of the existence of the yellow document. Today, I say: Those who hold possession of this document need have no fear of the emperor of Germany. The partnership I suggest has no other purpose than to get this yellow document into our hands."

De Tersy paused in the reading:

"It's madness," he cried. "And of what use could I be to Krampft?"

He went on with the letter:

"Where is this yellow document? That is what we must find out. Who is hiding it? I know of only three persons under suspicion. Colette, Monet, and the ex-Madame Bayen, who alas, is no longer Mme. Brigitte Ravignon.

"To sum it up: Colette and Monet are now actually in my power. I will tell you later how this came about. I will undertake to make them speak, but I do not know what they have done with Brigitte Ravignon. I fancy you know, or at least can find out. I also think you will not refuse to help in the undertaking. Whether it be Colette, Monet, or Brigitte who has the document, we must join together to make them speak.

"Think it over. I will come to see you soon, and I expect to find you ready to second all my efforts."

The letter was signed:

"Your very devoted, Krampft."

De Tersy put the letter down.

He was clever enough to see the advantages of this partnership.

He would not mind betraying his father, but would he be able to find Brigitte Ravignon?

Suddenly he raised his head.

The door opened and a man entered the room.

How could Wolff, his orderly and spy, have allowed him to pass?

While this question went through his mind, like a flash, he sprang to the mantelpiece and seized his revolver.

"Who are you ? What do you want? Stand still or I'll fire!"

The bastard of William II stared at his visitor. The man was of uncertain age and his face was so horrible that one could not bear to look at him. His cheeks were merely bleeding and terrible wounds. The bone of his nose was laid bare and his lips, half torn off, showed his teeth.

De Tersy repeated:

"Who are you? What do you want?"

The visitor seemed in no hurry to answer. He carefully shut the door and advanced a step.

"Monsieur de Tersy, you have drunk from that glass?"

He pointed to an empty glass.

De Tersy nodded, too amazed to reply.

The monster continued:

"If you have drunk from that glass, I warn you that it will be quite useless to threaten me. You have every reason not to kill me—for you are at my mercy."

With a trembling voice, de Tersy repeated:

"Who are you? How did you get here?"

The monster took a chair and sat down.

"Who am I? I shall not tell you. A man who revenges himself— that should be enough. How did I get here? Because I have been hidden in the loft of this house for twenty-four hours. Your orderly watches the door, but neglects the attic. What do I want? The yellow document."

Had an earthquake happened, de Tersy would not have been more amazed.

Again he lifted his revolver, but the monster stopped him:

"Remember, Monsieur de Tersy, you have drunk out of this glass."

"You have poisoned me?"

"Yes. But I can save you. Put down your revolver and listen to me."

De Tersy was so overcome that he did not dream of disobeying. The monster continued:

"This is exactly what you are to know. I may add that it would be useless to question me further or try to soften me by a prayer.

"You have drunk a terrible poison, Monsieur de Tersy, a poison unknown in France, but quite common in the colonies. I have given you a dose sufficient to kill you within three days: Therefore you have three days of life ahead of you in which to find the yellow document and give it to me."

The stranger spoke in the most nonchalant manner, while de Tersy began already to imagine the effects of the poison he was supposed to have drunk.

The monster went on:

"I may add that if you place the document in my hands in the three days, you have my word of honor that you will not die. The poison I have given you has its counter-poison, known only to me, and all your father's 'Herr Doctors' could never discover it. Give me the document and I will save you."

The monster rose and bowed.

De Tersy sprang up and lifted his revolver.

"Nothing can frighten me," the monster added, lifting a warning finger. "I am not afraid of death, so you would be wise to let me go freely and in peace. If harm should happen to me you won't get your antidote. Think it over!"

In truth, the monster seemed to have marvelously calculated the details of his fantastic enterprise. Paul de Tersy allowed him to go without a struggle. This man alone could save him and no torture would force him to speak if he decided to remain silent.

The sole means of getting the antidote would be to procure the yellow document.

What a strange and horrible visit!

What a terrible demand!

The young man sighed:

"The yellow document! I have three days to find it in."

On the floor lay Krampft's letter.

Krampft also wished to get possession of the document.

The maddest ideas went through de Tersy's mind. Who has this document?

It must be, as Krampft said, in the hands of either Monet, Colette, or Brigitte Ravignon.

And then he recalled what Krampft had written.

Monet and Colette were prisoners of the spy, and it was a great piece of luck that Krampft had made him this proposition.

And now another doubt arose in his mind.

Suppose this man had lied? What proof had he got that it was not a trap laid by the Kaiser himself to prove his devotion? What was he to do?

He must, evidently, sound Mme. Bayen.

He must, equally, wait for Krampft.

Above all he must not risk angering the emperor.

After a long meditation, the bastard rose with determination.

He pocketed his revolver, then, bareheaded, he rushed out of the house and ran to the other end of the village.

There, Doctor Karl, the doctor-spy had his quarters and attended to the dangerously wounded coming from the front.

This was the man de Tersy wanted to see.

When he stood before him, he spoke tremblingly:

"I beg of you to listen to me. I have a terrible mission for you, but I cannot say what it is until you have promised secrecy." He hastened to add:

"It will be worth a fortune to you—help me and you will be splendidly recompensed."

Doctor Karl listened as though utterly bewildered:

"What do you want?" he asked.

"Have you, too, some poison?"

"Have I too? What do you mean?"

"I have need of a deadly poison, similar to those used by savages to poison their weapons and which kills at the slightest scratch.

"Can you get me such a one?"

Then in a tone of anguish:

"But I implore you, swear to keep this a secret! Nobody must ever know what I am going to tell you."

The doctor smiled, and in a voice of apparent cordiality, answered:

"Don't be anxious, I promise you to hold my tongue—as for the poison, here it is."

He searched in a medicine chest and brought out a small bottle without a label.

"What use do you want to put this to?"

De Tersy did not answer.

Now that he held the bottle of poison in his hand he seemed reassured.

"Will you answer me frankly?" he asked.

"I am always frank—you mustn't doubt my word."

"Then I'll tell you this. You've heard about the yellow document?"

"Yes," replied the doctor after a brief hesitation. "I know what you are talking of."

"And I know where the yellow document can be found!"

The doctor evidently knew the value and the importance of the document.

He grew excited:

"You know where the yellow document is! Then what are you doing here? You must go and get it. You must—"

"You are mistaken," interrupted de Tersy coldly. "My duty is to stay here and obey my father's orders. But you can go. I can send you after it. Listen to me, these are my orders—"

6. Beaten

While so many formidable intrigues were being plotted among the infamous German spies, all dealing with the yellow document, while Rauerdt, Krampft, de Tersy, William II himself were fiercely struggling to recover the terrible paper, what was happening to the heroic fiancé of Colette, the unfortunate Louis Monet? Rauerdt had told the truth to the Kaiser. He had saved the young lieutenant from death by loss of blood, as he lay unconscious in the landau.

Thanks to the secret passages in the royal villa, Rauerdt had been a witness to the meeting of Monet and Colette. And thanks to his powers of detection, he had no difficulty in recognizing Monet under his priest's disguise.

When the latter had regained consciousness he experienced a strange emotion.

"Where the devil am I?" he murmured.

The reply to this question was, alas! simple and tragic.

He was in a prison cell.

Then suddenly he became the prey to a mad curiosity.

He remembered everything, that was sure, but why was he able to remember?

All the details were clear in his mind. He had had Colette's ring on his finger, now it was gone.

Whoever found him had bound up his wound and stopped the hemorrhage.

And then, in a flash, Louis Monet understood.

In losing blood he had also eliminated the worst of the narcotic from his system.

For a number of days Monet was left to his sad thoughts.

And then one evening his cell door opened and a man appeared: Krampft.

"How are you?" began the infamous German.

Monet looked at him with such an air of contempt that the wretch exclaimed:

"Why are you looking at me like that? Come, give me a welcome, for I bring you good news."

"Nothing you can say would give me any pleasure."

"Not even that you are going to make a change of residence?"

"Where are you going to take me?"

In spite of himself Monet had asked the question and Krampft burst out laughing.

"Ah! I thought that would interest you. But now you are too curious. I cannot tell you. It is true that I bring you further news—and I hope you are going to he sensible."

"What do you mean?"

"You would he wise to tell me where is the yellow document."

Monet shrugged his shoulders:

"That you will never know."

Krampft burst out laughing.

"'Never' is a big word. We shall see."

He went on pitilessly:

"Just think, I am charged by the emperor to make you speak. Yes, that's the way it is. For the sake of Germany, the yellow document must be found. Therefore all means are good. And here you are, both my prisoners. Colette will speak."

"Colette! Is Colette alive?"

"Very much alive—and in my hands."

The happiness that Monet felt on learning that Colette had escaped the horrible death she had been threatened with quickly gave place to despair.

Was not her present position worse than death? Krampft must have guessed the thought that passed through Monet's head, for he approached the officer:

"Thus it is," he insisted, "either Colette or you will speak. I give you my word on that."

"We shall never speak."

"That makes me laugh."

"We prefer to die."

"To die, perhaps. But before death there will be torture! Oh, there is no hurry, you have still some hours before you. I just dropped in to say 'howdy do.' Your journey will begin tomorrow. The torture will follow!"

Krampft grinned and left the cell with an ironical "good day."

The officer felt at the end of his strength.

That night he tossed sleeplessly, his brain filled with horrible visions.

At length, towards dawn, he dropped into a torpor from sheer exhaustion.

He must have had a long sleep, for when he woke Krampft had returned, accompanied by two men, doubtless two spies.

Between them they carried an enormous box. Into this box they put Monet, shut down the lid, and nailed it securely, after having gagged him in a most thorough manner.

What did these strange preparations mean?

Monet made no resistance, refusing to show either anxiety or surprise.

"I am at their mercy," he said to himself. "I won't give them the satisfaction of showing my feelings."

What were they going to do with him? And how was he to be transported?

He guessed that the box had been placed on a heavy wagon drawn by fast horses.

Then he felt himself being transferred to a baggage car.

Where was the train going?

Monet could not determine.

The journey lasted a long time. Finally after many stops, he realized that his box was being taken out and placed in another wagon. Again the box was unloaded and men were busy unnailing the lid.

A moment later, Monet was roughly dragged out.

Where was he?

He saw the thick and high wall of a kind of chateau.

He was in the courtyard of this building which he noticed had two tall towers.

Doubtless this was to be his prison.

A man came to meet him.

He held a large cap in his hand and smiled hypocritically:

"If Monsieur will follow me?"

Monet shrugged his shoulders.

"Have I the right to refuse?"

The man laughed:

"Ah! I see Monsieur likes to joke. Certainly Monsieur cannot refuse, because I have been charged by Herr Krampft to make you obey. But that is no reason why we shouldn't get on well together. I am a jailer, but that doesn't prevent me from having a soft heart. Monsieur will find in me a friend."

"Do your duty and hold your tongue," growled Monet.

He was in a hurry to be left alone.

They might put him in a dungeon, but at least he would be away from that man.

The jailer took the rebuke in good part.

"Monsieur is nervous," he said, "and that I can understand. But Monsieur need not remain here long, I think."

Monet was on his guard. The man would find some difficulty in gaining his confidence.

For the second time, the officer ordered:

"Do your duty and hold your tongue."

While speaking, Monet had glanced at the chateau. It was a sinister looking place.

The courtyard was narrow, shut in by the two high towers, and paved with heavy cobblestones where neither moss nor any form of green thing grew.

Monet quickly sized it up.

"To escape from here is impossible."

"I will take Monsieur to his apartments."

The man had replaced his cap on his head and this disclosed a large revolver which he had kept hidden.

Monet, seeing this, shrugged his shoulders, resigned.

In any case, the thought of attacking the man was out of the question. He knew very well that Krampft had taken every precaution.

"I am ready," he replied.

His jailer led the way to a small door in one of the towers.

"Monsieur has only to go up."

Monet obeyed. But he could not repress a shudder at the sound of the door closing behind him.

Was he not entering what was to be his torture chamber and his last dwelling on earth?

While he climbed the narrow and twisting stairs, the jailer kept up an incessant chatter.

"Monsieur will be very comfortable. We have given him a well aerated room and the necessary furniture."

But Monet was not listening.

He suffered acutely from hunger and thirst and it took all his remaining strength to climb the interminable steps.

Finally, he reached a landing and saw before him an open door.

"Monsieur will go in," ordered the jailer.

Monet entered what was evidently the top room in the tower. It was more of a cell than a room, and furnished with a bed, chair, table and wardrobe. A looking-glass hung on the wall. Monet's attention was immediately fixed on the window which was heavily barred. Below appeared an apparently bottomless precipice. The chateau had undoubtedly been built on the summit of a gigantic rock.

The country seen in the distance was impossible to recognize.

Monet recoiled with a sensation of giddiness.

At this moment the jailer questioned:

"Does Monsieur like his quarters? I may as well tell Monsieur that upon payment Monsieur can get some extras; for instance, I can bring him something to eat right away."

"I have no money."

"Then I am sorry but Monsieur will have to wait till tomorrow."

And without waiting to hear the protests of his prisoner, the jailer left the room.

Alone, Monet fell into the depths of despair. He murmured:

"I am lost—I am beaten."

No hope and no illusion were longer possible.

The idea of escape was out of the question.

And then a sudden rush of energy made him spring up from his couch where he had flung himself.

He was not yet beaten because he was still alive.

Was it not his duty to struggle to the end in spite of the odds?

"The first thing is to try and discover where the spy has taken me," he pondered.

He went to the window and peered through the bars, but it was already getting late and the evening fog was settling over the land.

The silence was complete, absolute, total.

"I do not even know if the other tower is on my right or left. Perhaps there are more prisoners in it!"

Then a sudden idea came to him.

Monet took down from the wall the small looking-glass and held it at arm's length through the bars of the window, though he scarcely expected to see in it more than the reflection of the interminable wall of the tower.

But after one glance he gave a loud cry of joy:

"Colette! It is Colette!"

He had seen the charming face of his fiancée in the glass.

She was leaning at a narrow window talking to someone. Probably she occupied the corresponding room in the other tower.

With beating heart and haggard eye the young man maneuvered the glass so as to get a better view and then suddenly a cry of horror escaped his lips.

He staggered back and the glass fell into the depths below.

He burst into choking sobs.

What had he seen?

7. Between Traitors

For twenty-four hours, de Tersy had found no time to be bored. In fact, he looked back upon his previous monotony with regret.

The wretched man could not close an eye, nor escape from the haunting fear of the poison he was supposed to have taken. He was constantly on the alert to discover the first symptoms of his approaching death. He felt a slight pain in breathing. Were his lungs becoming congested? To forget his agony he busied himself in an extraordinary way.

Upon the table he placed his revolver after examining the cartridges one by one.

When assured that it was in good working order he then got out the small bottle of poison given him by the doctor. He drew the cork and with the thick brown liquid it contained he covered some long pins which he then placed about the room on the furniture.

The day passed without incident, then followed a night of horrible nightmares, and finally the morning of the third day dawned.

Karl had not arrived.

Krampft had given no sign of life.

Now, as eleven struck, de Tersy sprang up suddenly. Somebody was coming upstairs.

And the footsteps were not those of Wolff, the orderly with the face of a spy.

Livid, with beating heart, de Tersy awaited the approach of his visitor. A knock and the door opened. It was the doctor.

A cry of relief escaped him.

"Well!"

"Well, I have been successful."

After regaining his breath, Karl rubbed his hands, smilingly triumphant.

De Tersy exclaimed feverishly:

"You have been successful! Have you the yellow document?"

"Yes. I have the yellow document."

"Ah! My friend! My dear friend! It can't be possible!"

"On the contrary, it is quite possible."

De Tersy rushed to the doctor and wrung his hands, stammering:

"Never can my father thank you enough!"

The bastard did not forget the necessity of lying even at the moment he felt himself saved.

"Now I shall be able to hand over the yellow document to the monster," was his real thought.

"Karl, your fortune is made! I shall tell his majesty—"

He stopped abruptly, seized by a fresh fear. Would the doctor give him the yellow document?

De Tersy ordered:

"Show me the document."

"I am only too happy to obey the orders of your excellency."

Undoubtedly the spy was convinced that his wisest course was to obey the natural son of the emperor.

He drew from his pocket a large yellow envelope and handed it to the bastard.

As soon as de Tersy glanced at it, no doubt remained in his mind.

He was in possession of the most precious of all treasures. It meant life to him.

"Aren't you going to open the envelope?" inquired Karl.

A strange smile passed over the lips of the Kaiser's bastard.

"Doctor, I respect secrets. But how did you get it?"

It was necessary to know the details. The monster might ask questions.

"It was quite simple," declared Karl. "First of all I made inquiries about the fate of Mme. Ravignon. I heard that she had been taken off in a special car by rail—they could not tell me to what place. Naturally I next went to the station, there I found a trace— or rather, I thought I had."

"Thought you had? What do you mean?"

"That I had followed a false scent. I felt sure I was following Mme. Ravignon, but I was quite mistaken. After a long trip I reached a kind of chateau-fortress built upon an inaccessible peak of the Vosges, and which I learned belonged to Krampft."

"To Krampft!"

"Your excellency may imagine how surprised I was. And fresh surprises were in store for me. It was not difficult to reach the prisoner. My relations with Krampft put me in possession of his passwords and his methods. I succeeded in winning over the jailer without much difficulty. I will skip the details and arrive at the morning when the cell door opened and I found myself face to face with the prisoner."

"Who was it?"

"Colette," answered the doctor calmly.

De Tersy remained dumb with amazement.

There could be no doubt of it, Karl was speaking the truth, for Krampft himself had written telling de Tersy that Colette was a prisoner.

"And then? Go on!"

"Then, I had the happy inspiration to present myself before Colette as an emissary of Monet. I told her that she must absolutely give me the yellow document to save Monet from being tortured."

"And you succeeded in convincing her?"

"The proof is that you have the document."

"Nothing else happened?"

"Yes. While I was talking to the prisoner I heard a loud cry and a noise as though something had fallen into the ravine. I don't know what it was."

The doctor's glance was now directed to the bottle of poison on the table and which he naturally recognized.

He did not see the expression in Paul de Tersy's eyes.

The Kaiser's bastard was furious. He was saying to himself:

"This man is lying."

He knew Colette well enough to feel sure that she did not deliver up the yellow document thus easily.

Karl must have taken it by force.

Possibly he had killed her.

"You have nothing further to tell me?" he asked.

"Nothing. Except that I am tired out and desperately sleepy."

While speaking the doctor watched every movement of de Tersy.

Was he afraid that the Kaiser's bastard would use one of the for-midable needles against him, for which he himself had furnished the poison?

He would not have been surprised.

"By the way," said de Tersy, "one more question. What would be the effect of this poison?"

The doctor smiled.

"It would cause immediate paralysis and death would come within the hour."

De Tersy bowed amiably.

"Well, it will be very useful to me."

Then he added:

"Doctor, sleep well. The yellow document will be delivered and when you wake the emperor will reward your services."

Karl stepped backwards to the door.

He saw de Tersy put his hand in his pocket but took no notice of this simple movement.

And yet it meant death.

The revolver, carefully prepared, did its terrible work.

De Tersy, a wonderful shot, fired through his coat and the body of the doctor fell shot through the heart.

De Tersy went near.

"My ambassador was a fool. I'm not sorry."

But as he bent over the body, he began to tremble.

It was his first crime and he was afraid.

"I was wrong!" he stammered.

Then he pulled himself together.

"No. I wasn't wrong. I had to kill him. By showing his body to Krampft I can avoid bringing his vengeance upon me. I shall say the doctor betrayed us, that he admitted having stolen the yellow document but I shall deny that he gave it to me. I can say he attacked me and that I had to kill him. Krampft will be grateful and may help me to dispose of the monster."

He burst into laughter.

"The monster!—I need not fear him now!"

And he added, aloud:

"I shall poison him by and by."

De Tersy took hold of the body intending to hide it under the bed.

At this moment the door opened and the monster entered the

room.

How had he been able a second time to slip into the house past the watchful eyes of Wolff?

In a manner extremely simple.

He had never left the house after his interview with de Tersy. He had merely returned to his hiding place in the attic.

Had he heard de Tersy's threat against him?

Did he know of the terrible poison?

He said simply:

"Evidently I run a risk but what does that matter? It is my duty!"

With assurance and in a calm voice he announced himself.

"Good morning. You are not afraid of murder, I see."

De Tersy became livid; he stuttered:

"Ah! I was waiting for you. I was afraid."

The monster took a seat.

"You were afraid? Why? I promised to come and I am here. An honest man keeps his word."

A hideous smile froze the blood in de Tersy's veins.

"Have you the yellow document?"

"Have you the antidote?"

The man shrugged his shoulders.

"You are suspicious?—And you are wrong. Give me the document and I will save you."

"Very well," replied de Tersy. "An honest man keeps his word. I believe in you. Here is the document."

The hands of the stranger trembled.

Who was this mysterious individual?

De Tersy thought he had found out. He must be a messenger from the emperor.

The emperor wanted to test his son's fidelity.

"If this is so," thought de Tersy, "my father will take vengeance upon me, for in giving up this document I am betraying him."

And then he shrugged his shoulders. There would be no occasion for vengeance. He would give up the document and then he would poison this messenger of William II.

The stranger held the document in his hands for a long minute. His face expressed nothing. At length he made up his mind.

"I ask your attention," he said. "You are sure this is the yellow document?"

"I am sure of it," answered de Tersy.

The monster opened the envelope.

Alas! It was not the precious document but some blank sheets of paper that he took out.

Colette had not betrayed her trust.

8. A Mysterious Disappearance

A cry of rage escaped the monster, and a cry of fear came from de Tersy's lips.

"That is not the document!" exclaimed the latter.

"Tricked," replied the monster calmly.

He seemed angry but not surprised. Had he foreseen that the envelope contained only blank paper? That was his secret and one he had no intention of confiding to the Kaiser's bastard.

Quickly he turned to de Tersy.

"You see?"

"I see," said the trembling wretch. "I am lost!"

"You are lost? Why?"

De Tersy began in a tearful voice.

"You cannot wish for my death. I have not been at fault.—You will save me?"

The monster smiled.

"That is true. You haven't forgotten the poison in your blood."

"Oh, don't say you cannot save me? That can't be true!"

And then he fell on his knees.

"Have pity upon me! Do not condemn me to death—this antidote—"

The fear of death had conquered him. He would gladly have agreed to become the servant, the slave of the man who had the power to save him.

"Get up," commanded the monster. "Don't you remember that I told you—an honest man keeps his word? Be satisfied—you are to live."

And as de Tersy could scarcely credit the good news, the monster continued:

"Oh, I know it's not your fault if I haven't got the yellow document. I know you did your best to get it. That is why I shall not kill you."

De Tersy was about to break into thanks, but the strange individual stopped him:

"Wait. I shall not kill you, but I shall tell you all the contempt I have for you."

"Then be pitiful. Hurry! This frightful poison is already burning me. Save me! What must I do? What drug—"

The monster laughed. He seemed to be greatly amused over something.

"I assure you you are quite mistaken. Do you really feel symptoms of poisoning?"

"Yes!"

"Are you in great pain?"

"At certain moments."

"And yet, de Tersy, your sufferings are quite imaginary. What a coward you must be to be caught in such a childish trap! I never gave you any poison. The story I told was merely to scare you into obeying me."

The monster continued to laugh while de Tersy, white with anger, sprang forward.

Could it be true that he had never taken the poison?

"Scoundrel!" he cried.

"Ah! You call me 'scoundrel' now! And a moment ago you were at my feet! Certainly I have tricked you, but in doing so I alone ran any risk. I fight squarely, de Tersy, I am not a murderer like you. Goodbye."

The stranger turned to leave the room.

De Tersy now felt certain that the man had come from his father and that he would return and report the whole story to the emperor.

This dissipated his last scruples. With a quick movement he seized one of the poisoned needles and threw himself upon his visitor.

"Fool!" he cried, as he plunged the needle into the monster's shoulder.

And then with a quick bound, he sprang back and drew his revolver, aiming it at his victim, now collapsed in a chair.

"Well! You won't insult me again, I think! The shoe is on the other foot! You have found your master!"

The man did not answer. He appeared to be unable to move.

De Tersy continued:

"Really, you are as simple as a child! You come in here freely, but how have you planned to go out? What? You don't answer?"

A groan came from the lips of the monster:

"I am in great pain."

De Tersy laughed louder.

"You feel the way I thought I felt just now. I am not an honest man like you. I don't pride myself on keeping my word! On the contrary, I boast of being able to lie cleverly. Do you hear?"

De Tersy bent over his victim.

"Oh! You will last some time yet. Death will come to you slowly. You can no longer speak! Slowly and by degrees you will stifle. Ah! You will taste the vengeance of the Kaiser's bastard! And that you taste it to the full you shall die here alone, without friends, without even the presence of an enemy! Alone! You understand? Funny what the prick of a needle can do for a man! Think over that—it will entertain you! You may have an hour more to live! Goodbye!"

And de Tersy went out.

In spite of his atrocious and cold wickedness the bastard of William II was at the end of his string.

It was his crime that drove him out.

*   *   *   *   *   *

The following evening Paul de Tersy was questioning Rauerdt in Berlin. So upset was he that it never entered his mind that the chief of the secret service might lie to him.

"So you don't know this monster?"

"I don't know him," Rauerdt replied phlegmatically.

"You haven't an idea who he can be?"

"Not the least idea."

"And it was not you who sent him to me?"

"I hadn't the least idea you would receive his visit."

"So it was not you who removed his body?"

"I assure you it was not."

"I shall go mad!" murmured de Tersy with a sigh, as he left Rauerdt.

How did it happen that the Kaiser's bastard dared to tell the master spy of the monster's visit and how he had been led to kill

Karl and later the other?

De Tersy had simply become panic-stricken after quitting the tragic room where he had left the two bodies. At first he rushed madly away, but after awhile he stopped and, with an effort of will, deliberately retraced his steps, determined not to go without the necessary baggage.

"I'm not going to run away from two dead bodies," he said to himself.

But no sooner had he entered the room again than he gave a cry of fright.

One of the bodies had disappeared!

Someone had carried off the body of the monster.

De Tersy had at first suspected Rauerdt. That was why he hurried to Berlin and questioned the spy.

Now Rauerdt had sworn he was innocent. He was not concerned with the removal of the body nor with the visit of the monster.

Then what was he to think? What conclusion could he come to?

But if de Tersy went away a prey to anxiety, Rauerdt, on his side, was no less worried.

Naturally, he had not been surprised to hear that the monster had visited de Tersy, but he had been more than upset by the events which followed.

"Monet and Colette cannot know much," he thought, "or in any case they won't speak.

"So now the emperor must win the confidence of Mme. Bayen who alone is able to give us any information. But to gain Brigitte Bayen it will be necessary to set Monet and Colette at liberty. After all, why not? If it were arranged properly."

At this same time, another person was busy thinking of the consequences of the monster's visit to Paul de Tersy.

And that person was Krampft.

Krampft had joined the bastard as the latter was leaving the ministry. He had listened to de Tersy's recital of what had happened.

And without doubt Krampft had genius. Without hesitation he guessed what Rauerdt must be thinking.

He turned abruptly to de Tersy.

"If you want my opinion, I think you were wrong to tell all this to Rauerdt. I'll wager the result will be that I shall be ordered to release my two prisoners."

De Tersy did not understand.

Krampft, however neglected to give him any explanation. With a shrug of his shoulders, he exclaimed:

"Well, it can't be helped. If they must be allowed to escape, they shall escape in the way I choose."

9. The Price of Blood

What had happened in the room where de Tersy found it necessary to resort to crime to extricate himself from what he considered a dangerous situation?

Was the body of the monster really stolen?

Paul de Tersy had simply been completely taken in. As soon as he had gone away the monster rose to his feet.

"That was a lucky escape," he murmured. Then bending over the body of Karl, he added:

"As a matter of fact it was this spy who saved me by giving the Kaiser's bastard a harmless liquor instead of poison. His reason for doing so was probably that he feared de Tersy would attempt to kill him."

The monster laughed at the thought.

And, in fact, he had guessed the exact truth.

When de Tersy had asked Karl to undertake a secret mission and then to furnish him with a deadly poison, Karl had divined to what purpose the poison would be put.

"A lucky escape!" repeated the monster. "And a fortunate thing I overheard the doctor explain the probable effects of the poison, otherwise I would not have been able to deceive de Tersy."

"And now what is to be done?" he asked.

"I have no time to lose. Since Karl could not procure the yellow document, and since Karl sent this spy to Brigitte, it means that it is not in Brigitte's possession."

Alas! the monster had guessed wrong this time. He had only caught the final words spoken by Karl. He did not know that it was Colette whom Karl had seen. And it was, doubtless, due to that mistake that he suddenly exclaimed:

"I must save them! I will save them! And I will do my duty to the very end."

The following day a strange scene was taking place in a wine shop at Saales, not far from the French frontier.

There, in an atmosphere saturated with tobacco, two men were talking and drinking.

"You are a poor man," said the first of these individuals, "and consequently you have the right to enrich yourself. Think it over! Fifty thousand francs."

The other man shook his head.

"To have my head on my shoulders is useful too!"

"With fifty thousand francs you can leave Germany and go to America. There you could live comfortably for the rest of your life without any fear."

The second man hesitated.

"Does Krampft pay you a fortune that you can despise fifty thousand francs?"

"Krampft?"

How did the name of the spy enter into the conversation?

The man who urged the argument of a fortune wore thick bandages over his face. His large hat was pulled down over his forehead, and his coat collar turned up so that nothing could be seen of his features but his eyes, and these were hidden behind dark glasses.

His companion would have been easier to recognize.

If Monet had seen him, he would have identified him as his jailer.

"Fifty thousand francs, cash down! And all for a job you can do without risk or danger!"

"That's all very well, but if ever my master—"

"He will never know."

"But I understand this young man is mixed up in some espionage affair?"

"Exactly. And that guarantees you from all suspicion. It will be thought that other spies planned his escape."

Monet's jailer drank a glass of absinthe at one gulp.

Was he hesitating?

Suddenly he shook his head.

"No, no, it can't be done. I should be caught and killed."

"By whom?"

"By Krampft, of course!"

A silence ensued. The two men watched each other.

"All right, so much the worse for you. We'll say no more about it."

The jailer took another drink.

"It wouldn't be so bad if I knew who you were."

"My name would mean nothing to you."

"If I could see your face."

"It would scare you."

"Who are you then?"

"A monster."

The jailer became more troubled.

"Fifty thousand francs is too little."

"What is your price?"

"A hundred thousand."

"You want too much."

"I should need it to get away."

The other shrugged his shoulders, made a move to pay the bill and get out.

The jailer put his hand on the other's arm.

"Look here, you're in too much of a hurry—let me think—it's a big thing you are offering."

"I will pay you fifty thousand francs."

"Cash down?"

"Cash down."

"In advance?"

"No. After the escape."

"How?"

"You will find the money at the end of the rope."

"How do I know you are not lying?"

"You must trust me as I trust you."

"Has he been warned?"

"You will warn him."

"How?"

"By hiding a small sealed case in his bread."

"Has he the money on him?"

"No."

"I don't know what to think."

"You needn't think. You must accept or refuse. Yes or no."

"Are you in a hurry?"

"He must escape tomorrow."

"Then he must be told tonight?"

"Yes."

"Have you the case with you?"

"I have."

"All right, give it to me. I accept."

The monster could not repress a movement of relief. He exclaimed:

"Then it's understood?"

"Perfectly. I'm to slip the little case into the prisoner's bread this evening. Tomorrow night, I give him a rope and he escapes by the window. At the end of the rope I find fifty thousand francs. Why not make it sixty?"

"No, fifty."

"And you will put the money there yourself?"

"No. Monet will do that. What difference does it make to you?"

"None."

The man passed over a small metal case which could easily be hidden in a piece of bread.

"Go along!" he ordered.

"All right, all right! I'm going," and the jailer went out, staggering.

No sooner was he left alone than the man dropped his head in his hands, exhausted:

"God help me! I shall have done the impossible! Can I save him?"

Outside, it was a dark, obscure night in the wooded, mountainous country.

The slopes of the neighboring hills were in deep shadow. There were no stars in the sky and the wind howled in the branches of the firs.

With heavy footsteps the jailer made his way along the narrow streets of the small village; he then cut across fields and soon gained a path which wound around the base of a hill.

The man was thinking:

"Fifty thousand francs! That's a big sum! But what I have to do is terrible! It will be easy enough to give the man a rope but if ever my master should know..."

The jailer stopped short.

Now in the darkness suddenly appeared a figure with out-stretched arm.

"Stop!"

Terrified by the sound of the voice, the jailer stammered:

"Krampft! Herr Krampft!"

"Answer me, frankly! Where have you been?"

"In Saales."

"What were you doing in Saales?"

"Nothing! Nothing!"

"You were drinking."

"That isn't forbidden, Herr Krampft."

"It is forbidden to keep me waiting."

The jailer crossed himself. He thought his last hour had come. Krampft took him by the arm.

"Now, listen to me. Can I trust you?"

"Surely."

"Are you anything but a brute? Will you help me?"

"I will do anything you want, Herr Krampft."

"Anything? Will you commit a crime?"

"A crime? Why yes, of course. But why?" Krampft laughed.

"Why? You will soon know. Now, pay attention to what I say; if you succeed there will be fifty thousand francs for you."

"Fifty thousand francs!"

The jailer repeated the words in utter bewilderment. So Krampft also offered him that sum!

"Speak! Speak!"

"This is what you have to do and you know that your life depends upon your obedience. Tomorrow you must kill the prisoner in the tower."

The jailer drew back.

"Are you afraid?"

"No."

It was not fear but amazement that staggered him.

A few moments ago he had been offered fifty thousand francs to let Monet escape, now he was offered the same sum to kill him.

"You want me to kill this young man?"

"Yes. I order you to do so. He is in my way. But I wish his death to appear an accident. This is what you must do: You will wait until he is asleep then throw yourself upon him. He is weak, sick. You are strong. It won't be difficult. You will then bind him, saw one of the bars of the window and push the body into the ravine below. A fall of two hundred feet—he won't escape from that!"

"And you will give me fifty thousand francs?"

"As soon as the work is done."

"You may count on me," said the jailer.

10. For France! For Colette!

Alone in his cell, Monet for long days struggled against his despair.

He was caught in the terrible net of German espionage and he was beaten. All his attempts to fulfill his mission had come to naught.

He kept repeating to himself:

"The yellow document has been given up! Colette has betrayed me! There is nothing to live for now. My work is done. I have the right to die."

Doubt was no longer possible.

He had seen Colette in the looking-glass, talking with a stranger, unquestionably an emissary of Krampft's. He had seen her take one of those large and old fashioned bracelets from her arm, break it and remove from its hiding place a yellow envelope which she gave to her sinister visitor.

How was he to know that it contained nothing but blank sheets of paper?

Convinced of her treason, he had been prepared to give up the struggle, to give up living. And now, he was pacing feverishly up and down his cell.

What had happened?

Simply that he had made an unexpected discovery. In breaking the bread supplied with his dinner he gave a cry of amazement.

In it was hidden a small metal case.

To open it and take out the paper it contained was the work of a moment.

Somebody had been able to send him a message unknown to Krampft.

What message?

The paper he held in his hand was a check for fifty thousand francs with a German signature.

A smaller piece of silk paper next appeared.

The letters which were printed in handwriting read:

"The jailer is bought. He will furnish a rope, saw your bars, climb down. You will be met. Fasten the check to the end of the rope."

Monet was at first so astounded that he did not take in the significance of the words.

Was it possible that somebody had planned his escape?

And then, the first moment of joy was quickly followed by a reaction. After all, he did not want to live. His whole being revolted against the thought of life without his love and without his mission. At this moment the key grated in the lock of his cell door. Instinctively Monet slipped the check and the paper into his pocket. The door opened and the jailer appeared. The man's face was deathly pale and he avoided meeting the lieutenant's eyes.

"Good day."

Monet did not reply and the jailer repeated:

"Good day."

"What do you want?"

"Nothing, nothing."

What was going on m the obtuse brain of Krampft's servant?

Had he made up his mind to earn the fifty thousand francs for the easy crime, or the fifty thousand francs for the escape?

He had delivered the message. Did that mean that he had decided in favor of escape?

"What do you want?"

"The weather is bad."

And as though speaking with difficulty:

"It's—it's the right sort of weather for your escape."

He tried to laugh, but the laugh sounded false.

"What's that?" said Monet, angrily.

The jailer's face took on a look of amazement. The very word escape seemed to anger the prisoner. He continued:

"Such a chance may not happen again. You'll have to saw one of the bars, and with a rope—"

Monet had drawn back and stood against the wall. With folded arms and lowered head, he reflected.

Should he live?

Suddenly he decided to face death bravely. He took a step towards the man and ordered:

"Get out!"

One glance at Monet's face and the cowardly German quickly disappeared. It might be said that he fled.

"What does it mean?" he cried. "A man who expects to be killed is told he is free and he refuses to go!"

The wretch could not guess the thoughts in Monet's mind.

Fifty thousand francs to save him—and fifty thousand francs to kill him! Well, he would have it!

The jailer rushed down stairs and out of the door. The storm had redoubled in violence.

The pine trees in the neighboring woods bent under the gusts of a furious wind.

After having gone about a mile, he reached the shelter of a rock.

There a man was waiting for him. It was the monster.

"Well?"

"Well, I gave him the little case."

"What did he say?"

"I went in to see him."

"What then?"

"I thought he would kill me!"

"You say he wanted to kill you?"

"Yes. He drove me out of the room."

"Didn't you explain that his escape was planned?"

"Yes."

"And he wasn't willing?"

"He wasn't willing."

In spite of the storm, the monster quitted his shelter.

"I wish him to be saved!"

"I have done your bidding," replied the jailer. "I have earned my fifty thousand francs."

"You shall have them when he is free."

"But I can't drive him out!"

"Listen! You must obey me. You will return to him."

"No, no, I won't! I'm afraid."

The monster repeated:

"Fifty thousand francs."

The jailer was silent.

"Can you get me into his cell?"

"No, that is impossible. I am not the only man on guard. There is a patrol. If I could have taken you to him, I could have let him out of the door."

The tone of the man was so decided that the monster didn't insist further.

Besides, the young man had thought it over by this time. Probably he regretted having thrown away the chance he had been offered.

Let the jailer but renew the offer and it would be accepted.

But Monet had decided quite differently.

After all, he had acted bravely. To live would have been a piece of cowardice.

The captain of a sinking vessel goes down with it. The commander of a fort does not survive its capture by the enemy.

Monet approached the windows. He pressed his burning forehead against the iron bars.

How the wind howled!

"I would like to die tonight," he thought.

Suddenly he started.

He must have been dreaming! His senses had deceived him! He could not have heard aright! Monet listened with all his soul.

And again, the echo of a distant voice came to him through the storm.

"For France! For Colette!"

Who could have shouted these words?

The moment before he was ready to die. Now he wanted to live.

Was it not cowardice to seek forgetfulness and peace in death?

The war was beginning. Men were needed to protect country, women and children!

The mysterious person who had cried, "For France! For Colette!" had discovered the only words able to touch Monet and drag him back to life.

And then a fear assailed him.

Just now he had refused the jailer's offer.

He had noted the man's scared face. Would the man dare to return?

"I was a fool!" he cried.

Krampft himself might appear at any time, might stand him up against a wall and shoot him.

And the jailer had said the night was favorable.

The storm and the darkness would prevent him being seen.

Monet stood listening. After what seemed an interminable time the door of his cell opened suddenly and the jailer reappeared.

"Good evening."

This time the young man ran to meet him.

"Good evening, good evening! Come in."

"Ah! you feel better."

Monet put his hand on the man's shoulder.

"I want to live! I want to escape!"

"Yes, that's natural. Only you must tell that to Herr Krampft."

"No, to you! You will help me to escape."

"You are mad!"

The jailer shrugged his shoulders.

Monet had no time to say more. The jailer hurried out of the room and shut the door. Monet, in terror, asked himself if he had been mistaken in thinking the wretch was willing to help him.

And then the door opened again and the man returned.

"Well, your way of talking is not very discreet."

Monet smiled.

"Were you afraid someone would hear us?"

"I should say so!"

"You agree then?"

"I agree to nothing."

"I will pay fifty thousand francs."

"That's easy to say, but what proof have I got?"

"You will find the money at the end of the rope."

"What rope?"

"The one you are going to give me."

"You have the fifty thousand francs?"

"Perhaps," replied Monet. "But I can destroy them so easily that you would never find them if you pulled down this prison stone by stone. Give me the rope."

"And how about the bars of the window?"

"You will give me a file."

"But—I haven't one."

"You have one in your pocket."

The man suddenly came to a decision.

"Very well, I trust you and I'm sorry to see a young man like you in prison. You belong out in the fresh air. Besides, I must live—the fifty thousand francs will be tied to the end of the rope? You swear it?"

"I swear it. Give me the rope."

The jailer no longer hesitated.

He took off his coat. Around his body was wound a slender line. "Here it is."

"Is it strong?"

"Very strong. It is made of pure hemp."

"Is it long enough?"

"It is. The end of it will be only six feet from the ground."

"All right. Be off!"

"You must hurry. The patrol will be passing in three hours time." He threw a small file on the table and opened the door.

"Good luck! The fifty thousand francs at the end of the rope!"

The German closed the door and hurried down stairs.

He was trembling with fear.

"Upon my word, I'm sorry. Still fifty thousand to save him and fifty thousand to kill him! And then there is Krampft!"

11. Monet's Vengeance

While the abominable German gloated over his gains, Monet set himself to work to saw through one of the bars of his window.

He realized that the least delay might have fatal consequences. He must be far away before the next round of the patrol.

Besides, Krampft himself might appear unexpectedly. Monet would have been still more uneasy had he known the struggle taking place in the jailer's mind, that a second fifty thousand francs had been offered for his death.

The young man worked with desperate energy, but the bars were strong. It seemed to him as though the file made no impression on the iron.

At length, after ceaseless effort, he threw down the file and seized the bar with both hands. With a violent jerk he succeeded in breaking the iron.

Monet leaned out of the window, drawing in deep breaths of fresh air.

Nothing was visible but the somber wall of the tower. Whether he would land in the courtyard or beyond in the moat he could not determine.

Once more he examined the rope and found it strong. Then fastening one end of it to a bar, he began lowering himself into the void below.

Accustomed to plenty of physical exercise, he experienced no difficulty at the beginning of his descent.

But when he reached a point where the full fury of the wind struck him, the rope swayed in a perilous manner.

At each gust he was blown against the wall and his wounded shoulder began to pain him horribly.

"I shall never get to the end," he exclaimed.

But at the moment he began to give way to despair, he grew angry with himself, accusing himself of cowardice.

Again he repeated:

"For Colette—for France."

The words brought him fresh courage. He descended some distance further, tearing the skin from his ankles and hands.

And then, as if the wind were not enough to contend against, the rain came down in torrents. The rope grew slippery and his speed increased in spite of the desperate grip of his hands.

Suddenly he no longer felt the rope between his ankles. He must be near the ground.

But before letting himself go he must keep his promise. He must give the jailer the fifty thousand francs.

With the utmost difficulty he extracted the small case from his pocket, then hanging by one hand, he tied a knot at the end of the rope.

Now, as he took the check out of the box, his hand slipped and the box fell, and in falling it struck a stone several seconds later. Then it rebounded and again struck the wall. Finally, after a longer pause, he heard it splash into the water.

His heart ceased to beat and the sweat came out on his forehead.

"Good God!" he cried. "There is still a terrible void below me!"

In a flash he understood.

The rope was too short!

Krampft had wanted to get rid of him, and with the aid of the jailer had played this sinister trick upon him.

If it had not been for the box he would have been dashed to pieces on the rocks below.

And now, what was to be done?

He was at the end of his strength, and even if it were possible to climb up again, death would be ready to meet him at the other end.

His bleeding hands and weary muscles would no longer support his weight.

He was on the point of letting go when suddenly a vision appeared before his eyes.

Two women were walking hand in hand.

And these two women typified to Monet all the love that was in his heart.

One was the France of yesterday and the France of tomorrow.

The other was Colette.

This hallucination was the one best calculated to restore Monet's ebbing will.

The unfortunate man braced up.

"I will climb back!" he cried.

He glanced upward and what he saw appalled him.

The black wall appeared to reach the sky.

"I shall never succeed," he said to himself, "but I shall die in doing my duty."

Each foot he gained caused him intolerable pain. It was a fantastic attempt.

And then rage gave him endurance. He would be revenged on the jailer. If he could reach his cell he would spring at his throat and strangle him.

Slowly, patiently, he went up inch by inch. At length he realized that he had accomplished the feat. He was able to seize one of the window bars, to get his knee upon the ledge, finally to drop into the cell, more dead than alive. How long he lay in a semiconscious condition he never knew.

He was recalled to his senses by the sound of footsteps on the stairs.

"The jailer!" he murmured, springing to his feet.

He picked up the file which, in the hands of an exasperated man, became a deadly implement. Crouching by the wall, he made ready to attack.

*   *   *   *   *   *

At the moment when the lieutenant hung suspended at the end of the rope and found it was too short, the infamous jailer was drinking glass after glass of absinthe.

His face expressed a drunken delight.

"That was a good idea of mine," he thought. "And luck was on my side, too. Fifty thousand francs to save him—so I give him the rope. Fifty thousand francs to kill him—and the rope is too short! In that way they both will be happy, Krampft and the other—"

The wretch took another drink.

Krampft could not complain because the young man killed himself by falling into the ravine.

The monster would never know that the rope had been too short. And the fifty thousand francs must be now dangling out there!

"I must hurry and get them," he exclaimed.

And then to give himself courage, he finished the bottle of absinthe in one gulp.

He had scarcely reached the stairs when loud knocks were heard at the door.

"Krampft!" he muttered.

He hesitated to open. What would he say to his master?

"I'll tell him to search for the body in the ravine. He will never guess the money is fastened to the end of the rope."

The knocks redoubled.

"Is that you, Herr Krampft?" he asked.

A dark form appeared in the doorway.

"It is I! Don't you know me?"

The jailer stifled a cry of alarm.

It was not Krampft who stood before him, it was the monster who wanted him to save Monet.

"What do you want? Why are you here?" he stammered. "Herr Krampft may come! Fly!"

"I don't care about Krampft, I am armed. Obey me!"

The man raised his arm and the gleaming barrel of a revolver pointed at the jailer.

"Now, answer me! Why hasn't he escaped yet?"

"But, he must have escaped! He certainly went down the rope."

Then a bright idea struck him.

"If you want a proof, come up with me. I will pull in the rope and if he has kept his word the money will be tied to the end of it!"

"Go ahead!" answered the monster.

What new villainy had entered the head of the German?

While climbing the stairs, the jailer thought:

"I'll go into the room with him—I'll get the fifty thousand francs—and then—I'll rush out and lock him in. What wouldn't Herr Krampft pay to get this man!"

"It's a climb, isn't it?" he exclaimed. "You'd think you were mounting to the skies. You're all out of breath! Courage, we're nearly there."

The two men had reached the top of the tower.

It was at this moment that Monet became aware of the footsteps and, file in hand, prepared to wreak his vengeance.

With a gesture, the jailer opened the door and invited his guest to go in.

12. I'm Nobody

Monet was in no condition to reason. Instinct alone spoke to him. The instinct of revenge, born of the agony he had gone through. Upon seeing the door open, he crouched and sprang.

A man entered the room.

He felt so sure that it was his would-be assassin who confronted him, that without hesitation and without pity he struck with all his strength.

The man received the blow full in his chest and with a loud cry he fell.

The monster lay on the ground as though dead.

Behind him, unaware of what had happened, the jailer entered and saw the body.

"Good God!" he cried.

And then he saw Monet, menacing, ferocious. He would have retreated but the wind had partially closed the door of the cell. He stuttered:

"I came—I—I thought—"

And then he stopped, terrified.

"Wretch! Scoundrel!" shouted the lieutenant, driving the file with one blow to the jailer's heart.

The man fell without a cry.

And then, the anger which had sustained Monet and enabled him to strike the two blows, left him exhausted, panting, incapable of movement.

"I—I have killed them!" he murmured, as he fell unconscious on the floor of his cell between his two victims.

Silence reigned in the room where death seemed triumphant.

Suddenly one of the bodies sat up, and in a shaken voice asked: "Ah! What has happened?"

His hands now felt under his coat, as though to find the wound he had received.

"Ah!" he exclaimed, "I was wise to take precautions. My chain armor has saved me!"

It was the monster.

The mysterious individual had not only escaped death, but he appeared to be not even wounded.

He rose to his feet and with a cry of terror noticed Monet's body.

"Why! he has not escaped!"

Bending over the prostrate lieutenant, he listened.

"His heart is beating," he exclaimed with a sigh of relief, then with a grim laugh:

"If he lives, the game is not up!"

As for the jailer, he pushed his body to one side with his foot. The man had only got his deserts.

All the monster's attempts to revive Monet were unavailing.

What was to be done?

To remain here was impossible. But how could they escape?

He crossed to the window, hauled up the rope and measured it with his arms.

"Ah! that's it! The rope was too short!" he muttered.

And now began a strange proceeding. After taking off his own clothes, he removed the jailer's coat and trousers and put them on. Then taking the man's cap, he placed it on his own head, pulling it well down over his face.

"That will do for me!" he thought.

Then, wrapping Monet in the bed clothing, the monster lifted him in his arms and flung him over his shoulder.

"If I don't meet the patrol, it will be all right," he murmured. "The door can easily be opened from the inside."

Bent under the weight of his burden he began the descent of the narrow stairs. He had reached halfway when a voice hailed him.

"Hello! Is that you?"

What was to be done?

To keep silent would be to attract attention.

To answer might be to betray himself.

While he hesitated the voice again questioned:

"I say, is that you? Why are you continually climbing up and down stairs tonight?"

The monster swore in a gruff voice:

"Hell! What's that to do with you?"

And he continued his journey noisily.

The ruse was successful.

The same voice replied:

"Ah! You are drunk! That's all right only look out that Herr Krampft doesn't come!"

At the sound of this name the monster shuddered. However, he reached the door in safety and was soon out in the night with his burden.

During a half hour he struggled through the woods. He was utterly exhausted by the time he reached a cave concealed by thick undergrowth.

After placing Monet upon a bed of dried leaves he struck a match and lit a lantern.

A gun rested against the stone wall. Further away, a box without a lid disclosed a supply of boxes of preserves and a kettle half full of water.

The monster searched among the provisions and with a sigh of relief picked up a small bottle which he quickly uncorked and held beneath Monet's nostrils.

"He has fainted from exhaustion," he exclaimed, "but he has no mortal wound. I shall be able to save him."

And suddenly he added:

"Yes, I shall be able to save him—but Colette? What about her?"

The lieutenant at this moment opened his eyes:

"Where am I?"

"With a friend," replied the monster. "Don't stir—rest, you are safe."

But instead of obeying this good advice, Monet sat up.

"With a friend! I have no friends! Who are you?"

"Somebody," answered the monster.

Then raising his lantern:

"You will not recognize me."

Monet could hardly restrain a cry of horror.

"You cannot recognize me."

"You are in the service of Krampft?"

"I hate Krampft."

"Are you the accomplice of his jailer?"

"I paid the man to let you escape."

"To let me escape! The rope was too short! You wanted to kill me!"

And again Monet asked.

"Who are you?"

"The person who cried: For France and for Colette."

At the name of his fiancée Monet could not help a groan of pain.

"Colette!—my poor Colette!"

"I will save her."

"You lie!"

"I will save her as I have saved you."

"You have not saved me."

"Yes. You are free."

"Free!"

Monet repeated the word. He could not believe it.

Free! He would soon see.

He rose, expecting the monster to attack him.

"You are free," repeated the monster. "I will give you a proof. Take this weapon."

He handed Monet a revolver.

"I'm not dreaming!"

"No," replied the monster gently, "but you have a bad fever. Calm yourself; rest. You are free, but you are on German territory. France is far away. And you must be able to fight again. Sleep, I beg of you—for France—for Colette!"

The soothing tones of the monster had their effect.

"Colette—Colette is still a prisoner."

The stranger must doubtless have been under the stress of a great emotion, for his voice changed, became sharp and clear:

"Lieutenant Monet, I will save your fiancée, I give you my word of honor—my word as an off—"

The monster did not finish.

At the sound of this voice Monet started:

"I'm going mad!" he shouted. "You are—what is your name?"

"Hush. I am nobody! An unknown. I forbid you to recognize me."

And he added:

"Lieutenant Monet, I order you to sleep! You must regain your strength and courage! Goodbye. Wait for me!"

Before Monet could speak the monster had disappeared.

Outside, the storm continued.

Quite indifferent to the elements, the monster walked rapidly with bent head, as though the events of the night had had no effect upon his strength.

From time to time, he muttered:

"I will save her! Yes. I must! It is my duty! Poor child. And the yellow document must be found. Ah! luck is with me!"

Twenty minutes later the monster reached the mysterious chateau and approached the door of the tower in which Colette was held prisoner.

Alas! the door was locked.

He searched in the pockets of the jailer's clothes and a cry of joy escaped him. A large bunch of keys, the keys of the chateau, were in his hands!

13. Love's Treachery

A moment later he growled:

"Not an instant to lose! It is he!"

What had he heard?

The sound of an approaching automobile.

Who else would be coming to the prison at this hour but its sinister master, Krampft?

Hurriedly trying one key after another, he finally succeeded in unlocking the door and entered the tower.

As he rapidly climbed the stairs the monster thought:

"Krampft will probably first visit Monet's cell. Finding the jailer killed he will make inquiries, and this will give me time to rescue Colette."

Suddenly he stopped short.

Two flights below him he heard voices.

"So each tower has its own watchman?"

The voice belonged to a woman and seemed to affect the monster strangely.

"Yes, Mademoiselle."

The second voice evidently belonged to another jailer.

The monster ground his teeth:

"Certainly luck is against me this time," he declared.

"The visitors must have come directly to this tower, and the jailer is not aware of his colleague's death."

The monster proceeded rapidly and with extreme caution. When he had reached the floor below Colette's he paused. If he continued up he would inevitably be trapped, for each floor contained only one room, and Colette's was the top one!

"What a fool I am!" he murmured.

He had the keys, why not open the door of the cell on the floor he was on?

He might be able to hide in it. At worst, the danger could not be greater.

He found the right key and unlocked the door. The room was without furniture and quite empty.

"Saved! I am saved," he sighed.

Above his head he could hear the nervous steps of Colette.

And he thought:

"If the persons behind me are on their way to see Colette, I shall be able to overhear everything they say."

The monster was right.

Alone in her prison, Colette was resigned, knowing herself condemned to death and expecting to be punished by torture for having given the blank paper instead of the yellow document.

"How are you, Mademoiselle?" cried the jailer as he opened her cell door.

Then he ordered:

"Come in, you—Herr Krampft will decide your fate during the day."

Colette wondered if she could be dreaming.

Behind the rough and brutal jailer she saw a young, dark-eyed woman with pale face and red marks left by thongs on her wrists. She had evidently been recently bound.

Who was this woman?

When the jailer's footsteps had passed out of hearing, Colette went towards her with a spontaneous movement of sympathy.

"Who are you? Are you a prisoner as I am? An enemy of Krampft's? Do you know why you are here and what they will do with you?"

The strange woman looked at Colette, but did not answer.

In fact, her silence became alarming and Colette wondered if she were not in the presence of a madwoman.

"I beg you to tell me who you are!"

In a strange voice, the woman answered:

"But who are you? I seem to know you. Still, it can't be possible!"

"You recognize me?" exclaimed Colette.

"Yes. I am sure now. Your name is Colette! You were Lieutenant Monet's fiancée!"

The young girl was astounded.

"Yes! I am Lieutenant Monet's fiancée! And who are you?"

The woman's face grew bitter. She made a movement toward

Colette.

"Who am I? You want to know! Well, I will tell you. I am the woman you ought to hate!"

"I don't understand."

"Must I explain further?"

"I beg you to do so."

"Is the lieutenant's fiancée so stupid she cannot guess? My name would mean nothing to you, unless you have already heard of your fiancée's mistress."

The strange creature threw back her head and burst into a sinister laugh.

"You didn't expect to hear that, stupid child! And still it's the truth. For a long time I have suffered from Monet's attentions to you. I love him! And he pretended to love you! I am his mistress and he told you he hoped to marry you! Oh, you have good cause to hate me! That is my revenge! Do you understand?"

Colette listened, white as death. The woman went on:

"I am prettier than you. He would have been mad to prefer you to me! But I'll tell you the truth. You passed for the daughter of Krampft—Ravignon. Monet has been mixed up in espionage for a long time. He had to have a reason for going to the mayor's house. Well, you were made that reason! And that's all you were!"

Colette, at first overwhelmed by this onslaught, now stiffened up.

"I don't believe you!" she cried.

A laugh greeted her words.

"You are lying! No, I don't believe you. Monet is not capable of such infamy. Monet really loves me. He was my fiancé. I do not know if he knows you, but I do know he would hate you if he could hear what you have dared to say!"

Again the woman laughed.

"You don't believe me? Oh, I know what you are going through! One never believes that one is betrayed—that the man one loves can repeat the same words of endearment to another woman. It is a fact, however, and I shall oblige you to believe it!"

"Never!"

"Then why am I here if I haven't fallen into Krampft's hands because I was Monet's mistress? Why should I want to see you suffer?"

"Leave me alone!" cried Colette, staggering back.

"So you believe me, eh? Besides, I have a proof to offer! Perhaps you know this ring?"

The woman took a ring from her finger and held it up.

Colette bowed her head.

"You thought yourself condemned to death—you were to be walled up alive—you gave this ring to Monet when he came to see you, disguised as a priest, to make sure that you would not betray his patriotic secrets. Well, this same ring he gave to me. Do you still doubt me?"

Alas! No! She no longer doubted.

Oh! the horror of this last and greatest treachery!

Colette laughed bitterly:

"Very well. I believe you! Monet prefers you and you are worthy of his love! The great love of a faithful heart!"

Monet's mistress seemed to be weeping.

"I beg your pardon," she murmured. "I have been cruel. I love him and you have made me despise him."

After a long silence, Colette asked in a trembling voice.

"In the name of your love, tell me truly. Are you really the prisoner of Krampft?"

"What do you mean?"

"I implore you to tell me! Do you think you can get away from here?"

"I am sure of it," answered the woman. "Krampft only seized me because I am Monet's mistress. But he has no motive to hold me prisoner. My liberty is certain; besides, I am sure Monet is doing everything in his power to deliver me."

"You know where he is?"

"I don't care to tell you that."

"Not even if I ask in the name of your love?—in the name of his life?"

"I don't understand you."

And, in truth, the woman little knew what motive was urging Colette to make this prayer.

The young girl was performing the cruelest and most sorrowful of noble duties.

She answered:

"Swear to me that you love him!"

"Don't you know that now?"

"Then swear there is nothing you would not do for him." ·

"Do you think one counts the cost when one loves!"

"Then, listen to me. If you are sure to be released, certain you can rejoin Monet, tell him that he must look at this ring with a magnifying glass—he must examine it carefully."

"I don't understand."

"Just tell him that. He will understand."

"Do you take me for a fool? It is just some trick of yours to get your lover back. No, Monet is mine and I shall keep him."

"Monet is not yours. First of all he belongs to France."

"France has nothing to do with it."

At these words Colette seized her rival by the arms.

"You are a demon," she cried. "But I will make you do what I want! Some words are scratched with the point of a needle in this ring."

"Yes, I have already seen them. 'For France!' It is a motto, I suppose."

"It is not a motto. It is the title of a picture that hangs on my wall. Ah! you can't understand—but Monet would have understood, if he hadn't given it to you without ever looking at it, without putting it on his finger as a token of our love!"

Colette spoke these words and with them went her strength. She grew pale and fell unconscious in the arms of her enemy.

Two hours later, an automobile was speeding away from Krampft's chateau.

In the automobile sat a woman and the woman was Carlotta.

"Caramba!" she laughed. "I played my part well! Rauerdt will be pleased. Mamma Mia! I can become an actress if I choose! Wasn't she taken in? She believed every word I said! And her jealousy opened her lips! Ah! Rauerdt is clever."

La Carlotta laughed again.

"It's a pity he scares me, I could almost love him!"

La Carlotta had the soul and heart of a prostitute; ready to love the man who terrorized her.

14. 32 + 4 = 36

"Thirty-two and four make thirty-six! I was thirty-two days in my prison in Berlin, and I have been here four days; add four more and that makes forty. So in four days I must say goodbye to the things of this world."

The person who had made these calculations, paced up and down his cell.

"It's not very amusing to die, but to die as I am to die is frankly rotten!"

The individual sat down, yawned, then sprang up again.

"I'd better get out of here! Why the devil did Rauerdt so kindly announce that he would have me drowned in forty days? To give me time to get the full taste of it, l suppose! That Boche is quite capable of it!"

The prisoner continued his pacing.

"And what would the lieutenant think of me if I let myself be murdered like an idiot?"

The man was silent for a moment, then in a strange voice, he continued:

"I've loafed long enough! From now on I shall spend every minute trying to escape. And as sure as my name is La Flemme, I'll get out of here before long!"

It was indeed La Flemme, Louis Monet's devoted orderly, who had been condemned to death by Rauerdt after finding that nothing could be drawn from him.

La Flemme rose and tapped the walls, but they were found to be solid throughout.

The prison was the cellar of a country house and was capable of resisting every effort.

Suddenly he gave a shout:

"Saved! I'm saved!"

A moment after he had climbed on an old barrel and began to examine a pipe he had just discovered.

The question he asked himself was this:

"Is it a water pipe or a gas pipe? If it is a water pipe I am lost… If it is a gas pipe I am saved."

What had he planned to do?

It would take a man like La Flemme, ignorant of fear, to have thought of such a thing.

He said to himself.

"I shall cut open the pipe. If it contains gas, the gas will escape and fill the cellar. I shall then set a light to it and blow up the house."

Blow up the house! But that would condemn him to the most horrible death!

The orderly knew very well the risk he was taking. But one chance was left him.

At the moment of the explosion, he would lie flat on his face.

Had he not read that the force of exploding gas went upwards?

La Flemme did not hesitate.

With the aid of an old penknife, he began hacking at the pipe. After five minutes' work he ascertained that it was really a gas pipe. In a few moments more the cellar began to fill with gas and the air became difficult to breathe.

It was time to set a light to it.

La Flemme searched in his pockets. And then he grew pale, overcome by the discovery he had made.

The unfortunate man suddenly remembered that his matches had been taken away from him.

"No matches!" he muttered, in an agonizing voice. And already he felt suffocated. Already a buzzing in his ears and a fearful head-ache warned him of approaching asphyxiation.

"This time the game is up!" he thought. "I am lost!"

But suddenly he recalled the lieutenant's advice never to give in, to struggle to the end.

"If I had flint and steel! The blade of my knife might answer, but where to find the flint?"

In the meantime his breathing became more difficult; he swayed and put a hand to the wall to steady himself. At the touch he give a cry of triumph.

"Saved! Saved!"

What had he discovered?

La Flemme found that the wall was partly made of pebble-stone.

Against this he struck the knife. A shower of sparks and a for-midable explosion followed. The house had blown up.

Stones and dust and flames settled over the ruins.

Had La Flemme perished in the catastrophe?

15. You

What was in Rauerdt's mind while he answered so casually to Carlotta's enthusiastic and breathless recital of how she had duped Colette?

The head of the Secret Service at first exhibited the keenest attention to Colette's reference to the words engraved on the ring—"For France"—and to their being the title of a picture hanging in her room.

Their significance was evident. Colette had hidden the yellow document in the frame of the picture.

"Caramba," cried the spy, "I thought I should never reach Berlin. What a voyage!"

"Really?"

"When we started off, I supposed the difficulty was all over, but it was only just beginning."

"Why?"

"I've just told you."

"That is true."

The head of the Secret Service was playing with a paper knife, his eyes fixed on his desk.

Carlotta continued, anxious to gain more interest:

"Just think, the car had one breakdown after another!"

"I am sorry."

"My chauffeur had hardly left Krampft's chateau when he found we had no more gasoline, and then followed a blowout! Fortunately we met another car, and I had to say I had just said goodbye to my husband who was leaving for the front. And that wasn't all!"

"You don't say so!"

"After a couple of miles something went wrong with the engine. I thought of your anxiety. I was in a hurry to tell you where to find the yellow document. Fortunately the railroad station wasn't far away. I managed to walk to it and caught a train and here I am!"

Carlotta burst into laughter, adding:

"I hope you are going to reward me!"

"You will be splendidly rewarded."

For the last fifteen minutes, Rauerdt had been thinking while apparently listening to Carlotta's chatter.

"I have no further need of this woman—what shall I do with her?"

In his crooked and Machiavellian mind a plan was already forming.

If he were certain to recover the yellow document within twenty-four hours and give it into the hands of the Kaiser, Rauerdt calculated that he might act boldly.

"I have beaten Krampft," he thought. "At first I saved him because he might be useful in discovering the document. Now, I see no reason why I should not finish with him."

But this was not an easy matter.

What were the exact relations between this wretch and the Kaiser?

He was afraid that the emperor had taken him into his confidence.

If that were so, it would be necessary to go carefully. To avoid attacking him until he was again compromised and his ultimate disgrace assured.

"I think I see an excellent chance," he exclaimed. "I will begin by bringing about a meeting between Carlotta and Krampft."

Krampft had asked to see him this morning.

"Why not let him meet Carlotta in the ministry? He will be furious to find her there. There will be a fight between them, each one will betray the other and I shall profit by the misunderstanding."

He turned, smiling, to Carlotta.

"I thank you for what you have done and I repeat, you shall be well rewarded. I am going at once to Cirey to get the yellow document. By the way, I shall be obliged to keep you prisoner until my return. Oh, do not be alarmed, it will not be for long, a special train will take me there and bring me back."

Rauerdt bowed, gave some orders, and went away. At five in the evening Paul de Tersy's mistress, who had been taken to a small salon and given some illustrated papers to read, gave a cry of alarm.

The door opened and an agent announced:

"Kindly step in here. The chief will not be back until later in the evening."

The individual who entered the room had occasioned Carlotta's cry.

It was Krampft.

For a moment they looked at each other in silence.

But when the agent had disappeared, Krampft sprang at de Tersy's mistress.

"You! Am I dreaming? What are you doing here?"

"What are you doing here yourself?" retorted Carlotta.

"That is none of your business. I am working for the common good. But how did you meet Rauerdt?"

Krampft was shaking with anger.

He guessed that she had betrayed him.

And Carlotta was afraid of him, she felt she was lost!

But an idea came to her.

"Oh! Monsieur Krampft, have pity; don't force me to say what you must have already guessed. Caramba! De Tersy would kill me if he knew."

"Rauerdt is your lover?" said Krampft in a surprised tone.

"I love nobody," replied Carlotta evasively.

And then she watched the effect of her words upon Krampft.

It was a clever idea to give the excuse of a love affair for her presence in the office of the Secret Service.

And it wasn't a serious matter to allow Krampft to think she was deceiving de Tersy.

In any case it would be better than letting him suspect her of being in the pay of Rauerdt.

But would Krampft believe her?

Carlotta felt reassured.

The ruse, so simple and so likely, had succeeded perfectly.

Krampft gave an amused laugh.

"Oh, I see," he murmured. "I thought—"

He stopped and shrugged his shoulders.

Carlotta laughed aloud.

Men were all the same. Each one a bigger fool than the next.

Krampft, in spite of his cleverness, had been fooled like a

schoolboy.

Carlotta went on with the game:

"I may count on your silence?"

"Naturally."

The spy laughed again:

"You know that very well. It's always funny to find one's friend deceived by his mistress. By the way, why not return with me? I shan't wait for Rauerdt, your lover. Now, I'm dining with de Tersy. Why not join us? I offer you one lover in place of the other! Isn't that nice of me?"

Carlotta smiled.

"All right. I will dine with you."

"Come on then!"

But suddenly she paused:

Would she be allowed to go out?

Taking Krampft's arm she passed along the halls of the ministry and gained the street.

"I was a fool," she thought. "Krampft is known to the Secret Service. Of course, they would let me pass with him."

When Carlotta reached Krampft's house she was beaming with joy.

Alas! five minutes later, a fearful anguish awaited her. Upon arrival at the head of the stairs, Krampft opened a door:

"Come in."

La Carlotta entered the room.

And then Krampft's voice suddenly changed. It became furious.

"And you will only get out of here to die!"

And he banged the door shut.

Not for one moment was Krampft a victim of Carlotta's game. He merely thought:

"This woman must be made to confess her treason! De Tersy must be warned. Only I must first get her out of here."

Now that Carlotta was a prisoner, Krampft could safely give way to his anger.

He rushed towards a small anteroom.

A cordial greeting met him.

"How goes it? What's new? Have you seen Rauerdt?"

It was William II's bastard.

After his adventure with the monster, Paul de Tersy had remained at Berlin with the permission of Rauerdt. He saw Krampft openly, supposing, with his naive credulity, that Rauerdt was a dupe of his comedy, that Rauerdt was ignorant of his connection with Krampft.

De Tersy started at the expression on his accomplice's face.

"What is the matter?"

"The matter is that your mistress has deceived you and she is going to die."

"What, Carlotta?"

"She is a wretch."

"You must be dreaming!"

"I tell you I caught her in the act. She was at Rauerdt's house."

The bastard became livid.

Of all men, he was most afraid of Rauerdt.

"Good God! What was she doing there?"

"I don't know."

"You must find out."

Krampft smiled.

He walked up and down the room; then stopped and examined the chimney.

"Oh, you will know!"

"She will refuse to tell us."

"We shall make her speak."

"How?"

"By a method that is very old."

Krampft had by this time taken off the screen disclosing a coal fire already laid and only waiting to be touched off with a match.

"What are you doing?" questioned the bastard.

"Surely you are not cold in midsummer?"

Krampft repeated:

"I swear to you that Carlotta will speak."

And he lit the fire.

For several moments de Tersy asked himself if he was not the plaything of a horrible nightmare. What did Krampft mean?

Why did he light the fire?

Besides, would it not be better to escape instead of wasting time?

If Carlotta had betrayed them, Rauerdt would know their plot against the emperor, that they were trying to steal the yellow document for themselves, and he would certainly be revenged.

Krampft asked abruptly:

"You have your revolver?"

"Certainly."

"Take it out and come."

The spy was also armed with a Browning. Together they quickly made their way to the room occupied by Carlotta and opened the door.

Krampft covered her with his weapon and cried:

"Not a movement! Not a cry!"

Then he ordered:

"Come!"

More dead than alive, Carlotta did not dream of resisting. Krampft directed himself again to the salon. There, he placed his revolver on the table.

"You have three seconds in which to make up your mind," he declared. "You see that fire? Well, I have made it for you. Listen to me, Carlotta! I swear you must either tell us everything or I will burn you alive. First of all I will burn your hands, then your arms. I will burn you bit by bit with horrible torture. Will you speak?"

"Never!"

"Very well."

With a sudden movement he sprang at her.

"Help me, de Tersy!"

Carlotta was thrown to the ground and gagged.

"Put her hand in the fire!"

Carlotta felt as though she would die of fright.

Krampft asked again:

"Will you speak?"

And this time she yielded.

She yielded as she had done to Rauerdt, as she would always yield, this woman of cowardly spirit.

In broken words and hesitatingly, she confessed everything.

She recounted how she had been forced into the Secret Service of Rauerdt; how she had kept him informed of the bastard's doings and finally, of her last commission and the success attending it.

"The yellow document," cried Krampft. "You have told Rauerdt its hiding place!"

De Tersy stammered:

"We must go! We must get there before Rauerdt!"

"Nonsense! Rauerdt has two hours' start of us! Get up, Carlotta!"

He then took out his watch.

"Ten o'clock—we have time—we must do nothing before midnight!"

"Midnight?"

What new plan had Krampft conceived?

De Tersy questioned him:

"Explain!"

Then, calmly and seemingly ignoring Carlotta's presence, Krampft began:

"The yellow document is lost to us—and that means we are beaten unless we can still struggle against Rauerdt."

Krampft paused as though to weigh his words:

"I am aware that Colette is to be taken to Brigitte Ravignon. Probably the emperor wants to gain the good will of my ex-wife, of the woman who is really Mme. Bayen. Now William II does not do things without a purpose. He knows that Brigitte knows the contents of the yellow document. Well, we must get Mme. Bayen into our hands!"

"But Mme. Bayen wouldn't tell us what she knows."

"What does that matter?" replied Krampft.

"She won't speak."

"She won't speak because we shall kill her. You see, it matters little whether she tells us or not—the essential is that we can swear she has spoken. One doesn't need to know a secret if one has the appearance of knowing it. We shall be the masters of William II if we can make him think we know the contents of the yellow envelope."

Surely Krampft must have lost his wits to speak this way before Carlotta!

16. For the Love of Monet

"Half-past eleven! Time to be serious!"

Undoubtedly Krampft was joking, for the three diners seated at the table had taken their meal in a most anxious and painful frame of mind.

Krampft brought the conversation to a sharp close:

"We have work before us tonight."

The Kaiser's bastard and his mistress were quite aware that they could not hope to argue with Krampft and that it would be best for them to blindly obey him.

Krampft rose:

"You understand me, my friends? You know what we have to do?"

But seeing the look of bewilderment on their faces, he added:

"It's perfectly simple. A reception will be held tonight at the Potsdam palace in honor of the taking of Liège and the capture of General Léman. We are to take advantage of this occasion to abduct Brigitte Bayen. Brigitte has an apartment in the palace where she is living as a semi-prisoner. Every night at midnight she takes a long walk in the park, where it will be a simple matter to seize her."

De Tersy thought his accomplice had gone mad.

"Abduct Brigitte Bayen! Explain how it is to be done!"

"Very well," replied Krampft in a matter-of-fact tone.

"The only difficulty will be in getting her out of the park."

"That is an impossibility," answered De Tersy.

Krampft continued:

"I happen to know that Brigitte Bayen is free to use the northern end of the park. There is a small door nearby, always guarded by a sentry. The whole difficulty—you hear, de Tersy—difficulty and not impossibility—is to get rid of this man and then persuade Mme. Bayen to escape and fall into our ambush."

De Tersy, carried away by Krampft's air of confidence, nodded:

"The problem is quite clear, but how are we to solve it? How get rid of the sentry? Who will persuade Mme. Bayen to escape?"

Krampft gave a look of contempt at de Tersy, then pointed:

"Carlotta!"

"I!" exclaimed de Tersy's mistress.

"You. You will do it to pay the debt you owe us."

"I don't understand. How would I go about it?"

"I'll tell you that by and by. To begin with, you will have something more urgent to do. I am quite sure you will not betray us this time."

Krampft leaned towards her:

"You will obey us this time because I shall first make you write a letter to Rauerdt in which you will state clearly that you are responsible for the abduction of Mme. Bayen. Rauerdt will never forgive that. Consequently, when you have quarreled with him you will have every reason to remain faithful to us."

Carlotta did not reply.

She had an inner vision of the fantastic and tragic struggle which was taking place between these two men, both scoundrels: Krampft and Rauerdt.

"I'm tired out," she sighed. "I should be able to do nothing tonight."

"Very well, we will give you a stimulant. De Tersy, pass me that box of white powder."

The young woman shuddered:

"Poison, I'm sure it's poison!"

Krampft shrugged his shoulders.

"Then I shall poison myself."

He took a pinch of the powder and swallowed it.

"Now are you satisfied? Unfortunately, the effect of this stimulant rapidly wears off, so I shall prepare a dose of it for you to be taken at the moment you enter the palace grounds."

Then turning to de Tersy:

"Just give me those capsules. Carlotta must be well doped, as you can see!"

Krampft himself was as good at acting as the woman. He seemed quite paternal and good-natured as he spoke the words.

*　　*　　*　　*　　*　　*

That evening the Potsdam palace was en fête. A grand dinner had been given in honor of the taking of Liège and the people had joyfully acclaimed the Kaiser and his family as they appeared for a moment on one of the balconies. The people of Berlin little guessed that their idol would, a few moments later, give a sinister proof of his infamous character.

William II, escaping from the applause of the crowd, furtively and alone, made his way to the park.

There, the poor prisoner, the wife of the unhappy Colonel Bayen, was walking in a secluded path.

Brigitte Bayen, transferred to Potsdam, certainly enjoyed greater liberty, but she was still tortured by her ignorance as to what was happening in France, and by the prayers of the Kaiser who seemed determined to gain her pardon.

The emperor, on this evening, became more pressing, while his victim scarcely answered him.

"I have good news for you, Madame."

"Sire, your majesty does not refer to the triumph of your troops, I suppose? The success of Germany is a defeat for me!"

The emperor bowed.

"I know that, Madame. I respect your feelings as a Frenchwoman. We are enemies. Well, it is to my enemy that I announce good news as a pledge of my sincerity."

"Will your majesty deign to speak, in that case?"

"The German troops are victorious in Belgium, Madame, that is something everybody knows. But you alone, in Berlin will know this: The German troops have been beaten in Alsace. The French are on the road to Colmar."

"Ah, Sire!"

For the first time, Mme. Bayen felt a spirit of gratitude toward the man who tortured her.

"I thank your majesty."

"Tonight you will have further good news."

"What do you mean, Sire?"

"I mean that I have perhaps found the way to gain your forgiveness. Some time ago I gave orders to allow Louis Monet to escape. I have given another order, Madame."

"Will your majesty tell me?"

"Madame, in a few moments you will see somebody who is very dear to you—your daughter, Colette."

"Colette is coming here? I cannot believe it!"

"In a few moments you will have the proof."

"In a few moments?"

"Yes, when you have made me a promise."

"A promise! Ah! I am afraid!"

"You must promise to listen to Admiral Von Tirpitz who has a communication to make to you. He will inform you of the decision I have taken. He will tell you that you must show me where the yellow document is to be found."

"The yellow document, Sire?"

"Yes, Madame. Oh, do not pretend you don't understand. You know what this document is—you know it is an electrical machine which projects Hertzian waves that are capable of exploding powder at a distance—you know that the possession of this invention would enable me to blow up all the arsenals, all the munition stores in France from my palace."

William II grew excited at the thought of this infernal discovery which he hoped to make use of. Ah! to fight in safety, to disarm the enemy at a distance was indeed pleasing to the German character. The consequences little mattered to him. The destruction of the civil population of an enemy country left him unmoved. The voice of Brigitte Ravignon drew him out of this dream:

"Very well. I shall pretend no longer. Yes, I know all about this yellow document. I know that the description of this machine is in France—I know where it is. Ah, Sire, I also know that you would not hesitate at any violation of international convention. And that is why I shall remain silent. Nothing you can do will drag this secret from me."

"We shall see about that, Madame!"

William II bowed, turned abruptly and left her.

Then Mme. Bayen wept.

She guessed the horror in store for her.

A few moments later the infamous Von Tirpitz appeared, the man who prided himself on the organization of the submarine warfare, the campaign of piracy.

Von Tirpitz spoke briefly and to the point.

"Madame. Your daughter Colette will be here in a minute or two. Either you will bid her an eternal goodbye and she will be executed tonight as guilty of lèse majesté, or you will confess the hiding place of the yellow document."

Without giving Mme. Bayen time to reply Von Tirpitz moved away, saying:

"Think it over, Madame. Here is your daughter."

Turning her head, the heroic and unhappy woman saw Colette. The young girl flung herself into Mme. Bayen's arms.

"Mother—my dear mother!"

"Colette—my darling Colette!"

Without further words Mme. Bayen drew Colette into the depth of the park.

She knew very well that the imperial garden was surrounded by high walls and the thought of escape never entered her mind, but she wished to be alone with her daughter.

The two women hurried down a path, almost running.

And then, suddenly they stopped short. Something moved in the shadows and a figure appeared before them.

They were frightened, terribly frightened.

In the silence of the night which carried to them the distant refrain of a waltz, two cries rang out.

*   *   *   *   *   *

Five minutes earlier the sentry on duty at a small door, seldom used, was startled by the arrival of a young officer who hurriedly gave the password, "Kultur and Civilization," and then passed through the door without a glance at the soldier who had come to attention and saluted.

"Another officer attached to the Secret Service," he thought. "No one else enters this way."

But the sentry was mistaken.

The officer was visibly unacquainted with the imperial park.

Scarcely had he found himself well inside when his attitude changed. He seemed very much afraid, and took the greatest precautions to keep close to the shadows.

Where was he going? What did he meditate? Who was he?

Two cries had rung out.

Oh! no doubt of it Brigitte and Colette were nearly dead of fear.

And now the officer rushed up to them.

"Quick! Quick!" he begged, "follow me!"

He then threw back his cloak and seized Brigitte by the arm.

"Come quickly. Don't waste an instant!"

But Brigitte resisted.

"You don't understand. I have come to help you both to escape. I am doing this—for love of Monet!"

For love of Monet!

Colette now seemed to understand the unexpected appearance of the mysterious savior.

"A woman! You?" she cried.

Colette had recognized her. She had seen her while a prisoner in Krampft's chateau.

This woman disguised as a man was Monet's mistress!

Carlotta, frantic with impatience, repeated:

"Come! A second's delay may spoil everything!"

17. The Trap

What had happened to the monster after the tragic moment when he had entered Krampft's chateau for the second time?

With a beating heart he had listened to the conversation between Carlotta and the unhappy young girl.

Doubtless the monster knew the two women and was even aware of the mysterious importance of the yellow document.

White with rage and with clenched fists he muttered:

"Lies! Lies! Always lies! The very spirit of Germany!"

Not for one moment had the monster been taken in by the game played by Carlotta.

And Colette had suffered so greatly by Carlotta's words that she had been convinced of their truth.

"This woman has been sent here by Rauerdt, I would swear to it!"

Then he smiled grimly:

"Very well, it is between us two, Rauerdt!"

The struggle was to be fierce, a fight to a finish!

No doubt Carlotta would hurry back to Berlin. She would notify Rauerdt of the hiding place of the yellow document! Rauerdt would consider the victory won.

But he would find himself mistaken!

With an exclamation of anger and joy, the monster swore:

"When Rauerdt reaches the hiding place of the yellow document, it will no longer be there!"

And then the mysterious individual began hurried preparations.

Danger did not exist for him. For a long time he had held his life cheaply, had resigned himself to any sacrifice in the cause of duty.

"Whatever happens," he thought, "I must get hold of the yellow document without a moment's loss of time. That must be done even before I see Colette or Brigitte."

Contemptuous of the danger of leaving his hiding place, the monster opened the door and listened.

The tower was absolutely silent.

"Luck is on my side," he thought. "If I don't meet the jailer I shall be able to slip out."

And indeed it seemed as though Chance would favor this enigmatic individual.

He left the tower without hindrance. Furthermore, he uttered a cry of joy:

"Ah! Carlotta's motor!"

Not far away a superb automobile was stationed by the side of the road. The monster drew near it.

"Carlotta will take longer than she thinks to reach Berlin."

With a smart blow the monster punctured the gasoline tank and the gasoline began to leak slowly, drop by drop.

"That won't be enough," he murmured. "They can get more gasoline. I must put it out of business!"

He then picked up a handful of sand and mixed it with the lubricating oil.

As he was about to move away he gave a sudden cry and threw himself on his face in a ditch. He was just in time, as at that moment the chauffeur appeared, hands in his pockets, and smoking a cigar.

"This man may belong to the Secret Service, I mustn't let him see me," he exclaimed.

And now luck seemed to be turning against the monster. He had done everything possible to delay the arrival of Carlotta in Berlin so that he might have time to get the yellow document himself.

And here he was, obliged to remain hidden while the precious time slipped by.

As evening drew on the monster at length saw Carlotta appear accompanied by the jailer, who stood hat in hand.

Carlotta appeared to be giving orders.

"Tell your prisoner to get ready. You are to take her to Berlin; tell her she is to meet her mother."

Twenty minutes later the monster reached the cave where he had left Louis Monet.

As he entered, the young officer sprang towards him. He was still weak from fever but his voice was eager.

"Ah! Where have you been? Why mustn't I recognize you?"

"Because I am no longer myself," replied the monster, simply.

"From the moment war was declared, Lieutenant, I knew that my duty was to disappear. I have disappeared. That is all."

"But why? Why?"

"I killed myself because otherwise I would have been killed."

"Ah! Colonel!"

What was Colette's fiancé thinking of? Why did he call this man colonel?

"Lieutenant, since you have recognized me there is no longer any reason for denying my real identity… I am indeed Colonel Bayen! My story is a simple one. I will tell it to you.

"When I gave you the yellow document I knew war to be inevitable, and I also knew that immediately mobilization started I had to disappear. Lieutenant, I pretended to kill myself. I left my clothes on the river bank to give the idea of murder. And then—I vitrioled myself."

"You did that, Colonel?"

"Yes, Lieutenant."

"But why?"

"Because I had to go to Germany and to reach there I had first to disappear, and then reappear, with a new face, a face which nobody in the world could recognize. Not even a German spy! Colonel Bayen is thought to be dead and the monster is unrecognizable. I betrayed myself to you by forgetting to disguise my voice."

Monet was overcome by such heroic courage.

What sublime devotion!

"Ah, Colonel! You did more than your duty!"

"No, Lieutenant. One never does more than one's duty, when it is a question of devotion to one's country."

But the colonel no longer wanted to think of the past. Above all, he no longer wanted to think of himself.

"Lieutenant, the yellow document is incomplete. It is merely the description of a mechanical apparatus, a sinister discovery which our enemies would not hesitate to make use of. Ah! What agony I have gone through for twenty years. The person who knew how to manipulate it could destroy munitions at a distance. If the emperor of Germany possessed it, he could disarm the Allies with a single gesture—a gesture which would kill millions of beings and deliver France to his mercy. He would have only to pull down a handle.

"What a struggle has raged over this document for twenty years!

"I was attaché when I treated with the inventor. I bought his secret at the cost of my entire fortune, but that was not enough—the Austrian wanted millions. Then he planned an infamous piece of trickery. He only gave me the description of the apparatus in the yellow document. He did not tell me how to use it; that he told Krampft, Fantômas of Berlin."

"I don't understand," cried Monet. "Does Krampft know this secret?"

"Yes, Lieutenant, he knows it, although he denies that knowledge, and that was the beginning of these espionage intrigues which have lasted for twenty years. I know the secret of the machine—Krampft knows how it functions, and Krampft has tried to murder me for twenty years as he murdered the inventor, in the hope of becoming the master of the world, the master of his master, the emperor."

"Colonel, suppose Krampft should discover the mechanism of the machine?"

"If he should do so, he would not live an hour longer!"

And the colonel spoke in a manner which left no doubt to what lengths his devotion would go.

"Lieutenant, after buying the secret of the machine, I went to France to raise money to purchase the rest of the discovery. It was then that Krampft poisoned the inventor. The man died at my house and my wife was with him at the end. Since then, I have never seen my wife."

"She was murdered!"

"She died, so far as it was known—by the will of the Kaiser—but she lives for France! Lieutenant, Brigitte Ravignon is called Brigitte Bayen—Brigitte is my wife! For twenty years she has been a prisoner of the Kaiser—for twenty years she has been willing to pass for Krampft's wife. And during that time she has been ready at any moment to kill him should he succeed in reconstructing the mechanism described in the yellow document."

"Colonel—and Colette?"

"Colette is my daughter—my dear daughter; and I have never held her in my arms. She does not even know she is my child."

Colonel Bayen had buried his face in his hands. Suddenly he

raised his eyes.

"I know your love, Monet. You are worthy of Colette. May you one day get your reward!"

*   *   *   *   *   *

At midnight Monet was walking along a road bordered with large trees.

The young man was on his way to Cirey to find the yellow document before Rauerdt had a chance to steal it.

The colonel expected to be able to reach his wife, Brigitte Bayen. Was he not a spy in the eyes of Rauerdt?

He would find his wife! He would save her! And then he would be free to settle matters with William II—to square the debt that had been owing for so many years.

Alas! Was not fate once more to intervene in the plans of Colonel Bayen?

Would Monet arrive in time to save the yellow document?

In spite of his fatigue, Monet traveled rapidly.

He avoided the highroad whenever possible and was careful to give the farmhouses a wide berth.

He recalled the colonel's warning: "Remember that the German spies are all powerful and all daring!"

It was dawn before he drew near Cirey. Finally he reached the garden railing and saw the little house, formerly so cheerful, now blackened with smoke, the shutters torn off, the furniture scattered on the lawn.

Tears came to his eyes.

But it was no time for vain regrets. His first duty was to recover the yellow document.

The garden was deserted. Not a sound could be heard from the house.

"I am in time," he murmured.

He entered the hall and made his way to the first story. He reached Colette's room and rushed in. With a cry of joy he saw that the picture was still in its place. "For France."

He seized it and examined the frame.

This time he gave a cry of rage. The hiding place was empty!

Who had stolen it? Who had taken it away?

Mad with anger and more than ever determined to fight to the bitter end, Monet was now in haste to return to his chief for further orders.

As the officer ran down the garden path, suddenly he staggered and fell. Something heavy had fallen upon him.

In a moment he realized the trap he had fallen into.

Looking up he saw a man above him on the branch of a tree, who with a sardonic laugh had flung down an enormous fishing net, completely covering him and preventing the slightest movement.

"Ha! Ha! Lieutenant Monet, you thought you had won! You thought you had outdistanced me, that you could escape with the document! Fool! You should have known it was risky to show a light in Colette's room! Now, I've got you—you are beaten!"

The man who jeered at Monet was Rauerdt.

But before Monet could answer him, a shot rang out.

With a cry, mortally wounded, Rauerdt let go his hold and fell to the ground.

A cheery voice now exclaimed:

"Say, Lieutenant, a bit of a boaster, that chap! Don't you think so? But apart from that I'd like to know what has become of you all this time. I've been growing old waiting for you!"

The man who spoke was La Flemme.

18. Vengeance

"The chief is not here. He has left no instructions."

The door closed and Colonel Bayen was obliged to take his departure.

This news was serious. The absence of Rauerdt interfered sadly with his plans.

Alone, and walking along the deserted streets of the great city, Colonel Bayen thought:

"Carlotta has certainly arrived. If Rauerdt is not here it means that he has gone to Cirey after the yellow document. If only Monet gets there first."

Quick action was necessary.

"I must manage without him," decided the colonel.

But how would it be possible for Colonel Bayen to enter the Potsdam palace?

How could he reach the unhappy captive of the emperor?

The officer hailed a taxi and gave the chauffeur an address.

And while the car carried him rapidly toward the royal residence, Colonel Bayen made up his mind to make a desperate attempt, to take the most forlorn chances.

After dismissing the taxi, he stood outside the wall of the park.

"Brigitte and Colette are there," he murmured. "Brigitte knows the secret of the yellow document—and Monet loves Colette. I must get to them at any cost."

The officer put his hand in his pocket. He made sure that his Browning was ready for use.

Would he have recourse to violence?

What could he do alone against the guard of the imperial palace?

Colonel Bayen had quitted the road and now was walking on a strip of grass which finally led him to the extremity of the park.

Suddenly he sprang behind a tree.

He had caught sight of a powerful automobile standing with

lights extinguished.

After a moment, he dropped to the ground and crawled forward noiselessly.

"Krampft," he murmured. "That is Krampft's car. What is it doing here?"

It did not take him long to guess the truth. Krampft, too, was attempting to carry off Brigitte Bayen.

What was to be done?

The heroic officer had one of those ideas which seemed to be mere madness.

He crept up to the car and crawled under it between the wheels.

After waiting ten minutes the park door opened and a figure appeared.

Immediately two men sprang out of the car.

"Well?" they questioned.

"It's all right. Let's get away."

Colonel Bayen could hardly repress a cry. He recognized the two men. They were Krampft and de Tersy.

He also recognized the voice of the third person. It was the voice of the woman who had called on Colette in the tower.

But what costume was she wearing?

"Colette is here?" asked Krampft.

"Yes."

"And Brigitte Bayen also?"

"Yes. They are waiting inside. I said I was coming out to see if the coast was clear. You have only to seize them."

Colonel Bayen realized that his guess was correct. Everything had been prepared for an abduction.

"I arrived just in time," he said to himself. Suddenly a woman's figure appeared in the doorway. Scarcely had she taken a few steps outside when de Tersy sprang upon her, threw her down and gagged her.

And then, another form issued from the park, apparently carrying a burden in her arms.

"Help me, Krampft," whispered Carlotta. "Brigitte Bayen is half dead."

"Half dead?"

Carlotta placed the body on the grass and the three figures bent over her.

"I don't know what's the matter with her," exclaimed Carlotta. "I was afraid she would faint, so I gave her the capsule you prepared for me. I made her take it and when I got back—"

"Mein Gott!" suddenly swore the spy. "She has taken the capsule! Then she will die!"

He then seized Carlotta by the wrists.

"It was for you!"

"But it was not poison. You swallowed some of the powder before me!"

"The powder! That was nothing! But the capsule was filled with cyanide of potassium."

And he added:

"All the same, you won't escape, Carlotta!"

With a sudden movement he seized her by the throat. His fingers tightened more and more and then he let go.

Carlotta collapsed and lay motionless on the ground.

"She has her deserts," exclaimed the ruffian.

"Oh! never mind my mistress," shouted de Tersy. "Time is precious, Krampft! What shall we do with Mme. Bayen? Shall we take her with us?"

"No, no! Her body will only be in the way! We must leave her in the park. She will be found tomorrow and William II will suppose she was murdered."

De Tersy and Krampft lifted Mme. Bayen and carried her back to the park.

And then Colonel Bayen left his hiding place.

Rapidly he unbound Colette.

"Save yourself," he cried. "Run! No matter where—but go!"

But the young girl had fainted.

"Ah! I must save her."

Close at hand Colonel Bayen noticed a thick underbrush. It was the work of a moment to transport Colette in his arms and hide her in the thickest part of the brush.

"De Tersy and Krampft will never find her here," he thought, "and I shall have time to reach Brigitte."

Colonel Bayen ran to the park. A few yards away Krampft and de Tersy passed him on their way out; and he had the courage to let them go. It would have been imprudent to attempt to kill them.

He would find them again later on.

He would punish them as soon as he was free to act.

Krampft and de Tersy had scarcely left the park when Colonel Bayen was on his knees by the body of his wife, Brigitte Bayen.

The unfortunate woman was dying.

A white froth was on her lips.

A terrible poison was this cyanide of potassium! And its effects were immediate and overwhelming.

"Brigitte! Brigitte! Can't you hear me? It is I—your husband! Oh! speak to me! You must! For France!"

For France!

The magic words again performed a miracle.

Brigitte Bayen stirred. A light shone in her eyes—her lips attempted to frame the words.

Did she recognize her husband? Yes, without doubt.

The dying woman had just the strength to murmur:

"Krampft must be killed. He has found the secret of the mechanism!"

*   *   *   *   *   *

A short distance away in the park a man sprang forward. It was the emperor.

And his face was convulsed with rage.

In truth, the Kaiser had just received the worst of news. A telegram in cipher had arrived, short, laconic.

"Our troops have been decimated. At any cost make Brigitte Bayen speak.—HINDENBURG."

The emperor had immediately rushed in search of his captive to force a confession from her.

But where was Brigitte Bayen?

After a five minutes' search, the emperor called his lackeys and ordered them to scour the park.

Suddenly as William II reached the park wall, an electric pocket lamp was flashed in his face.

"Stop, Sire! Your victim is here!"

"My victim!" exclaimed the emperor, springing back.

"Your victim, Brigitte Bayen. She whom you have tortured—she who has just been murdered!"

Pale with terror, the Kaiser could not speak for a moment.

He wondered if it was not a supernatural apparition that addressed these sinister words to him. Was it possible that in his well-guarded park a stranger, an enemy, could find his way in?

"Who are you?" stammered the emperor.

"Who am I, Sire? A Frenchman—a judge—a man who seeks vengeance. My name is Colonel Bayen! I am the husband of that poor woman that your people have just killed. Sire, remember that at the first attempt to escape, the first call for help I shall shoot you as I would a criminal, a murderer!"

"Pity! Pity!" wailed the Kaiser.

"Look, Sire, there are your lackeys, your officers searching for you. You see their lanterns moving away; they have taken the wrong turning! Ah! don't call them or I fire!"

"Mercy! Mercy!"

"A man does not pardon the murderer of his wife! A Frenchman does not spare a treacherous German in wartime! A soldier has no pity for the Kaiser."

Then he ordered:

"To your knees, Sire—beside your victim! I give you three minutes to repent in."

The Kaiser collapsed rather than kneeled.

From his throne he fell into the mud, and it was in the mud that he would doubtless die.

"Three minutes," repeated the colonel. "In three minutes, on my soul, I shall blow out your brains."

But was the wretched Emperor of Germany to die that way?

"Only a minute left, Sire," said the officer, slowly.

19. The Last Battle

"Well, Lieutenant?"

"Well, La Flemme?"

"We are almost comfortable. We can have a chat."

"You want to talk, then?"

"I should say so! Think! eleven days of silence! After blowing up the house and getting away, I waited eleven days for you at Cirey. And I don't like holding my tongue."

"So you want to make up for it now?"

"Yes—but hold on, Lieutenant."

La Flemme was obliged to shout at the top of his voice.

Why?

The orderly went on:

"You weigh 150 pounds. I weigh 148. The fat chap there about 180—and we are carrying 800 pounds of bombs!"

But Monet did not answer.

He pointed his revolver and ordered:

"Go straight now! Don't try any tricks or I'll blow out your brains!"

Monet shifted in his seat, and La Flemme bellowed:

"Careful, Lieutenant! You make me giddy. Forty-five hundred feet! Take a long staircase to get down!"

What did it all mean?

The orderly and the officer were traveling in an airplane and the pilot wore the Kaiser's uniform.

And it was towards the imperial palace at Potsdam that they were speeding through a starless night.

What had happened?

Released from the net by La Flemme, Monet had immediately searched Rauerdt's body.

With a cry of joy he found the yellow document in his pocketbook.

And then he realized that the document was not safe.

He was still behind the German lines!

What was to be done?

And then La Flemme had calmly made his suggestion.

"There are three Boche aviators less than a mile away. The pilots have orders to be on duty. One or the other of them is always on guard. I found this out while waiting here for you. Now, this is what I suggest: We'll creep up and stick a gun under the nose of one of them. When a Boche is under dog he soon gives in. We'll make him take us in his airplane."

"At midnight," said Colonel Bayen, "I shall be at Potsdam. I shall try to save my wife, Brigitte, and my daughter, Colette."

"Then it is to Potsdam I should go and deliver the document into Colonel Bayen's hands," thought Monet.

"Your plan is a mad one, La Flemme, but we will try it."

They had tried it and they had succeeded.

Would they arrive in time?

Could it be possible that this fantastic flight to the imperial palace of two French soldiers in a Boche airplane might be crowned with success?

In the park, hurried footsteps, a breathless run—the impossible had been accomplished!

A few seconds earlier the Boche airplane had landed on one of the lawns surrounding the Potsdam palace.

"Find out what is happening," whispered La Flemme. "I'll look after our pilot. It's not enough to have brought us, he'll have to take us away too!"

And Monet set out, trusting to chance.

How could he find his way in these immense gardens?

By the sound of voices? Shouts for help?

"I thought I heard that," thought Monet, "at the moment we landed. Was I mistaken? And can it be Colonel Bayen they are looking for? I saw some persons carrying torches!"

He ran and ran.

Suddenly a figure stood before him.

"Who goes there?"

It was a woman's voice, gentle and sweet.

Monet clutched a tree so that he might not fall. His joy was beyond words.

He could only stammer one name:

"Colette! Colette!"

And it was a cry of joy which answered him:

"Monet! My love—is it you?"

Chance had guided the officer to his fiancée!

At that moment, a few feet away, Colonel Bayen repeated:

"Only a minute, Sire."

The officer felt strangely calm.

It was an act of justice he was about to perform.

The revolver with which he covered the Kaiser did not tremble.

The master of Germany once again cried:

"Pity!"

And then, with an agility one would not have thought him capable of, he sprang up.

Oh! the necessary precautions had been well taken. The sovereign assassin had more than one means of defense installed in his park.

Before Colonel Bayen could fire, the Kaiser had reached the pedestal of a marble statue.

His hand touched it.

A loud explosion followed.

And then, the ground seemed to open—a flame of fire rose skyward.

The Kaiser had set off a mine hidden under the path.

Flung to the ground, Colonel Bayen lay bleeding with torn breast.

At the sound of the explosion, Monet and Colette rushed forward.

"Hurry! Hurry!" cried Colette.

"Too late," replied the officer.

Around a bend in the path lay a body.

"Too late!"

At a glance he had recognized the man whose chief claim to glory was in being a monster.

Monet knelt by his side.

"Colonel! Colonel!"

The dying man opened his eyes.

"You, Monet? Oh! tell me, have you the document?"

"Yes, colonel, yes!"

"Then destroy it—when you have killed Krampft. France does not use such weapons!"

"Colonel, let me—"

"Kill Krampft—burn the document—victory—"

He did not finish. His soul took its flight. Colonel Bayen had died as a soldier.

"This way!"

"No, this way!"

"You are wrong, counselor."

"I know what I'm saying—I heard a noise—and look! Look!"

From all sides of the park, servants, soldiers, officers arrived pell-mell.

What had happened? Where was the emperor?

Why had the mine exploded?

Some of them affirmed that they had seen an airplane land on one of the lawns.

Krampft, who had retraced his steps and entered the palace grounds, was certain he had seen the airplane.

"There!" he cried. "Listen!"

And, in fact, the whirring of an engine became audible at that moment.

A hundred persons made a rush for the lawn.

By the side of the airplane Monet and La Flemme were seen.

"Start, La Flemme! Start off!"

"Without you? Never!"

"Yes, take Colette, save her!"

At the moment of Colonel Bayen's death, Colette had fainted and Monet had been obliged to carry her in his arms to the airplane, where La Flemme had dragged her on board.

"I must remain here," declared Monet. "I must find Krampft and kill him!"

"Hands up! Surrender!"

"Fire!"

Monet heard the balls whistle about his ears but he paid no attention to them.

His eyes were fastened on a man who was aiming at him, slowly and methodically.

It was Krampft.

Monet raised his Browning and fired.

He saw Krampft—the enemy—Fantômas of Berlin—fall dead, shot through the head.

And then he was seized by the shoulders.

"How obstinate you are, Lieutenant! It's lucky I am here!"

The machine started.

La Flemme with one hand held his revolver at the head of the pilot and with the other hauled Monet on board and flung him down beside Colette.

*   *   *   *   *   *

Three months later the *Petit Journal* announced the marriage of Captain Monet and Mlle. Colette Bayen, daughter of the regretted colonel.

The *Petit Journal* added that the young officer, decorated with the Croix de Guerre and the Legion of Honor, had obstinately refused to be transferred to the Ministry of War and asked to be sent back to his place at the front.

THE END.